THE MISSING LINK

A GIL YATES PRIVATE INVESTIGATOR NOVEL

By Alistair Boyle

ALLEN A. KNOLL, PUBLISHERS

Cover photo: Garden of Phil and Mitzi Bergman, San Diego, CA
Courtesy of the Southern California Palm Society

Publisher's Cataloging in Publication Data

Boyle, Alistair.
  The missing link : a Gil Yates private investigator novel /
Alistair Boyle.
  p. cm.
  Preassigned LCCN: 94-78009
  ISBN 0-9627297-3-6

  1. Yates, Gil (Fictitious character)--Fiction. 2. Private investigators--California--Los Angeles--Fiction. 3. Detective and mystery stories. I. Title.

PS3552.0896M57 1995   813'.54
                                        QBI94-1739

Typeface is ITC Galliard, 11 point
Printed on 60-pound Lakewood white, acid-free paper
Case bound with Kivar 9, Smyth Sewn

Okay, I admit it. It was a crazy thing to do.

But, who said uncompromising, pathological sanity was the key to life?

I would have to rank myself as the least likely person I know to venture into detective work–or any endeavor, for that matter, that required any daring, chutzpah, risk. People I knew referred to me as Caspar Milquetoast when they thought I wasn't listening.

That must be why I wanted to do it.

It was a beautiful day for raising palms. The sun was gentle, the sky was friendly and the fires of autumn had passed me by. I should have been outdoors.

Instead, I drove up the coast to a meeting of the Southern California Palm Society, in Bernuli, an inoffensive seaside town where you could stop for lunch between here and there without getting mugged.

The last sound I heard going out the door was the inimitable thrust of my wife's longshoreman's gravel-pit voice.

"You be back here by five."

I always felt like saluting when she spoke.

Between my wife and her father, they had a pretty good grip on my life. I was confident that those who knew my situation at home would understand my harebrained fantasy.

I pulled into the Bernuli Junior College parking lot

and started fumbling around, looking for the meeting room.

The campus had a lot of low-slung buildings that started out as temporaries and wound up permanent. The rooms had a numbering system that would have flummoxed Einstein.

At best they call us palm collectors; at worst, palm nuts, but we are mostly nuts. To get a bunch of people who are passionate about plants in the first place, you have a pretty strange menagerie. Mainly they are folks who eschew the interpersonal contacts our society has deemed normal. When you put together palm enthusiasts, you are teetering on the edge of the whacko scale.

Cycads and most palms are the slowest growing plants in the world, so you should start young. I didn't. Twenty-five is about the optimum age, as far as I can see. That way you can diddle around with seeds and, if you take reasonable care of yourself, you might live to see a real palm tree. To buy the big unusual stuff you need big bucks. It goes without saying I didn't have big bucks. Yet.

I finally found the palm meeting room. I arrived early. I always did. I was a careful guy. Frightened of being looked at for coming in late. We met in an amphitheater-type setup like the medical students use to look down on the slicing of a cadaver. We were looking down on palms, some of which would become cadavers in my garden.

Being more introverted than the run of the palm nuts, who are a pretty introverted group to start with, I chose a seat in the back row, hoping my fellow nuts would keep their distance.

Wrong. A guy with dark, curly hair, woman's length, and a pair of glasses hanging around his neck with an elastic band not only sat down, but struck up a conversation. I wondered where he thought he was. At some sporting event perhaps.

He saw I was reading THE NEW YORKER and asked how I liked the change (of editors).

I had the magazine folded over, so he could only see the arrangement of type. This told me: One, he had winner eyes without his glasses, and, two, he was a pretty erudite guy.

That's the thing about palm nuts, they come in all sizes and shapes, sexes and schooling levels.

The president of the group is a genial chain-smoking D.D.S. We have lawyers, professors, housewives and just folks like me–a beleaguered property manager in my great and powerful father-in-law's robust enterprise.

Some of those adjectives describe my wife. You'll figure it out.

A few years ago I would have mumbled something the palm-meeting intruder couldn't hear so he would get the buzz-off message, if sitting alone in the back row with my nose in a magazine wasn't enough to do it for him. But age has softened my social phobia and I was fairly pleasant, for me.

He certainly was fond of talking. More than I am fond of listening. And of all places to experience logorrhea, a meeting of palm nuts should rightfully be near the bottom. There is zero communication with palm trees. Oh, a lot of people talk to them, but there is no documentary proof that any of them have ever talked back.

My new buddy is a gardener for one of the super-rich. Mr. Rich's got a whale of a palm collection, so Jack Kimback is here to bone up.

Now Jack gets to the meat of the thing. His boss, who is just too famous, in an illicit sort of way, to mention, is looking for a private detective to find his daughter.

He has interviewed every known agency, tried a few, and doesn't like any of them. He is apparently a very picky man, as can be seen in his hiring this erudite, well-spoken young man to tend his palms.

Said Megabucks has also had it with the cops and the missing persons folks. A man that rich, his gardener says, is used to buying what he wants, but his money, this time, isn't cutting the ketchup.

If you have ever felt possessed by the devil, you know how I felt when I heard the following words come out of my mouth:

"Oh, I just happen to *be* a private detective."

Jack's eyebrows hit the ceiling. You could tell he was skeptical that a mealy-mouthed guy like me would be in such a macho line of work.

It seemed like a harmless tease at first. I didn't look on it as a lie, exactly. A lark. I thought it would go no further. Any time now, I would set him straight–tell him I was only joking. But the more he told me, the more intrigued I became, and the less impetus I had for telling the technical truth.

You know what the "technical truth" is. It is something that only serves the science of mathematics. Every other human endeavor is necessarily fraught with nuances, with shadings, with spared feelings, with personal aggrandizement. Call a spade a spade? Only when you are playing cards.

"I'll give him your card," Jack said, putting his hand out for a card, as though that would be an easy end to it.

"I don't have cards," I heard myself say, "that's for small-timers."

His eyebrows were on the rise again.

"Well, give me your name and office address, he'll have somebody check you out."

"I'm not a guy who sits in an office," I said, astonishing even myself with the dire depths of my deception. "Results is my middle name. And," I added with just the right touch of hauteur, "my phone is unlisted."

"So how do people get a hold of you?"

"They don't," I said. "I call them."

Now the dark eyebrows went whacko. "You don't know my boss," he said.

"And maybe I'd be just as well-off getting through life without knowing him."

He frowned and gave a curt nod that he must have thought was noncommittal.

"Tell you what," I said. "Let him know we talked. I'll call you in a couple days. If he's interested, I'll meet him." Then I added, unknowingly, the clincher: "By the way, I work like the ambulance-chasing lawyers: I don't find his daughter, I don't get paid."

A smile crossed his face, like a man realizing the razor being held at his neck was just for shaving. "He'll like that," he said, writing his phone number on a photocopy of a walking tour of the palms at Bernuli Junior College. "Sometimes he's so tight, he squeaks."

2

He had given me the time and address on the phone in hushed tones, as though it were a secret.

I hailed from Los Angeles County. My destination was Santa Barbara County–a nice place to visit, but I couldn't afford to live there.

Driving our freeways gives you a perfect opportunity to see what a desert we live in. A land fried by persistent sun, too little rain, and occasionally fire. Green and brown, with the emphasis on the latter. And it's a pallid green–not macho like the East.

California, they say, *does* have four seasons: fire, earthquake, flood and drought.

I am driving in one of the smallest cars produced in the continental United States–by Americans, for Americans. Little Americans.

I found the house by process of elimination. It was between higher and lower visible numbers. The front gate spanned the driveway to keep the riffraff in their place. I pushed the button on a white stucco post. A door opened in the wall, revealing a television camera.

"Who's there?" a voice inquired. It was singularly lacking in human warmth.

"Gil Yates," I said, trying to put some punch in my thin, trembling voice, giving him the phony I had settled on. He wouldn't remember Gil Favor and Rowdy Yates from *Rawhide*. He wasn't in the country when it aired. The gate swung open and for the shortest moment I felt important. After I started up the long driveway, I saw the tiny address carved in a piece of redwood on a metal stand–as though it were moved to a visible position on the street and back again as struck the owner's fancy.

I didn't think hiding the address for my visit was a good sign. They would have to put it back for the mail delivery. Unless they were expecting a bomb.

Sometimes, fantasizing about getting a glamorous job can be more fun than the job itself. If you get the job, the thing is often not quite what it was cracked up to be. Instead of glamour, you are stuck with drudgery. The fantasy scoops off the cream. I should know–I am a guy whose fun moments have been more fantasy than fact.

Even my passionate hobby of palm growing can be more anticipation than realization. Most palms and cycads grow so slowly, you are forever anticipating what they are going to look like. And when they finally do grow to maturity they are so tall all you can see is the trunk–the least appealing part of the tree.

I had fun fantasizing about being a private eye. It was, I reasoned, the most outlandish of my fantasies. But here I was, anyway, trying to see how far I could push it.

Getting to the house from the street was as uneventful as a smooth crossing of the Atlantic Ocean. And almost as long.

The driveway to Michael Hadaad's house was a wonder to behold. It was a half-mile long and had three generous hairpin curves in it. The land was skillfully planted with bushes and tall trees so that when you arrived at the house via this circuitous route you didn't realize that you were only 50 feet from a side street that could have given you a short, straight-shot at the front door. But what kind of impression would that have made?

On the edge of the cliff dropping off to the Pacific Ocean sat the splendiferous digs, which I recognized in an instant. It was featured in those glossy, glitzy magazines–every last one of them–and each in its multi-paged garish display of wealth mentioned what a private person the owner was.

The house was a Moorish castle, not to say boorish, fashioned out of studs, plasterboard and stucco, whacked here and there to give it just the right Moorish curves and arches, balconies and turrets. It was spread all over the place, with one story here, two stories there and three stories over there.

I parked my Plymouth in the driveway: Palm Springs gold stones, one of the chichi mags pointed out, named for their outrageous cost. My Plymouth was issued to me by my father-in-law, in whose legitimate employ I was. You've seen the ad:

Handles well in tight
financial situations.

And my father-in-law is the tightest financial situation known to man. He drove a Chrysler New Yorker. He was nuts about Lee Iacocca, who didn't share the feeling, because he didn't know him. I always secretly suspected that if Iacocca *had* known my father-in-law, he still wouldn't have shared the feeling.

There were two carved front doors, either one big enough to drive my Plymouth through. A cheeky mag told how many Moors it took to carve the doors. It was obscene.

There were palms everywhere, giant ones, not pipsqueaks like in my garden. I thought I was in heaven, and I had to fight the impulse to wander, because somehow I got the feeling that I would be asking for a bullet between some sensitive organs.

I grasped the bronze knocker—shaped like a horseshoe, with the side up that held all the luck in it, and was suddenly seized with an irrational urge to spill the luck out.

The door was opened, after an executive-style wait, by a guy who put me in mind of Quasimodo without the charm. He stood about nineteen hands high and coincidentally weighed in at about nineteen stone. But somewhere in that assemblage of bone and muscle and little else, his neck had disappeared and his earlobes just sort of rested on his shoulders.

"This way, please," Quasimodo said. At least, I saw his lips move. The sound of his bass-heavy voice seemed to be coming from a sophisticated sound system in the ceiling. The way he said it, I was grateful for the "please."

As I followed his back down the half-acre corridor to the master's chamber in the rear, I made a mental note not to cross this monster. And that went in spades for his boss.

A gentle rap on the door with hard-as-brass knuckles elicited a "Come in" response in a hoarse-breezy voice that paled next to his functionary's. Quasimodo opened the door and nodded for me to enter–but it was such a foreboding nod that I had second thoughts–the kind of nod that said, "Go on in–if you have the guts." Guts was something I might be fairly accused of being short of. Finally I thought, what the heck, it's only a lark anyway, and I started the trek to the business end of a capacious library.

The desk seemed as far from the door as Catalina Island. As I swam toward it I realized how naive I had been. This smallish figure sitting at a desk the size of a Civil War battlefield was dressed to kill, and that's what I was afraid of.

As I drew closer I caught the nautical thrust of the garb: a blue blazer with a white shirt, blue silk cravat sprinkled with red and white semaphore flags, and when he finally stood to greet me I saw the white slacks with creases in them as sharp as samurai swords.

He put out his hand in greeting. He was swarthy-handsome with black eyes that could kill. Close up I saw that his costume was perfect for one of the glitz mags that featured him as the private-person-of-the-month. Bandbox pure.

"I'm Michael Hadaad," he said. "Thank you for coming."

Michael Hadaad was not the name he gave me. Nor is it his real name. It isn't even close, so don't try to guess. I don't want any repercussions.

"Gil Yates," I said, and checked those kamikaze eyes for sign of suspicion. I saw nothing there you wouldn't find in the eyes of an everyday Joseph Stalin. I tried to break the ice I felt enshrouding me.

"Is that a *Chrysalidocarpus lucubensis* by the front door?" I asked.

He looked at me as though I were speaking a foreign language, which, in a way, I was.

"The palm," I said.

"Oh, the palm. I'm afraid I don't know the names, just what they cost."

"A pretty penny for that one, I'm sure," I said, my voice quavering in the hope he would share his fabulous secrets with a fellow palm nut.

"I daresay," he said. "If they don't cost 'a pretty penny', as you say, I don't buy them. There is no sense in having money if you spend it like the common folk."

"I daresay," I said, and immediately regretted it.

He looked at me as if to determine if I were mocking him. He was short and stood erect like Hitler and Napoleon had.

In case you were liable to miss the point, our meeting was to be in this two-story library–the second-story bookshelves were accessed by ladders and catwalks.

My host's desk was at the end of this splendor. "Stunning in its magnificence," *Architectural Glitz* trumpeted, as though hyping some B-movie.

The neat white cap with the gold-braided anchor, front and center, perched atop the desk like the crown jewels. It had a shiny black visor covered with the scrambled eggs of a very-high-ranking naval officer.

I chuckled to myself–a nervous chuckle. "This is some place," I said. "You get it from the Hearsts?"

"No," he said, putting an effective cap on my inept small talk. Being a slow learner, I tried again:

"Fantastic library. These leather-bound books look smashing. Are they all first editions?"

He waved a hand of insouciance. "The interior deco-

10

rator picked them for the colors and the sizes."

I gave up. Sooner or later he would tell me what he wanted, one or both of us would fall asleep, or one or both of us would up and skedaddle. He was staring at me as though checking for minute physical flaws. I had plenty and would have been glad to catalog them for him myself if he had asked.

I guess my main flaw was I was about six inches taller than he was–he was about five and a half in those elevators and I was a notch under six when I straightened up, which was seldom. Surely he could not accuse me of lording my height over him.

Others might say I am flawed by my subservience to my in-laws. I work for my father-in-law and, they say, live under the thumb of my wife. I rather think of it as a go-with-the-flow kind of life. I made my pact with the devil many years ago and I have pretty much stuck with it. Call it a flaw if you want, I'm loyal to a fault.

Sometimes because I don't push or argue I am accused of being henpecked. Sometimes because I work for my father-in-law I am considered without ambition. Palm growing or gardening in general can be successfully done by the mentally deficient, so wouldn't it follow that I was if not exactly deficient, no Einstein either?

In keeping with my laid-back personality, I don't argue with the charges. You know what they say: "A man convinced against his will, is of the same opinion still."

"Sit down," he said at last, and waved me toward the wooden plank bench that faced his desk. He took his seat behind the battlefield.

"Would you like something to drink?"

"Oh, no, thanks," I said, and checked his face to see if I had pleased him. I couldn't see a crack in his inscrutable facade.

What is it about the super-rich that makes them so different? And yet much the same?

Strip them all and put them in a room full of just folks and don't let them say anything and you might have a hard time.

But with Michael Hadaad you'd pick him right out. He had arrogance in his eyes–unless he was trying to snow you. Then the eyes turned to a twinkle of charm. I was getting the twinkle.

"Now then," he said, and I wondered if he meant now or then–or perhaps both. Probably neither. "My gardener informs me you are a private detective..."

"Yes."

"*Very* private, I'm told."

"I am discreet in the extreme," I countered.

Michael Hadaad prided himself on his stone face. Inscrutable. But I saw a twitch of disdain. "How, sir, am I to verify you are a licensed detective without being able to check references?"

"That's easy," I said. "Call the state. They'll tell you I don't have a license."

"You *don't* have a license?" his left eye was drawing a bead on one of my eyebrows.

"That's correct."

"Why, that's *crazy*. How could I ever check on you? What control would I have?"

"Control?"

"Yes."

"What is your fear?"

"That I pay you a handsome sum and you deliver nothing."

"Oh, but you don't pay unless I deliver. Didn't Jack tell you that?"

"Oh, he told me. I didn't believe it."

"A thousand a day and expenses?" I said. "Terribly tacky."

The way his cheek hoisted his lips, scrunching down one eyebrow, I could tell he was betraying admiration. For nothing is so sacred to the filthy rich as the preservation of capital.

"All right," he said, "give me some references, people I can call who can vouch for your work, I'll get back to you."

I shook my head. "No references," I said as resolutely as any hanging judge giving the final sentence. I surprised even myself–but not as much as I surprised Michael Hadaad.

His palm hit his battlefield desk, I'd say inadvertently because Gotrocks Hadaad I pegged for a guy who fought to contain his emotions. "The last straw," he murmured.

"Would you want me to give your name and phone number as a reference?" I asked.

He stared at me with those ice-water eyes, as though I were plumb out of my mind.

I spread my hands in the air to say: "There you have it." "I don't work for people who would allow me to bother them for a reference," I said, putting the cap on the deal. And it was true. As true as if I had said simply, "I don't work for anybody." Was it my fault if he chose to interpret a different way?

A woman breezed into the room. About Michael Hadaad's height, with an expensive blond dye job, with the finest of full figures oozing out of a disappearing waist. She was adorned with the chicest ebony silk sheath and the rarest of jewels. Like everything else around the place, she was expensive.

She bent down to kiss his cheek.

"Darling," she purred, "I'm going shopping." She looked like she'd be very good at shopping and a lot of other things.

Hadaad didn't introduce me. I was strangely flattered by that omission. Any contact I had with a woman that gorgeous would be strictly fantasy. If I ran into her in a parking lot and she propositioned me, I would most likely faint dead away. Sometimes I think all of life is repressed sexuality. Chalk it up to another personal flaw.

As she left, I hoped that my staring at her sensuously undulating gluteus muscles was not obvious to my host. It was a forlorn hope. But rather than anger him, it seemed to please him. She had been chosen, I later realized, like everything else: because of her price.

"All right," he drawled, signaling his desire to return

to the business at hand. "Let me recap this. You have no license, no references and you don't charge a fee or expenses unless you complete the job to my satisfaction?"

I raised my hand to show the captain. "Now that's a loophole big enough to drive a battleship through. We agree in advance on parameters. I achieve that, I get my fee." I paused for my bomb. I had thought about this a long time–and it just seemed right for this pigeon. "And that fee will be four, five times what you'd pay a run-of-the-mill shamus."

He blanched. "And how much would *that* be?"

"Tell me what you want accomplished."

He sank back in his seat. The moment of truth for the captain. Will he really go down with the ship? When he started to tell me his story, I knew I was close to home.

"I have one child," he said wistfully. "A daughter named Alecia. I loved her very much."

I noticed the past tense, but held my tongue.

He frowned, then rubbed the back of his neck under his longish dark hair. Did he realize he used the wrong tense? "She had problems–I don't say they were any worse than your normal teenager's problems, and maybe I did overreact. It's so hard to know what the perfect response is to any challenge your kid throws at you.

"Do you have children, Mr., ah, what was it?"

"Yates. I have a girl and a boy."

"And a wife?"

"Alas, yes."

He seemed perplexed.

"Is that bad?" I ventured. It may not have been so hot from my standpoint, but I didn't see why it should bother him.

"No, no," he hastened to assure me. "It's just that, well, I thought most of you guys were single, divorced, foot-loose-and-fancy-free, hard-drinking sports."

I shook my head. "The small-timers, maybe. I don't even drink."

Was that admiration I saw on his stoic kisser?

"She was anorexic," he said softly, a little ashamed. "Bulimic. I tried to help her. I couldn't do anything. I put her in an institution. The best money could buy," he hastened to add, unnecessarily. He paused to control his breathing–to drain the flush from his face. "She escaped. Hasn't been seen since."

"How long ago?"

"Nine months or so."

"Been to the police? The FBI? Missing persons?"

He stared at me as though it were a naive question. "She's an adult. They seemed to spit on me. They went through some motions," he said. "Nothing came of it." Then he added, as though it surprised him, "I think they resented me."

"Why?"

"The way they acted. What do cops make now–twenty, thirty a year? Bound to be some resentment," he said, waving his hand to encompass his expensive property. "I never felt comfortable with them."

"Do you feel comfortable with me?"

He gave me the frozen fish eye. "I don't know yet."

"What is it you want? Just a notice that she is alive–or dead–or physical possession?"

He looked at me as though his nose were a gunsight. "Well, I would expect to see her," he said. "I mean, I don't doubt your integrity, but I'd have to have the physical evidence."

"Is it possible she won't want to see you?"

Darts came through the eyes. "Why would she not?" he faltered. I think I heard his voice break. "Of course...it's...possible." He put a spin on "possible," like anything was possible but he would just as soon not think it could be in this case. When he regained his composure, he asked, "So what would you charge?"

Here we were at the moment of truth. I had rehearsed my blasé response to this inevitable question in front of the bathroom mirror in our tract house. I had honed it to as near believable perfection as I was capable of bringing off. But now my tongue seemed to stick to my lower teeth. Michael Hadaad didn't let his gaze waver. Finally I shook my head, once. "Phew," I said with as much bravado as my thumping heart would allow. "Gonna be expensive."

"How expensive?" he asked, cocking an eye of suspicion.

"Not so simple," I said. "I bring her here and she's happy to come, I'd settle for two hundred."

"Two hundred dollars?" He thought he had gotten lucky.

"Two hundred thousand," I corrected him.

"Two..." he choked. "That's ridiculous!"

This is where my art came in. I nodded, the soul of understanding, and stood to leave. I nodded again, in acknowledgment of his hospitality, and said, "I quite understand. My fees are a lot higher than the run of the mill. There are many available for a lot less."

He just stared at me, as though I were the first person to ever walk out on him. For my part, I was not as bummed at the prospect of losing the case or the fee–it was a lark anyway–as I was of losing the opportunity to see his palm collection.

I turned to leave. I had not taken three steps when I heard the mighty Michael Hadaad say, "No, wait."

I smiled to myself before I turned. Now I cocked my eye–as he had done so expertly.

He answered: "You had the guts to get up. Most people can't see past their fee. Sit down."

I did.

"Is there room for negotiation?"

"I don't nickel and dime," I said. "I don't submit chits for meals and gas. But I'm afraid I've only given you the low side."

Up went the eyelids.

I nodded. God, I thought, is he buying this? But how could he? "If she doesn't want to come, it will be a half-million."

16

He sank back in his chair. I stood again, but faced him. "I quite understand your reluctance, Mr. Hadaad. I am used to working for the extremely wealthy, exclusively."

He waved me back into my seat, without looking.

"The good news is, if I don't find her, you pay nothing, not even my gasoline. If she is, well, if she is no longer living and I can document her death, it will cost only one hundred thousand." I noticed a show of approval on his face. That seemed his favorite option. Then he frowned, as if considering some ramification.

"No, no," he said hastily, in apparent defense to my take on him, "I want her alive. I want to make amends. I *love* her." This last came out as though an untrained actor were declaiming Shakespeare without really understanding it.

"Please feel free to shop around. I know of no one else as expensive as I." I paused, then tossed off, "Of course, I don't know anyone as effective either. But the choice is yours. I pegged you as a man who didn't stint on cost when the object was important."

"Yes," he said so distantly I thought he had left the room.

"Well, why don't you think it over," I announced boldly. "If you want to find your daughter, there is no one better suited to do it discreetly, efficiently, albeit expensively. In this world, Mr. Hadaad, we get what we pay for, do we not?"

He nodded abstractedly. His mind was elsewhere.

"Leave me your card," he said.

"I don't have..."

"That's right, you don't have cards," he said as if a matter of only minor annoyance.

"I'll give you a call," I said to cut him off from asking me for the phone number I did not yet have. Then, to get him completely off the subject, I asked if I might look at his palm trees.

"Sure," he said, recovering from what must have been a traumatic negotiating wipe-out for a man who was congenitally accustomed to having the last word. "Be my guest," and he stood to lead me through a side door from his library to the garden. "You know Jack—he'll be out here somewhere. Just help yourself," and, distracted, he went back into the house.

3

I gave it a day and then, from a phone booth near my father-in-law's office, I called Jack Kimback, Michael Hadaad's gardener. I missed him when I was ogling the palms.

"That's some palm collection," I said, as though that were the purpose of my call.

"The most extensive in the country. He's working on the World Cup now."

"Does he like palms?"

"Not so I could notice. He rarely looks at them. He's a sportsman collector."

"Sportsman?" I hadn't heard the term.

"He collects trophies," he said. "I'm glad you called. He wants to see you. I think you got his attention, whatever you did." And he gave me the master's unlisted number.

"How is he to work for?" I asked.

"Peaches and cream," Jack said with the wrong sort of inflection.

I called the number from the same phone booth. Quasimodo answered. Who needs an unlisted phone when you never answer it yourself?

"Ah, yes," he boomed out of the ceiling sound system

still, "Mr. Yates. Mr. Hadaad is anxious to see you. He would like to come to your office, at your convenience."

My heart was on a Ping-Pong table. A net ball. "I don't see people at my office," I said. "Confidentiality," I explained. "I do nothing that might breach it."

"I see," he said in the voice that told me he didn't. "I'm afraid his minimum requirement for the contract will be to have an address and a phone where he can reach you." He paused to listen to me breathe. "I do hope you won't find that unreasonable," he said unctuously. "You *are* asking a sizable fee, with no license and no references. Mr. Hadaad was impressed with you–I've no idea why–but he is a very careful man. So the ball is in your court."

My turn to listen to *him* breathe. "I'm in the process of moving," I said. "I'll call you in a couple days with my new number," and I hung up before he could ask where I was moving *to*.

Well! Apparently my performance with Mr. Gotrocks was as successful as I'd imagined, even though he wasn't quite ready to roll over and play dead.

If I was going to be a private detective, I thought I should look like one, rather than the junior high school biology teacher my looks have been compared with.

I don't know about you, but to me being a private eye means a trench coat with the collar pulled up to cover the ears and one of those narrow brimmed natty hats they call fedoras.

I already had the hat. One of those melodramatic dermatologists sliced what he called a "cancer" out of my cheek and told me in a quiet voice that it was not a life-threatening event. I did notice he seemed to enjoy calling it a "cancer" and in his loud voice he said I'd better wear sunscreen, 15 or stronger, and a hat might be a good idea too. The unspoken consequences of disregarding his advice would be a painful decaying death by the ravages of creeping, crawling skin cancer.

Having been something of a coward in my prime I bought the whole bit: tubs of sunscreen (25, just to be safe) and every hat I could get my hands on. I figured I could deduct the hats from my income tax as a medical expense.

I feel it is incumbent on me at this juncture to set the record straight vis-á-vis the hats. I wear them solely as sun protection for my face. The insidious inference by my wife and children–and even my father-in-law who should surely know better–that I wear the hats to cover a negligible bald spot is totally without foundation.

For the trench coat, I was not in the mood to go cheap. So I sashayed over to the Brooks Brothers in Century City to try on their version.

Fortunately, I had a very perceptive salesman who took one look at me in the tan trench coat with the collar pulled up to cover my ears and the gray fedora brim pulled down to cover my eyebrows and said, "If you will pardon my saying so, sir, you look dashingly rakish in the coat and fedora."

A man of that perspicacity deserved to make the sale. I wore the coat out of the store and flatter myself to say that I noticed quite a few women looking my way.

The phone company was most obliging. They would install two days after I told them where. They offered to answer my calls for a friendly fee. Voice mail they called it. So I wouldn't become dependent on yet another fallible piece of mechanical goods.

Now all I needed was an office. Nothing down and pennies a day. Rentals were soft all over Southern California.

I called Saul Jerome, a guy I met years ago at some real estate management course. Over the years we traded favors. Most recently I found a place in one of our buildings for his girlfriend, who wasn't aces with the credit bureau. It seemed like it was my turn.

I met him at this brick monstrosity in Hollywood. Hollywood was really Los Angeles, but the post office folk were liberal about delivering mail addressed to Hollywood, CA 90028. I thought it might have a reverse snob cachet.

Saul was a guy who liked his pastrami sandwiches, and he was past hiding it.

"You ask low rent," he said in greeting me, "you get low rent."

I groaned. "Low rent, yeah," I granted him, "but this place is low self-esteem."

"Malvin, Malvin," he said, "verily I say unto you, in this world you get what you pay for." He took me down the hall, where we descended some stairs to the basement. He opened a door and flicked his hand to part the cobwebs, and I beheld a dark chamber which could have been designed by Edgar Allan Poe.

"Saulie, Saulie," I said, "what is anyone gonna think, they see this hole?"

He shrugged his shoulders. "Eccentric," he said, with the kiss of a question.

I shook my head. "Brain-dead," I said. "Not to say dirt poor. Don't you have any spiffy buildings where I could rent a broom closet or something?"

He pouted, then drove me–in his BMW with very high numbers–to an elegant facade across town. "Best I got," he said.

"Now you're talkin' my language," I said. I always slipped into sloppy speech when I spoke with Saul. I don't know why–there was nothing wrong with his accent, even though he had dark ties to The Bronx.

"But now I'm talking rents in the arm-and-leg category. Nine bills a month for the worst. You want to pay that?"

"Not yet. Don't you have any broom closets?"

"They all got brooms in 'em."

"I don't mind sharing."

It was while he was showing me his minimal offering

that I got my inspiration. "Hey," I said, "what are these walls made of?"

"Studs and plasterboard," he said. "Why?"

I walked back out of the room to the hallway. It was carpeted in puce pile, the doors were dark mahogany with brass levers. We were at the back end of the second floor but it was well-lit with recessed lighting. The place was class, but $900 the month, $10,000 plus the annum, was completely out of the question at this juncture.

"Who owns this joint?" I asked.

"Bunch of guys in New York. What difference does that make?"

"Big difference. They don't come out here much?"

"Never."

"Perfect," I gloated, and told him what I had in mind.

He groaned.

"Look," I said, "the office is empty. The next guy won't notice any difference."

Saul started laughing, a Santa Claus kind of laugh. "You're nuts, Malvin, nuttier 'n a fruitcake." But Saul was a good sport, if nothing else, and the deal was made. Fifty a month, I pay the "alterations," and I could get one of those swell mahogany doors with a brass lever, with a mail slot, a lock and a sign that said:

Shamus
N. Andee

And I would be legit. Low overhead doesn't save *you* money, but it saves *me*.

The door was to go on the wall. We'd only have to take out one vertical stud and wouldn't disturb the wall behind it. If anybody wanted to verify my office, let them come ahead. Of course I wouldn't be there. Nothing fatter than spaghetti would fit in that space.

Of course I couldn't hire anyone I knew to do the work, so Saul saw to that. We brought it off for a shade under five bills, only I decided to go more sedate on the door sign.

**Gil Yates
Private Investigation
By appointment**

I decided against doing the phone number. Not only was I paying by the letter, I didn't covet any walk-ins–not in the practice I was building. Besides, if anyone walked into *that* office, they were going to need a nose job. My new office was only two inches deep.

I was ready for another go at the great Hadaad. On my way to see him, after fabricating a whopper for my wife, I realized the toughest part of this gig was not going to be dealing with a rich, powerful client who *always* had his way; it was going to be dealing with my powerful glass-blowing wife. Her name was not Tyrannosaurus Rex, but I called her Tyranny Rex for short–but not to her face. I had trouble enough.

Her father, my boss, would be no piece of cake either, since most of my investigating would have to be done on his time. But I have been a pretty loyal soldier over twenty-some annual reports, and he wasn't riding my tail like he used to.

Oh, he was still riding *me*, but it wasn't the same.

Back in Santa Helena by the Sea, a couple hours up the coast in my trembling Plymouth, I was delighted to see Hadaad's redwood address sign stuck on the street side of the gate. Maybe it was an omen.

Ever notice how when you finally get help in life, you don't need it?

I got inside the inner sanctum with a lot less fanfare this time. Hadaad and I were squaring off over the battlefield.

24

I gave him my new address and phone number. "I must warn you, these are nuisance formalities. I never sit in my office, or answer my phone. I don't have help, I don't want to chance any breaches of confidence."

He nodded in acceptance, not approval. "Do you want my attorney to draw up the contract?" he asked.

"That's up to you," I said with a careless casualness.

"How would you be sure of getting your fee without it?"

"Good question. Any guy who has lawyers to make contracts can get the same guys to get them out of it. I figure you must have a burning desire to see your daughter–or to know she doesn't exist anymore–for whatever reason. If I find her, I get my money before you get the girl. If she's, ah, deceased, I get my fee before you get the proof."

"What about the other option? If she comes willingly, I save three hundred thousand dollars. How will I be sure you haven't bribed her with half of that–to appear hard-to-get?"

"Mr. Hadaad, I think we both know getting your daughter back to you will take all kinds of legerdemain and chicanery. If she was willing to see you, she would have come back long ago. And your need, whatever its basis, must be worth a half-million to you or I wouldn't be here."

"It's love," he said, trying to soft-soap me again, but, if anything, it sounded even flatter than before.

"That's a lot of love," I said.

He fidgeted. I had angered him. "You can't put a price on parental love. A man of my resources. What's a half-million against the love for one's daughter? Why, this house cost six times that–so did the land."

"Yes," I said in a tone midway between "That's nice" and "You don't expect me to swallow that one whole, do you?" Instead I asked, "Do you have any pictures of her?"

He opened the middle drawer of the battlefield and pulled out a bound book and passed it over the table to me. I paged through it and saw it contained scores of pictures of one beautiful filly. She had the dark hair and eyes of her father and she held her head like a filly being reined in by a tough rider. "Where is her mother?" I asked.

Hadaad glared at me. "I do not wish to interfere in your investigation in any way, but if you make any contact with that despicable woman our relationship will be instantly severed."

"That bad?" I asked.

"Worse. In fact I think I will have the attorneys insert a clause to that effect in the contract."

"How long were you married to her?"

"Way *too* long," he said.

"You don't think she might help find the girl?"

"No, I don't. I expect her mother is the main cause of her disappearance in the first place." He waved a hand in disgust, chopping the air as though he held a grudge against it. "Oh, the cops found her in some hovel someplace. She didn't know anything. They just had to listen to a torrent of her hateful opinion of me. What's the point?"

"Well, she might give me some leads. Sometimes we swallow a little pride to get what we want–especially if we want it bad enough."

He shook his head. He was telling me with that grim head toss that the matter was closed.

To him maybe; not to me. Who could resist a challenge like that? What did I have to lose? I'd already seen the palms. And I really had serious doubts about getting the fee, even if I found the girl. O'Melveny and Meyers, at $500 the hour, would find a loophole. But who could, or would, give me the lowdown on the big mogul like the ex-wife–mother of the missing person?

I didn't know much, but I had a powerful suspicion it wasn't love that was behind his burning need to see his daughter.

With a little more cat-and-mouse sparring, and collecting all the helpful information he was willing to give me, I was cut loose from the battlefield and sent on my way. I promised to stay in touch, but for some reason wasn't looking forward to that part of it.

4

Now for the hard part. Working all this in with my job and my "marriage."

Back from Santa Helena, I swung the Plymouth into the parking lot of Elbert A. Wemple and Associates, Realtors. I found the last space, as far from the door as you could park. There was only one reserved space next to the door. That was for the big cheese himself, Elbert A. Wemple.

I left my trench coat in the car when I alighted. Nice word, "alighted." While I hated to be without the coat, I wasn't up to the ridicule I would take from daddybucks when he saw me looking like Sherlock Holmes. Besides I must remember to keep my P.I. persona separate from my high property management profile.

The building was a flat-roofed clump of earth-tone beige stucco. Inside, the place looked like any number of bloated real estate franchises in the heyday of California real estate, where virtually anyone with a real estate license could get rich.

Desk upon desk in a cavernous windowless room; a few, for the top producers and yours truly, the income property supervisor, were fenced in with nose-high (while seated) prefab blond wood walls.

The theory was that the nose height was so the boss could see if you were thumbing your nose at him.

It might be considered a tribute to my boss' estimation of me that my desk was still out on the floor with the peons.

My father-in-law is, for want of a nastier word, rich. He backed into real estate at the perfect moment in the history of the world and bought apartment buildings with the passion of William Randolph Hearst going after faux Greek statues.

He is the modern prototype of Sinclair Lewis' Babbitt, whom he never heard of because he doesn't read.

I read. And when I read *Babbitt*, I said, "There he is, that's my father-in-law, Elbert August Wemple."

So, you may ask, how come I work for him–and for twenty-three years? It certainly isn't the money. He still has his first nickle. Quite frankly, I was trapped.

Way back I was nuts about his daughter. Since I am not what you would call a forceful character, she did not seem to be quite as nuts about me. She reminded me often about the numerous opportunities she had, so I started promising things to stay in the running. Ridiculous things–stupid things. Like sure I would work for her father (real estate property management wasn't low on my list of careers, it wasn't even *on* the list). And like sure we would go into hock for the rest of our lives for that cute house she had to have. Her father took the mortgage and the commission.

Three points on the loan and a half-percent higher than the bank-rate. "High risk," he cited.

Oh, I've taken a lot over the years, but I've gotten little revenges, now and again. Like my palm garden. I got interested in palm trees five years ago. It isn't something you can explain, being a palm nut, it just grabs and consumes you. If you want to be realistic about it, palms are pretty absurd plants–the way they grow from a seed to a thing that looks like a blade of grass that can cost you a hundred bucks and just as likely as not conk out on you as soon as you put it in the ground. And they develop out of the ground headfirst, but one leaf at a time. That leaf pokes slowly up all bundled up in this lengthening cylinder, then bursts open to its full complex form. Then the process begins again. After five or six years you see the full head of the palm sticking out of the ground. Then the next thrill is watching the trunk develop. As it does, the head starts pushing its way to the sky and, before you know it (fifteen years or so), all you can see is the trunk and the bottom of the fronds. Unless you build platforms, like some palm nut I know. He walks on the platform to look down at his fifteen-foot-tall trees.

Well, I could fill a whole book with what I know about palms, and maybe a couple-dozen books with what I *don't* know about them.

Elbert A. Wemple, chief executive officer, president and sole owner of Elbert A. Wemple and Associates, Realtors, sat in an elevated portion of the building, in a glass cage, like the damn King of Siam. The glass shut out the buzz of activity from the forty-some desks on the floor, but afforded him an uninterrupted view of the water cooler, should anyone waste too much time drinking water.

Actually the water wasn't cooled. Daddy Wemple (as his charming daughter called him) was too cheap to cool it for the troops. Room temperature it was. His glass cube had the cooler. I always made it a point to help myself to some cold water when I was in there.

Tyranny Rex started calling her father Daddy Wemple after her exposure to Daddy Warbucks in *Little Orphan Annie*. Some of us at the office called him Daddy Pimple–just to be mean.

And now, though his wealth would make Croesus blush, he's still at it, tooth and nail, piling useless dollar on useless dollar. He who dies with the most money, still dies. The man is amazing. He can still pinch a nickel till it screams bloody murder.

My desk was uncomfortably close to his (the better for him to see me thumbing my nose). This may be looked upon as an emblem of my importance to the company. I rather think it was because he thought I, a salaried employee, needed watching more than the commission-only flakes on the floor.

The biggest disadvantage was there was no way to make it to my desk from anywhere without passing his. Most of the time I said, "Howdy." Some of the time he would grunt. Too often he would hail me into his presence for a piddly report on some asinine pretense.

Daddy Wemple was a stout-hearted man. Stout-gutted too. His hair was leaving him as fast as his compassion had, so he grew some muttonchop whiskers to take your mind off his higher vacancy factor. He was a man who enthused more than he engaged his intellect, who rationalized more than he reasoned. He was fond of brown suits that seemed more rumpled than they were.

Today it was carpets. "What about that carpet over on Broadway? Can we dye it?"

Here was a guy with more money than he could spend in his lifetime if he had been a young man, still worried about saving a few bucks on an apartment carpet.

"Sure," I said.

"What would you do?"

"Replace it. It will look a lot better, make a happier tenant, last a lot longer and won't cost that much more."

He seemed to consider my opinion a moment longer than usual.

"Dye it," he said. I returned to my desk and called the manager of the Broadway Terraces.

"Guess what?" I asked when she answered.

"Dye it," she said. And she had only been with us six months.

I took some computer runs out of my desk drawer and pretended to ponder them while I was planning my moves on my real interest: finding Alecia Hadaad. All I could think of was earning the fee and blowing this job.

At the stroke of six, the salaried employees (there were six of us) rose as one and exited the cavern in haste, I among them.

Daddy Wemple always looked grumpy at this action, as though we ought to stay and kick in some extra time gratis, probably in gratitude for the twenty-buck bills he passed out at Christmas time.

I ducked into his office, swiped a paper cup and filled it with chilled water, then planted the seed.

"I'm beginning to wonder about our rents in the South Bay. I think I'll be doing a lot of rental surveys to get a better idea."

"Finally taking my advice," he said gratuitously. Then he added as an order to a very junior officer, "Get a handle on it."

I made it the eighteen miles to the tract home I shared with my beloved wife, Dorcas, who I less than lovingly referred to as Tyranny Rex the Glass Blower, but never, as I said, to her face.

She was my wife of twenty-three years—to the minute the time of my appearing on the payroll of Elbert A. Wemple and Associates, Realtors. It was as though he wasn't taking any chances hiring me while I could still back out on the wedding. He needn't have fretted. They didn't call me the Gutless Wonder for nothing.

We signed the loan and escrow papers on our new house, between the wedding and the reception. It was all done through Elbert A. Wemple Escrow.

Now, at home, Dorcas greeted me in her glass-blowing apron and announced dinner would be on the tardy side tonight as she was firing up for one of her sidewalk shows and she wanted to have "simply an army" of her ridiculous little glass figurines.

They had, believe it or not, named her Dorcas. After some rich aunt, as I remember, who showed them by dumping, on her demise, all her cash on the Sierra Club.

But, in fairness to the elder Wemples, they named the kid Dorcas before "dork" gained currency in the language. I can't say it wasn't apt; I can't say I haven't called her a dork a time or two. Not to her face, of course. I'm not *that* insensitive.

The Dork was built like a glass blower. She had, they said, the lungs for it. I often wonder what I saw in her all those years ago. She had a happy-go-lucky giggle, an engaging smile and enough push to get me to the altar. I was so stupidly shy of girls and she was top-notch at making me feel desired and lucky to get her, simultaneously.

Before I lay on you the bare bones of my marriage, let me say that nothing encouraged me more than the hubbub over equal rights. I would die for equal rights. My wife has been treating me as an inferior for years.

Our daughter, Felicity, is going into her fourth year of college and any day now expects to complete her second year of work. Well, at least she's out of the house. Much as I love her, the kid's character has an uncanny resemblance to those of her mother and my father-in-law. That's not all bad, but very little in it is good either.

Our son, August, named for his mother's father (and my boss, against my tacit wishes), is a *ballet dancer*! And does that drive his grandfather up the wall! I couldn't be more pleased. So August just up and sashayed to the Big Apple, where he waits on tables with his fellow aspirers, dancing his shoes off and praying for the big break.

The tardy dinner tonight was Campbell's tomato soup–made with *milk*. As I crumbled my saltine crackers into the bowl of frothing pink, I casually said, "I'm going to be doing a lot of work the next couple weeks. May even miss a few of your scrumptious dinners."

"Remember my Scotland trip is in less than two weeks," she said.

Every year she went to some Scottish festivities for glass blowers. They were my best weeks of the year.

"That's too bad," I said. "I'll miss you."

"In the pig's ear," she said.

5

The telephone installer had been quite amused when he saw where my telephone jack was to be installed.

"I'll be damn," he said when I opened the door and pointed to the wall inside it. "How you planning on getting a phone in there?"

"No phone," I said.

"So why the jack?"

I shook my head. "Just trying to stimulate the telephone business."

"I'll be damn," he said.

Saul Jerome had just made an extensive rent survey of the South Bay, and he was happy to let me rip it off. In my own words, of course. I figured this bit of fortune freed me for a good two to three weeks from over-scrutiny on the home front.

I was pleasantly surprised at how helpful the missing-persons cops were. I heard all these clichés about nasty policemen, but I discovered right away they treat you pretty much as you treat them–like you, me and Alfred E. Neuman.

The atmosphere in the police station was not unlike that of my own work station. Colorless and impersonal.

The big difference, I decided, between a cop's lot and mine was the cop got a pension.

Of course Daddy Wemple would never let his fair-haired darling starve, but she was my pension. It was a further incentive to crack this case. Five hundred Gs would allow me to rise above the modest circumstances to which I had been reduced and enable me to spring for a couple nice-sized cycads.

I settled in with one Sergeant Weiss, who had done the foot work on Alecia Hadaad.

If Weiss was ever on traffic, I could see the girls stomping on the gas just to get stopped by this hulk with dimples.

If that appears sexist to you, remember that all sexism is not unrealistic.

We were at his G.I. desk. "Hadaad," he said. "Never found her. From the look of her pictures, I wish I had."

"How hard did you look?" I asked, then realized he might be insulted. He wasn't.

"We gave it the old college try." He seemed to be recalling something. "You know, it wasn't top priority around here. She's an adult and we couldn't find the slightest evidence of foul play–besides..." he trailed off to nothing.

"Besides what?" I prodded him.

The dimples creased. "You working for her old man...I'd better not."

"Go on," I encouraged him. "I hardly know him."

"Well, he's a little on the pushy side, wouldn't you say? Didn't take long to find that out. After a couple prods by Big Shot we were kind of getting the picture on why she would want to flee. You know what I mean?"

I nodded.

"Why are you in this thing?" he asked.

"Money," I said.

He nodded. "Best reason." Then he paused to consider. "I don't know what it would take in bucks to get me to throw that girl to that wolf. I hope you're getting a lot."

"Remains to be seen," I said. "You ever meet her mother–Hadaad's ex-wife?"

"Yeah." Then shook his head in somber reflection. "You meet her?"

"Not yet."

"A basically decent woman."

"Give you any theories?"

"Not really. Aside from the feeling we got that she didn't blame Alecia. There was this vital, intelligent, gorgeous young girl stuck away in a sanitarium for fruitcakes–well, she got away, which was no big deal seeing how lax the security was. What was surprising was how the trail had instantly frozen. No one at the home had any inkling of what happened to her. As though the earth opened and swallowed her.

"Alecia's mother came to see her. They went out for walks together. She came four or five times to the old man's one. He always looked so disdainful, they told me. I wasn't surprised. He always looked that way to me too. You?"

"Pretty much," I agreed. "What's your take on the funny farm?"

"The Bright Side Sanitarium? One of the best. Lot of rich stow their embarrassments there: drugs, booze, obesity, anorexia."

"Success rate?"

Sergeant Weiss shrugged his massive shoulders. "Some, I suppose. But you know it's the cause of these things that matters. You got to get at the roots, and the roots are usually underground. Rich, preoccupied daddy, psychotic mommy. The kids are often helpless victims. I really don't know what success they have–why don't you ask them?"

"Thanks, I will," I said. "Who's the best bet for info out there?"

He went to the next cubbyhole and opened a file drawer. He brought one of them back to his desk and leafed through the pages. "Here it is," he said. "Doctor Elsie Schaeffer," he said.

"Shrink?"

"With a heart."

"Thanks," I said. "Can you think of anything else I should know?"

He thought a minute. "Nah," he said, "it's nothing. Just a hunch."

35

"Hunches are often the best," I said, without saying the best what. Without, in fact, knowing anything at all about hunches. It just came tumbling out, as though I were a seasoned investigator who knew what he was doing.

"I always doubted his story–the father, I mean," he said. "Oh, it's not unusual to have them hiding something important, but the way he went on about this daughter, you knew two things: One, he was crazy to find her, and, two, he didn't care a fig for her personally."

I thanked the sergeant and promised to keep in touch.

Before I left he gave me the address he had for Mrs. Michael Hadaad. I didn't really want to cross my principal, but it seemed a little bizarre and silly not to consult the mother of the missing person.

6

The trees that lined the driveway to the low buildings of the Bright Side Sanitarium were fuzzy and warm. It gave me a real homey feeling just getting there. There were pines, mostly, no palms.

Once in the compound, I felt more like I was in one of those Polynesian Hawaiian hotels than a funny farm. Here and there were scattered the most common king and queen palms. They were the fastest growers. That's why they were so common.

Elsie Schaeffer set me straight. She greeted me in her office with hearty good cheer and made me feel like she had not a care in the world and no better way to spend her time than to squander her PR energy on a nobody detective.

You know how the guys said there were no really beautiful nuns? That inner-beauty stuff aside. That if a girl had a half-decent shot at getting married, she wouldn't sentence herself to life in some hidden damp-and-dreary unisex monastery.

Some of the guys said the same about girls who went to med school. But if you laid your eyes on Dr. Elsie, you wouldn't peg her for a nun–but maybe for med school. Big, rawboned and a sun-dried face, she probably would have looked younger had she shunned the sun. But the inner beauty was there in spades, and her beaming smile was as warm and fuzzy as the trees beside the driveway and sucked you unsuspectingly to her happy bosom.

We sat together on a floral-print couch she had against the wall. Probably her patients used the same couch. I wondered if she sat with them. I guessed she did. The whole thing was so damn democratic.

There were blues and greens in the couch flowers, which, along with the white background carried the color scheme for the room. It looked like it had housed two beds in its past.

"I'll tell you what I can," she lead off, "but it won't be much. I've been over this with all the agencies and your two predecessors."

That was news to me. No one mentioned other private investigators.

"I have a feeling if there is a key to this thing, it isn't here. She left us. She vanished. She had almost no associations among the guests. Very little interaction with the staff. A nice enough girl, but very withdrawn and private."

"Did you get a feel for her family situation?"

"I met her parents, of course."

"And?..."

"It's pretty easy to get cynical here. We get our share of parents at the end of their rope. Men and women, often no longer living together, who have washed their hands of their children. Alecia's parents seemed different. So did Alecia. Though she was sullen and defensive about her father, I got the impression that he truly cared about her."

"Did he visit often?"

She frowned. "That's the weak link. You put your finger on it right away. You must be a very intelligent and perceptive man."

She checked my face to see if she had scored a total ego knockout, and I did not have the defenses to hide it.

"Thanks," I muttered when I should have protested.

She beamed. I would henceforth be eating out of her hand.

"How long was Alecia with you?"

"Just under five months, as I recall. If you want that closer, I can look it up."

"Close enough," I said. "Why was she here?"

A grudging smile pursed Elsie Schaeffer's lips. "Why is anyone here? Because they are sick, or because someone puts them here. Sometimes both."

"In this case?"

"You want to know was she sick?" the doctor asked rhetorically. "Matter of definition sometimes. If you binged on food, then went to the bathroom and stuck your fingers down your throat to throw it all up, would you be sick?"

"What causes that?"

"Varies. Often it is low self-esteem."

"How do you get that?" asked a guy who lived a life virtually without self-esteem.

"You can only get it from yourself," she said. "Of course it is common to blame others, and we try to work that out with the patient."

"In this case," I asked, "she blamed her father?"

"Oddly not. She wouldn't blame anyone."

"She came here on her own steam, then?"

"Oh, no. Very few do that. First of all, very few could afford it on their own."

"Expensive, huh?"

"The *most*," she said.

"Are you an owner?"

She laughed. "Oh, my goodness, no. I am simply a hired hand."

"They are lucky to have you."

She inspected me for cracks in my sincerity. "Why, thank you."

"Are you lucky to have them?"

"Why not? I have a job. I like it here. I am a bleeding heart. I have to be helping people to survive. I think I'm helping people. Ergo, I am a happy woman."

"Did you help Alecia Hadaad?"

"I tried. I *did* try," she said, not seeming to know the answer. "She was no longer bingeing and throwing up when she left here, but I am hard-pressed to take any credit for that. Perhaps at best I was a conduit."

"Do you think she is a danger to society or herself?"

The doctor frowned. "I'm a psychiatrist," she said, "not a mind reader. In many ways she was a reasonable, functioning adult. In some ways, in darker moments perhaps, she was a lost little girl."

"What was she the last time you saw her?"

Dr. Schaeffer frowned and rubbed her forehead, more in weariness than thought. Perhaps I had asked one too many questions. Bound to happen, I suppose. "In my last meeting, I'd say she was both."

"Multiple personality disorder?"

Her eyebrows shot up. "My, are you a doctor?"

"No," I said modestly. "I read a lot."

"Well, don't become a victim of your reading."

"Did Alecia ever express her true feelings about her father... or mother, for that matter?"

Her finger went to her lips, as if to seal them. "Now you are getting onto shaky ground. Impinging on the doctor-patient relationship. I can't answer those questions."

"You mean you won't."

She waved a hand of concession.

"You have any notion of where she might have gone?"

She shook her head. "Nobody does. We've been over this ground many times with many people. Fellow patients, staff, family, cops, FBI, missing persons. Nobody knows any more today than when she left."

"Anyone else ever run away from here?"

"Sure. It's not unusual. We are very low security. No armed guards. No locked gates." She puckered her lips. "But every one of them was found. A lot came back on their own. Alecia is the only one to vanish."

"How did Michael Hadaad take the news she was gone?"

"He wasn't happy," she said. "He loved the girl, and his lovely girl disappeared."

"Could he have been the cause of her disappearance?"

"Why? How? You mean he set up a kidnapping?"

"Maybe."

"Anything is possible," she said, "but I don't really think so."

"Could she have been running away from him?"

"I wouldn't know why."

"Any sign of molestation?"

"None."

"She ever accuse anyone?"

"Not to me. Not to anyone I've heard from."

"Do you know how Alecia's father made his money?"

"I don't ask."

"Any ideas?"

She shrugged and offered her best guess: "Real estate."

I chuckled. "I guess anyone who owns a house can be said to be in real estate. And he's got quite a house."

"I've never seen it," she offered, gratuitously, I thought. Hmm. Two singles. He looked like a ladies' man to me. But could the doctor's inner beauty have been enough for him? I thought of him more as a trophy hunter.

"Why did you say real estate?"

"Oh, I don't know. You get a feel for the parents after a while. They seem to come in three broad categories: The professionals–doctors, lawyers, professors; the movie people; and the business people. The professionals are the most eager to keep up appearances. The movie people get dramatic and weepy, and the business people are always angling to get the most for their money."

"And Mr. Hadaad fit that latter category?"

She wrinkled her nose. She looked pretty cute doing it. "He questioned our charges more than most. But I still say he seemed to genuinely care about her. He asked a lot about percentages and success rates. Another sign of a businessman."

"Don't you have applications with a space for occupation?"

She shook her head. "We don't want to know. We have enough prejudices. Look at me, I've already generalized. That could mean three things. One, if you want us to know, you'll tell us, so why ask? Two, if it is important to the cure, the patient will tell us. And three, we can usually tell without asking, and not asking strikes everyone as being bloody democratic."

"Are you British?"

"No, I just like the word 'bloody.'"

"What kind of patient was Alecia?"

Dr. Schaeffer frowned. "Not ideal. She was often sullen, withdrawn, even hostile to the staff. She wasn't a lamb like some are. She didn't take it lying down."

"Didn't think she belonged here?"

"No, but they seldom do."

"Did she get along with the other patients?"

"She was pretty withdrawn."

"Any boyfriends?"

"Not that I was aware of. She actually could be quite personable when she wasn't resenting her overabundant life. And her father."

"Did you ever feel any of that resentment justified?"

She laughed. "It usually is, Mr. Yates. Funny," she added as an afterthought.

"What is?"

"Your name. It just occurred to me–Gil Favor and Rowdy Yates from *Rawhide*." She smiled a kittenish we've-got-a-secret smile. "Did you make it up?" she asked, wrinkling her nose. I decided that wrinkle-nose bit was her most engaging pose.

"That's the thing about TV and movie names. They're so common."

She cocked a green eye at me. "That doesn't answer the question, but I'll let you off the hook." I couldn't help marvel at *her* perspicacity. Could someone so intelligent get the wrong vibes from Michael Hadaad?

"What do you make of her mom?"

"Good person. Overwhelmed with making a living.

Visited often in her waitress costume that would have been happier on a younger woman."

Whoa, I thought. Maybe she did have designs on the man of the house.

"I did not get the impression," she spoke with slow care, "she was up to all the turmoil in her life. Seemed ill-at-ease. Like she was really a waitress instead of the ex-wife of one of the richest men in this country."

"You know her background?"

"I don't."

"Was there no cash settlement? No alimony?"

"I have no idea. If there were some settlement, there is no evidence of it I can see. Unless she actually *likes* being a waitress. Happens, I suppose."

I asked for Alecia's mother's home address. Dr. Schaeffer hemmed and hawed. Ethics, she said. Should get the woman's permission, blah, blah.

"Up to you," I said finally. "Just remember I'm on their side. I'm trying to help."

She nodded.

"Besides, I may not use it. If I don't need it, I won't bother her."

"I think you'll find she knows no more than her ex-husband. But I guess I can't dissuade you," she said, getting up from the couch wearily.

She went to her desk, opened the file on top, and with a fountain pen wrote in green ink an address on a pad, then tore it off.

"Careful," she said mysteriously, as she handed me the note. "Very careful."

Did she know Hadaad had forbidden me to see his wife?

She didn't say.

My exit was not as warm and fuzzy as my entrance. Those pines had taken on a foreboding air–as though they too were forbidding me to contact the former Mrs. Hadaad.

Well, I wasn't planning to contact her. Rather, to just observe. Maybe she would lead me to Alecia.

7

I drove over to the Wilshire District, in search of Helen Hadaad's abode. The district, at its extremities, ran the gamut from those holding tenaciously to luxury to those who never had it.

Hancock Park, on one end, housed the super-rich–but now older–families. The younger kids with bucks bailed this situation eons before. There is the nice palatial residence for the mayor, among Alzheimer dowagers and sedentary men and women rooted to what they saw as their ancestral home, though one generation was usually about it.

As the district moved west it began to fade. Apartment buildings, once *la crème de la crème,* now faded with the inevitability of overbuilding and the need to fill them up at any price. Managers all over winked at credit reports. Some took the hookers, pimps and pushers, anyone who could peel off a roll of hundreds for the rent and security deposit, which, you could tell by looking at them, they were kissing goodbye the moment they parted with it.

A little farther west, around the L.A. County Art Museum, an enclave of serious adherents to the Jewish faith abounded. Lot of oldsters were sitting on bus benches waiting for buses that didn't go anywhere.

Koreans and Mexicans, blacks and Vietnamese had filtered in on the Jews, and, except for isolated incidents, they all did a good job of keeping the melting pot from boiling over.

Helen Hadaad's pad was in one of those pseudo-Spanish stucco jobs on Farley Street, just a couple blocks south of Wilshire. Stucco houses have one reason for being: they are cheap to build. Most cultures build their shelter the cheapest, easiest way. The Spanish, who we are aping here in Southern California, are no exception.

There is a saying in my real estate game: "If you buy a stucco house, you are the stuckee." There appeared to be three families in this modest two-story stucco, so Helen Hadaad was probably a renter, not a stuckee.

It had what looked like an unseen flat roof and a parapet covered with red tile to give it that Spanish flavor at bargain-basement prices. *To wit*: Helen Hadaad did not seem to be living in the style which her ex-husband accustomed her to, nor in the style which he was maintaining himself. Why is it the women always become the paupers after a divorce?

I had checked the mailboxes surreptitiously and found the name "Helen MacDonald" on unit B, which appeared to be the back downstairs unit. Using her maiden name, or I had the wrong place. So not only was she in a fire-sale building, she had the bargain-basement unit.

I parked down the street and waited for something to happen.

Nothing did. I realized this was the hard part–the scut work you will find in any job. But though I must have realized it was inevitable, I was still ill-prepared. It drove me nuts sitting there. She had to come and go using the side-walk, unless she wanted to go through a neighbor's yard and climb a fence. There was no garage on the property. But nobody came or went.

Six hours was all I could handle. Three to nine, roughly. I figured almost any kind of job she had would put her home between those parameters. Maybe she went to the movies, visited a sick friend, was on vacation. It was dark outside and there were no lights on inside her apartment.

I went home to a robust interrogation on where I had been.

45

"Burning the midnight oil for Daddybucks," I said. "Some surveys in Mid-Wilshire. Hard to find anybody home in the daytime."

"I don't believe you," she said.

"Want to go along tomorrow?"

"No, thanks."

It was always a mystery to me why she was so eager to have me at home. Once there, she had as little as possible to do with me. Blowing little glass ballerinas was her thing.

Next day, I went back to Farley Street and settled down in my Plymouth for another round of boredom.

I arrived at ten, after putting in a cursory appearance at the office, paying my customary obeisance to Daddybucks. I just couldn't call him Daddy Wemple, nor could I call him Daddybucks to his face. It wasn't important. He did most of the talking anyway.

Today, I was armed with sufficient reading material. I get over thirty magazines a month, which is kind of a sickness, and am always struggling to keep abreast. Today I brought the *Smithsonian*, *The American Spectator*, the *New Republic*, *National Geographic*, *The American Scholar* and the *Palm Journal*. I also had Plato's *Republic*, which I was lumbering through at a labored rate.

I parked down the street from the Hadaad pad so as to not arouse suspicion. It was a tribute to my naiveté that I never considered what some observant neighbor might think of me sitting in my car six hours yesterday and camped out again today with a pile of magazines.

This morning I thought I saw movement in apartment B as I went for a stroll down the street to stretch my legs.

By noon, no one had come or gone. I was getting hungry, but I didn't dare leave. I was giving myself two and a half more hours today. Tomorrow I would come earlier.

Of course, I could have knocked at the door under some pretense, but I thought my plan was more subtle and had a better chance of being effective. I kept in mind my principal's strongly stated wish that I not contact his ex-wife, and I would have been happy to abide by that wish if I had any inkling of where else to turn. Remember, the real pros at this had come up with zilch.

I was looking at a particularly amazing *Euterpe edulis* in the *Palm Journal,* when I sensed some motion on the streets. From my vantage point down the block, I saw a woman in a brownish short dress and a white sweater emerge from apartment B. She turned right, heading toward Wilshire on foot.

She seemed to have a salubrious build and carried herself in a manner that hinted she was living in more modest circumstances than she might have been. But perhaps I was projecting my knowledge and hoping this was the real Helen Hadaad.

I started the car after she had gone a block and a half. I drove slowly, passing her as she turned left on Wilshire. I parked across the street, where I observed her going to the bus stop. In eight minutes a bus came. It was the 320, going west on Wilshire.

There is nothing easier than following a bus. She alighted some ten stops later. I parked (illegally in a no-stopping, we're-gonna-tow-the-pants-off-you zone), but I didn't leave the car.

She went another half-block and entered the trendy Diner Diner on Wilshire. It was one of those places you read about where some interior designer goes nuts and pours millions down the sewer to make it look kitsch, but not quite as kitsch as it looked before they dropped a dime.

Diner Diner prided itself on overcharging for simple food. It attracted a Hollywood crowd of plain-food devotees and a couple stars with the lure of comped meals. It soon became known as an *in* place.

Beverly Hills is not a friendly parking town. Now I see why all those guys I called small-timers get expenses. So they can pay eight bucks an hour to park.

I found a meter and reluctantly fed it a couple quarters. At my Wemple wage even fifty cents hurts.

So I had to walk almost three blocks, and better hustle back before my hour was up or I'd be paying fair Beverly Hills more than eight bucks in fines.

I sashayed into Diner Diner just like I was a regular. I'm sure I had them all fooled.

I sat in a maroon booth that was supposed to take us back to the fifties. At a little past three in the afternoon there was no arm wrestling for seats.

You could tell the tone of the place by the people they hired to wait on you. Some places had a sullen air, others overtly friendly. "Hi, I'm Wendy, I'll be your waitress today." To which I respond, "Hi, I'm Gil, I'll be your customer today."

That's what you are liable to run into in the kind of establishment that kisses you off with a "Have a nice day," to which I respond, "Thanks, but I have other plans."

Well, I guess by now you've guessed I don't *really* say those things. I don't have the nerve, but I *do* think them.

That's the kind of swashbuckler I am: a swashbuckler of the mind.

Diner Diner had friendly but not ridiculous women slinging the hash. They wore tags with fifties' names like Sally, Naomi and Helen. No Jennifers, no Tiffanys.

In this town, no one is a waiter/waitress by profession. They are all singers, dancers, actors, writers and directors, marking time until their ship comes in and dumps the Big Break on them.

When I can't avoid eating in a restaurant (an unbroken string of Campbell's tomato soup assaults will send me packing), I select my venue by the cut of the female wait-persons–how's that for impeccable political correctness? I no longer patronize eateries that employ males to serve the vittles.

A long time ago a premier ice cream maker told me "People eat with their eyes." And that's me in spades. I'd rather feast my eyes than my gullet. Decades of canned soup, you could say, have dulled the palate.

Once inside a restaurant, I speculate on what the real occupation of the wait-persons might be. In this neck of the woods (Beverly Hills) waiters are usually actors–too often men. As you move west to Westwood you get students. The owners or managers suffering under a misguided notion that men give the joint class. And, rising feminism notwithstanding, most of the checks are still picked up by men.

My first take on Diner Diner was the waitresses were between marriages.

My waitress was Ruth. She was, like the others I could see, sidling up to middle age, in good enough shape to wear the short dress and not look like the grandmothers at Du-par's, over on Fairfax.

I suppose the thrust of Diner Diner was if you set the decor in the fifties, it wouldn't do to have young chickies who never heard of the fifties parading around taking your mind off the past.

I glanced at my soda-fountain-style menu, skipped over the burgers and fries, steak sandwiches, hot dogs and cherry Cokes, and ordered a junk salad (render unto Caesar that which is Caesar's) and a chocolate malt.

I opened my magazine and pretended to read it while I watched Helen Hadaad, née MacDonald, putzing around at a station in back as though she were taking inventory.

I was surprised at how nice looking she was. No spring chicken, mind you, but she had kept herself in reasonable shape and there wasn't a trace of the demon Michael Hadaad hinted at.

She seemed to take her task rather seriously. Another waitress went to the station for the water pitcher, said something to Helen, who smiled and nodded.

I was about three booths from the station and I could get a better look at her features. Her face had some lines of living in it, her hair one of those frosting jobs. Did they do that in the fifties? I was too young to remember. I could see from here she had been a startling beauty, but now, with the severity of her haircut, which looked like it could have been chopped for salad by some unskilled kitchen helper, it was as though she were deliberately downplaying it.

Two guys came in and plopped in a booth between Helen and me. In the fifties we'd have called them hoods. Now, call them what you like, I wouldn't want to get in a car with them. You know the type: lot of scars, tattoos and muscle.

While I picked at my salad; the ham, the turkey, the cheeses, the egg, the anchovies, and sipped my chocolate malt, I got a peculiar, uneasy feeling that these chaps were taking an interest in me. My first ridiculous thought was that they were closet homosexuals who didn't take no for an answer.

Geez, I was starting to get uncomfortable. When Ruth came with the check, I asked her surreptitiously if she knew those gents. She didn't.

I paid the check and perused my *Smithsonian* magazine. A waitress with fifties red hair brought the unsavories two greasy hamburgers.

When the two bruisers took their first carnivorous bites, I slipped out of the booth and hastened to the door.

They were right behind me, still chewing.

8

It was times like these that made me pine for an expense account and retainer. If I had been willing to pay the eight bucks, I could have parked a lot closer.

I felt an unwelcome tap on my shoulder. "Hey, buddy, you got a light?"

I whirled and told him in my most menacing voice, "Buddy, a guy with your pea brain is better off in the dark."

Well, okay, I didn't say that, but I thought it. What I did was what I always did–pretend they weren't speaking my language or I was stone-deaf.

"Hey, buddy," he shouted so even the deaf would hear, "you got a light?"

New tack called for. I turned, confused, "No, sorry." I gave it a little sissy twist so he might think he had the wrong guy. I noticed he was alone. His pal was doubtless getting the car out of eight-buck hock. I kept walking.

So did he. I took some crazy turns and he seemed flabbergasted. How would his sidekick find him in this mess?

I got lucky. I saw a young woman go into a security apartment building, putting her plastic card in the slot to open the door. At the last moment I ducked in, to her surprise. It is a tough situation–for real security you shouldn't let anyone in, but what can you do when someone pushes in?

"It's okay," I told her, "just don't let this bozo in." She looked at man mountain who was at the door.

51

I sailed across the courtyard pool area and went out a back gate to a side street. Then I ran around the corner, doubling back to my car.

I had shaken him this time, but I was much shaken. What next?

When I got back to the office, I checked my voice mail. I had one. "Call me," it said. No mistaking the voice of the mighty Hadaad.

Daddybucks was away from his desk, probably inventorying paper towels for pilferage.

I put off calling until I could figure what my story would be. I should be outraged he had me followed. Trust is the keystone of my relationships. He wouldn't buy it. I didn't talk to her, I was just getting a feel. Want to watch her. Daughter *could* contact her. Doesn't he want me to do everything? I tried it all on him. Nothing worked.

"I know nothing about you," he said. "I am going to protect my investment." What was he talking about? He hadn't even given me change for the parking meter. "Now listen again, and listen good. You stay away from my ex-wife or not only will you be out of a job, you won't be in any shape to work for a long time."

Whew! What about that helpless-looking woman could flip this rich, powerful guy out like that?

Of course his adamance only made me, as old Lew Carroll would say, curiouser and curiouser. The ex-wife, the child's mother, was not only the next logical step, it was the only step that I saw. Despite his rancor, wouldn't Hadaad, who professed so much love for his daughter he was willing to pop a half-mil for her presence, be delighted no matter how I produced her?

Apparently not.

If nothing else, he had piqued my interest in Helen MacDonald. What was it about her that was so threatening? I felt like calling him back and saying, "I quit. I'm talking to Helen." But first, I didn't have the nerve, and second, I could hear him say, "You can't quit. You're committed."

I got back to Diner Diner the next night, toward the

end of Helen Hadaad's shift.

Quietly I asked for a table in Helen's section. I was shown to a dingy little thing that had room for a plate and a glass of water, if the plate wasn't too big.

There was a theory in the Southern California restaurant industry that the worse you treated the customer the better they liked it. I never caught on to that philosophy. Diner Diner was not an eatery I would be patronizing if it weren't for Helen.

I had been pretty observant on the way over and I didn't think I detected anyone following me. I surveyed the room from my chessboard-sized table (*portable* chessboard) and didn't see the two goons from yesterday, or any pair of goon-like men.

I realized he could have sent a single man, but the only other single man in the place was at the counter–nerdy-looking guy who didn't seem to take any notice of me. It could have been a couple, or half a couple–even a woman.

Of course, then it occurred to me he might have set me up. "No, no, you can't talk to my wife," when that is what he wanted all along. The cops didn't say they stayed away from her, *or* that she had any startling revelations.

Helen came to the table to ask if I wanted anything to drink.

I was tongue-tied. She was, up this close, a startling woman. One who seemed clothed in the wrong situation. She looked like she belonged in swell parlors and chichi boutiques–and here she was, in the garb of an indentured servant. Indentured? Wouldn't that denote a person with a scarcity of teeth?

"Just water," I said, "please," I added ingratiatingly. She nodded, not disappointed I wasn't running up the bill with booze, but not pleased either. It was more of an all-in-a-night's-work shuffle.

I could not write a book *How To Pick Up a Waitress.* I really have no idea how to get their attention other than, "Hamburger and fries."

Here was the whole crew in Diner Diner hustling

back and forth taking orders, delivering orders, clearing tables, writing checks. A lot of hustle-bustle. How was I going to get Helen MacDonald Hadaad to break her stride to chat with me? As the kids say, no possible way.

In the Navy I had a marine sergeant who said our marching looked like a Chinese fire drill. In retrospect, this is, I suppose, a racist comment, but I never came across a marine sergeant who was cognizant of racial sensitivities. I, myself, have been conditioned to more of this sensitivity and would never say the hubbub at Diner Diner reminded me of a Chinese fire drill, even though it did.

I'd like to tell you it was easy getting through to Helen H., but it was anything but.

First of all, she was busier than a one-eyed paper hanger (or was that a one-armed paper pusher?). Second of all, she did not seem like one of those relaxed, friendly sorts–she was, by my assessment, a closed book.

Helen came back and I ordered something and apparently ate it, because when she returned, my plate seemed to be empty.

The place was finally thinning out and Helen was moving at a slightly more relaxed pace.

"Dessert or coffee for you tonight?" she sang out, sort of like whistling Dixie.

"Well, yes," I said. I was getting braver and was able to answer a simple question simply. I was stuffed to the gills, but I wanted to dawdle and take her home. I was sure she would reject me, and was planning how I could get on the bus with her, sit next to her, and make myself generally irresistible.

I had something for dessert that stuck to the roof of my mouth. Helen was gracious about bringing me enough water to cleanse my palate of that sticky substance.

On each of her trips to my table, I tried to screw up sufficient courage to ask if I could take her home. It did not come easily. In fact, it didn't come at all, so I just kept her coming back on one pretense or another, like more lemon for my tea. I don't drink tea or coffee, but I had to do something to wait out the closing of the shop.

When I simply couldn't prolong it a minute longer–when I was the last soul at the trough, the doors had been locked and I got that uncomfortable feeling that the entire staff was glaring at me–I paid my bill in cash, leaving her a tip as though I were the Bank of America.

She smiled and brought me a whole pile of change, as though I'd made some mistake.

"No, no," I said, "that's for you. Thank you."

She smiled and cocked her head, inspecting my face for some sinister motive.

"If you'll pardon my saying so," she said, "you don't look like the type who can afford a tip like that."

I blushed. "I guess I can't," I said.

"Here." She pushed the tray toward me. "Take it. I'll get by."

"No, no, I want you to have it."

She cocked her head again. It was a knockout gesture coming from her. "Why?"

"Would you let me take you home?"

A quick laugh came at me like a bullet. "My home, or yours?"

"Yours, of course." I blushed again. "I'm not asking to come in," I said.

"Yet," she added with a troubling finality.

"I just thought it would be easier for you than taking the bus."

She frowned down at me. I got the feeling I was a humble supplicant in an audience with royalty–but then I always *did* idealize women.

"How do you know I take the bus?" she quizzed me. It was more like an interrogation.

"I don't," I said hastily. "I thought I saw you get off the bus yesterday."

"Hm. You here yesterday?"

I nodded.

"Hm. Well, thanks, but I don't mind the bus. I'm used to it." She looked at her watch. "Speaking of the bus,

I've got to run to catch it. Thanks for the offer."

She went into the back to deposit her apron and check out with the people she had to tip. It was then I noticed she had left the pile of money on the table. She didn't even help herself to a more appropriate gratuity.

I must have looked as dejected as I felt, because she came back to the table and looked me over.

"Here." I pushed the tray toward her. "Please take this."

"No, thanks. It's way out of proportion. Even if I thought you were rich, I wouldn't want a tip like that. Why, it's way more than your bill was."

"Really?" I looked perplexed. Something told me I should be playing dumb and vulnerable to appeal to this woman. Others would argue I didn't need to do any acting. I *was* dumb and vulnerable. My wife would be among them.

She was studying me from on high. I should have stood up, but something told me she wouldn't like that. There's that "something" again. And I was playing laid-back–unaggressive. Okay, I know what my wife would say.

"What do you say?" I pressed without, you know, pressing. "Let me drive you home. I won't get out of the car, if that's what you're worried about."

There came a sigh. "I should decline the honor. But you are, frankly, the most harmless-looking person I have ever seen."

"Thank you...I think," I said, and we both laughed. I could see we would hit it off right away.

9

As we left the restaurant, side by side, I sensed the eyes of the crew burning into my neck. Envy it was. Outside, the air was mid-fifties, nippy for Southern California. We passed a couple lean teens, and one said, "I'm freezing," and the other riposted, "Tell me about it." A quick breeze picked up Helen's skirt. I looked away after the skirt flopped back in place. I didn't fool her.

Up close you saw she wasn't the sort that was easily fooled. She had a full face, not out of whack from the sinister ions emanating from a TV set. A face you might find in a book once in a while. Oh, not comparative calculus maybe, but the better suspense books or, now and then, a soft-porn romance.

It wasn't a face you'd see in a fashion rag, teetering insouciantly atop the impossible body. It was a face that had lived, by God. A face with gentle nooks and crannies softened by a refusal to get worked up about them.

The hands had held more mundane tools than a silver spoon; the fingers just right for a wedding band. She was the kind of person for whom you'd cash the check and skip the I.D.

Her tastes ran to the main-line conservative-cut catalogues, not the high-end, designer delirium. She was a girl who still put the pennies in penny loafers.

"I guess I don't relish taking the bus on a night like this, after all," she said.

"Well, I don't blame you." I was Mr. Magnanimous. My immediate goal was to stretch the time with her so I could get maximum information without seeming unnaturally snoopy.

It would be ideal if I could count on her inviting me in for a two-hour chat, but that didn't seem in the cards. All I could think of was falling back on my non-sense of direction. We could get lost looking for the car, get lost driving the car–except for a couple things: One, she would not take kindly to too much walking after a long hard shift on her feet, and, two, she would certainly know how to get to her apartment.

It was all the smallest talk en route to my car. I wanted her to trust me, which precluded any precipitous moves or sudden questions on my part.

When we hit the sidewalk, I started with, "Good tips?"

"Yours was good. I don't know, till we get finished tipping out all we have to, it's just a living."

"You pardon me making an observation?"

"Hm?"

"You look like a woman used to a lot better."

She laughed. "I'll bet you tell all the girls that."

I blushed. "There are no other girls."

She looked at me again and nodded. "You know, I believe you. It's a terrible line, but I believe it."

"We believe what we want to believe," I said.

She sighed. "Don't we ever."

As our 42nd president used to say, I could feel her pain. "You ever believe wrong?"

"You could say that."

"Ever suffer for your beliefs?"

She wrinkled her nose. "Don't we all?"

"I don't know. Some more than others, sure. Depends, I guess, on how strong the belief is to start with. Mine were never too strong."

"Hm..."

"Were yours?"

She considered this for a long time. "I couldn't say," she said, "strong is a relative term."

"Very astute," I said.

"Phew," she exhaled the night away. "That's hard work."

"Why do you do it?"

"That's all I am, just a waitress."

"All?" I said. "It's honest work."

"Yeah. I guess work is honest."

"Why do you say *all* I am is a waitress?"

"I guess I've always thought of myself as a waitress. It was my first job, before I was married. It was my job while the going was rough financially, and it's my job now that it's over."

"Over?"

"The marriage."

We arrived at my car and I opened the door for her.

"How gallant," she cried, clapping her hands once. She was so happy I opened the car door for her I expected her to break into a jig.

"Say," she said after I started the car, "how come you didn't ask me where to go and you are headed in the right direction?" Her tone was more one of curiosity than of suspicion.

The old blush flushed my face again. "Sorry, I guess you are just so spellbinding I'm not thinking. East just seemed more...well, more likely than west, but perhaps I do you a disservice. You probably have a pad on the beach, overlooking that big ocean out there, what's it called?"

"The Pacific," she answered seriously, then caught herself and laughed. I joined in. I made a U-turn with the car. "Where are you going?" she asked.

"Go best, young man. Horace Greeley," I explained.

"Isn't that 'Go *west*, young man'?"

"Yeah, maybe, so that's where I'm going."

"But you were right the first time," she said. "I don't live on the ocean or anywhere near it."

"Wish you did?" I said.

After a minute she shook her head. "Used to," she said.

"Really?" I said, feigning my surprise. "Bother your arthritis or something?"

She shook her head, but did not elaborate. "Hey, but you're going west, now," she said.

"Yeah? I don't have much of a sense of direction," I admitted. "Face it, I don't have *any* sense of direction."

The laughter came easily to both of us. As though we were comfortable old friends. And that would have been jack with me.

Wilshire Boulevard always seemed to have a special half-light all its own. An unhappy share of businesses had folded, and I always felt for the failed proprietors, whose high hopes and delirious dreams were unmatched by any marketing surveys which might have given them a handle on just how unnecessary their enterprise was.

I was taking new measure of Helen, sitting beside me in the front of the Plymouth. She seemed less regal here, more down home but with suffering-fed strength and necessity-induced native intelligence. I knew I had no business taking any personal interest in her, but taking it I was.

In fact, she seemed so down-to-earth, I thought I could just blurt out, "Where's your daughter?" and she would give me her address and phone number.

"What do you say we cruise the beach, since we seem to be headed that way?" I asked.

She frowned. As though she would have any call to question my motives. "Thanks, but I'm kind of beat. I may be getting too old for my trade. Would you mind just taking me home and taking a rain check?"

"Oh, gosh, no. I'm sorry. I got carried away." I turned the car around and we made our way east. I remembered to say, "Tell me where to turn."

And she did. I had really gotten enough for one night. I just wanted to break the ice and leave the window open for another meeting.

"Thanks a lot," she said when I pulled up in front of

her triplex.

"May I see you to the door?"

"Oh, thanks, but it's okay. If it weren't so busy tonight and I weren't so old, I'd invite you in."

I beamed like a sophomore getting a wink from the prom queen. "If I weren't so old," I said, "you wouldn't have to invite me."

We both had a good laugh. "Say," I said, "you wouldn't give me your phone number, would you?"

"Why not?" she said. "I like to get calls." And she gave it to me.

How refreshingly candid she was. She put out her hand and I took it and shook it just as though we were long-lost fraternity brothers.

She darted into her place like the wisp of a disappearing dream.

It wasn't until I pulled away from the curb that I saw the man sitting in his car. He didn't follow me, which pleased me at first. Then I began to worry about Helen.

At the first gas station I came to on Pico Boulevard, I pulled in and threw in twenty cents (non-expense account) and dialed her number. It rang too many times before she answered. My heart was pounding, and when she finally answered, it took a couple moments before I could get my heart back out of my throat.

"Oh," I said, "you had me worried. Am I disturbing you?"

"Oh, no," she said, "I was just in the bath."

I wondered if the man in the car was waiting for her. I didn't ask. "I just couldn't wait to try out your number."

"How sweet," she said, as though she might have meant it.

"And..." I added casually, "I did notice some guy sitting out front in a car. I thought it a little odd. Would you check to see if he's still there? I think he was parked where he could see a sliver of your door."

"Oh, you silly," she said. "Whoever he is, he didn't come here."

"Can you see if he's still there? I mean, from inside. Don't go out or anything."

"Oh, Gil, really. Is this real paranoia?"

"Remember what Kissinger said about Nixon?"

"What?"

"'All paranoia is not unfounded.' Please look."

"Okay. Hold on. What kind of car? Where?"

"A big, dark thing. Other side of the street. In my blind spot when I left you off."

She was back in a minute. "He's gone. No sign. Thanks for your concern–'night." She said it all at once, run together like a freight train, then hung up before I could put her to any more trouble.

I still wondered if she bothered to look at all, or, worse still, if he was her boyfriend, waiting for her to come home.

I was dancing on air when I got home. I thought I could sneak into the family room and call my voice mail without Tyrannosaurus Rex being the wiser.

Fat chance. "Who are you calling?" came the inquiry, cascading down the stairs like an old pal in a barrel of cement. "And why are you so late?" She asked a lot of questions without caring to hear answers, so I ignored her.

The family room was festooned with glass-blown candles, fisherboys, ballerinas, pixies, gnomes, the seven dwarfs and Snow what's-her-name, and Tyranny Rex's *pièce de résistance,* the little boy urinating. I could look at that a thousand times and never understand its appeal.

Packing crates were cheek by bowel all over the place. She did a land-office mail-order business.

Peeking through the crates was a clear path to the television set, in front of which the great Dorcas did her "books." Adding up her take, and too seldom subtracting her mammoth costs.

"I did eight hundred this weekend," she would chirrup after a sale, and I would mutter, "Only cost you twelve hundred," under my breath.

"What did you say, dear?" she would ask, even though she didn't want to know.

"I don't want you using the family room when I'm prepping a show," she said. "You're so clumsy, you're liable to destroy my entire stock."

"Count your blessings if I do," I said *sotto voce.*

I decided to put off checking my messages until I could be assured of some privacy.

10

Next morning, when T. Rex was in her bath and I found she had left me a one-inch piece of banana for my cereal, I checked the phone company for messages. Another call from you-know-who was on my voice mail. I called him back.

"Who *are* you?" he asked after I identified myself.

"I told you," I said, getting a little more put out by his tone, in light of his ex-wife's revelations.

"My men went into a...what is it? Wemple Realty Company? and asked for Gil Yates. They never heard of you."

"Why is that surprising?"

"They saw you go in. *Some*one should know you."

"Saw me go in, huh?" I said, trying to pump a little disgust into my voice. "Following me again?"

"Yes, we are following you. I don't trust you yet."

"Think you ever will?"

"I don't know."

"I think you never will. I also think you are following me to cut me out of the deal. I am supposed to lead you to your daughter, then the goons take over and I'm left without change for the parking meter."

"The financial arrangements were your idea."

"Want to call it off?"

"Ha!" he snorted, as though he didn't believe I wanted to.

"Up to you, sir," I said, and when I was obsequious,

no one could touch me.

"You want to follow me, the deal is off. You trust the goons more than me, let them find your daughter. I got other fish in the skillet," I said, vaguely aware I had messed up the cliché, as I so often did.

"Well, are you making any progress?"

"Progress? Two days? I'm satisfied–but for my fee you don't expect instant results. Now, are you calling off the dogs or do I quit?"

There was a pause to perfect his breathing. "I'll call them off," he said.

"Good."

"On one condition."

"No conditions."

He didn't hear me. "You stay away from my ex-wife." And he hung up, as though that were that. Michael Hadaad was a guy used to having the last word.

So I can hardly be faulted for going back to see Helen. I did *not* agree I would stay away. I got careless. But the incriminating fact was, I was a tiny bit smitten with her. She seemed such a noble woman, I thought. Down-to-earth, hardworking. So why would Hadaad be so angry? She didn't seem to be getting any of his precious money. I would expect my father-in-law would have been ecstatic in the face of that kind of deal.

I put in a partial day at the office, making calls to the apartment managers to keep up the pretense. The fact was, the managers were a lot better at doing their jobs than I was, and a lot more interested too.

"Taut ships are glad ships," I told them, then realized later it went, "Taut ships are happy ships."

Daddybucks was on his platform, conniving how to squeeze another nickel from the poor.

About four I bid them all adieu.

"Little early, isn't it?" Daddybucks inquired as only he can.

"Few loose ropes out in the Valley," I said without looking back.

"Well, look who's here," Helen said as she saw me at my tablette. She seemed sort of pleased.

It was an easier evening for Helen and she said, "I'd like that," when I asked if this would be a good time to cash in my rain check for our drive to the beach.

We drove out Wilshire to Santa Monica, where I asked if she would like to stroll in the grassy park above the water.

"Why not?" she said.

We started walking and I paraded my repertoire of small talk. "So how long were you married?" I shot in out of the black.

"Too long." She shuddered at the memory.

"Have any kids?"

"Sort of," she said. It wasn't going to be easy.

"Sort of boys or sort of girls?"

"Yeah," she said, "how about you?"

"Sort of," I said, and we both laughed into the chill night air.

There were a lot of homeless people around, taking up space on the grass with their packaged belongings. We had to pay attention lest we step on them.

"Don't ex-husbands usually chip in a little to support their ex-wives?"

She stopped walking, examined my face as though she were looking for leprosy, then cast her gaze on the dark ocean.

"Some do," she said finally. "Some don't," she added with finality. Then added, as though she hadn't meant to, "I didn't want any of his tainted money. I'd feel unclean."

"What do you mean?"

"No, no," she waved me off. "It's not a pleasant

subject. Let's talk about you for a while. I have a suspicion you are married. Are you?"

"Oh, I wouldn't say that."

"What's that supposed to mean?"

"Used to be," I said. "It's not a pleasant subject."

She laughed, but I don't think she thought it was very funny.

"I can talk about my kids though," I offered generously. And I told her about August and Felicity. My hope was she would reciprocate. But she said nothing. For myself, I was troubled at misleading her. All part of the job, I rationalized. But already I was caring more for her than the job.

"About those kids?" I asked after a silence.

She drew in a deep breath of the night air. "One, but I don't know where she is."

"Really?" I perked up. "Estranged?"

"Not from me–from her dad. I'm just a side effect."

"Bother you?"

She sighed. She was good at it. "Too much."

"Never hear from her?"

She shook her head.

"How long?"

"Could you take me home now?" Helen asked–a true question, not a command.

"Sure," I said. "Something wrong?"

"This talk depresses me a little."

"I'm sorry."

"Oh, it's not your fault. I should be a big girl and overcome it. I try not to think about it, but it just eats me away." She took a last look at the black ocean. "Isn't it sad the time we waste in our lives dwelling on annoyances?"

I looked at her and nodded. There weren't two answers to that one that I could see.

There were a lot of silent stretches on the way home. I wanted to reach out so often and hug her. I wondered, during one of the long conversational voids, how she would react to that? I was afraid to find out. There seem to be so many strictures laid down by the moralists, the politicians, the clergy, the media about what you can do and what you shouldn't do that it's a miracle anything gets "done."

When we pulled up in front of her place and got out of the car, all I could think of was did I dare put my arm around her. Helen wasn't a woman who evoked sympathy, and yet I somehow felt protective.

So I just didn't see them, that's all. They came out of the bushes, the garbage bins, the walls, some place and they worked me over world-class.

Helen was screaming for help, but it wasn't forth-coming. The pain was startling–and no words were spo-ken–no hint given to the identity of my assailants, for which I was grateful. I didn't want Helen to know what was up. I'd never get any info if she did.

A couple curious neighbors showed their faces to check the damage after the bullies had fled. No sense stick-ing your neck out, you're liable to get it whacked off.

Helen helped me into her apartment with such care and expertise I could have taken her for a nurse rather than "just a waitress."

She laid me gently on her bed and went to get the stuff to mop me up. I didn't know what was broken–it felt like everything. At least they didn't kill me, and they certain-ly could have. Wouldn't have taken much more.

The room smelled so good. Like mild soap and fresh air. Helen returned and started to gently sponge the blood. The cool water felt good–better than the blows. A man never feels better than after he gets off a hot stove.

Through the slits in my puffy eyes I could see her frowning. "Are you tied up with my ex somehow?" She didn't relish the thought.

"How would I know your ex-husband?" I groaned. "He like to beat people up?"

"Nothing is beyond him," she muttered.

"Jealous? Why didn't you tell me? I'm a certifiable coward."

"He's not jealous of me," she said. "You in any kind of deals with anybody?"

"Hey, I don't even know any MacDonalds," I said.

She shook her head. "That's my maiden name. His name is Hadaad."

"Oh, man," I said, faking being startled by trying to sit up. She gently pushed me back. "Michael Hadaad, the arms dealer? That's your hubby?"

"Ex," she said.

"Ex," I confirmed. "Man, let me out of here. He's got a rep that I don't care to deal with. Hey, I'm just a property manager, and I wouldn't even manage his property if he had any." I was running off at the mouth to keep her off the track.

"Settle down."

"Easy for *you* to say. They didn't work you over. Why didn't you *tell* me you had a nutso husband?"

"Oh, Gil."

"No, really. These hotheads kill people at the drop of a hat. Lot of jealous hubbies in the hoosegow for terminating a rival. Not for me, thanks. Can you drive me home?" I asked, then sank back groaning in excruciating pain so as to erase all thought of moving me from her mind.

"Oh, why don't you just lie still till morning. I can tend to my maternal instincts and you can start to mend."

"Okay. If you'll talk to me. I'm afraid I might have a concussion, and you're supposed to keep people with concussions awake."

"What shall I talk about?"

"Anything. Tell me about your life. Your marriage–why this guy would be so jealous. Your kid? In-laws? Anything? Hey, wait a minute, really. You were married to one of the richest guys in the world and now you're–excuse me for using your words–'just a waitress.' How come?"

"It's a long story."

"So that's it. Tell me."

"You don't want to hear it."

"Yes, I do."

"Maybe I don't want to tell it."

"I'll fall asleep," I said, closing my eyes to scare her.

"I'll read you something. It's just not a story I tell anyone."

"People reading to me puts me to sleep," I said. "I need real conversation." It was a cheap shot, but it worked.

She started talking. Then she settled down in the bed, next to me, and drew me close to her. It was, after all, her only bed, and I was in no shape for hanky-panky, but with her so close I was feeling no pain.

11

It was easy. As soon as there was a lull in her narrative, I feigned dozing off. And she got right back to it. She didn't realize the pain was so intense, I *couldn't* go to sleep. I dearly wanted to block out the pain with sleep, but it wasn't in the deck of cards I'd been dealt.

"Where do I start?" she asked.

"The beginning. You were born somewhere."

"Oh, yeah. Texas. Small town outside of Dallas. Mom was a secretary, Dad was a cop. She ran a stop sign. He pulled her over but didn't 'issue a citation,' was the way he put it. I guess I was the result of that bribe, but I don't know for sure. I do know I was a very short-term baby. I came on the scene about four months after the simple marriage. I was just the beginning. They had a lot of kids, Mom and Dad. There were nine of us before they caught onto birth control."

"So how did you meet your irate husband?" I asked, trying to cut through to the important stuff.

She furrowed those silky, smooth eyebrows.

"That's a lot harder for me to talk about," she said. I pretended to fall asleep. She shook me gently. "Okay, okay. You sure are a pest. Why are you so interested in this boring stuff?"

"I'm interested in you," I said.

She sighed and started slowly, with a flat voice.

"I was going to UCLA and waiting on tables. I was

71

what I've heard called an indifferent student. I couldn't get that interested. I thought marriage and family was my true calling."

"What were you going to study?"

She gave me a short laugh. "Physical therapy," she said.

"Great," I said. "Stand us in good stead."

"Don't get your hopes up. I didn't get that far."

"Got a husband instead?"

"He came into the restaurant one night and I swear all eyes were on him. He looked like Omar Sharif in his prime, but his face wasn't as round. Swarthy he was, and he came in like he owned the place. He had that commanding presence you see when a celebrity walks into a crowd. Well, he was like that wherever he went. He just took over the room. I said a silent prayer the hostess would seat him at my table."

"And she did?"

She nodded. "My lucky day," she said with a sarcastic smirk. "When I went over with the water, he looked me up and down like I was one of those biblical sacrifices. I must have blushed from head to toe.

"When he ordered, it was just that, an order. He wasn't very nice, but was he handsome. Everybody wanted him, you could feel it in your bones. He had that smell of big success about him."

"What did he do?"

She laughed. "Oh, nothing. Prey on working girls, I guess. But he was a schemer. He always had some scheme going on. I think his family was supporting him. He was a student from one of those oil countries."

(She told me which one, but I am not giving any hints. No repercussions, remember? Can you blame me? Look at the fix I was in for just talking to his ex-wife.)

"My head was spinning the moment he asked me out, right through the obligatory seduction (not too long afterwards, I am ashamed to report), up to the obligatory marriage. I was three months gone. Like mother, like daughter.

"I shouldn't have been surprised he turned out to be a self-centered brat. I should have known–the Middle East isn't exactly famous for its women's liberation. But I could have taken it if I had sensed he had any regard for me personally. I was a pretty face for him to display. He's very possession oriented. And the baby was a possession too. He liked to show her off. She was so cute."

"Looked like you?"

"Oh, here I go, rattling on about looks as if they were important. You know what they say, if you are good looking, you don't have to talk about it."

"But you're beautiful."

She smiled and patted my hand. "Used to be passable," she corrected me gently, "in another life."

I started to argue. She let me know it wasn't necessary by cutting me off.

"As soon as our daughter displayed a mind of her own, Michael went ballistic. The poor girl kept getting these awful mixed signals. I tried to reassure her, but what is it about men that causes women to behave so irrationally?"

"Beats me," I said. I only wished I had experienced some of that feminine irrationality coming my way. The few women in my life were commandingly rational. Maddeningly so. *Especially* you-know-who.

So her daughter had one thing or the other: bad grades, smoking in sixth grade. Her first sex at 14.

"What was Daddy up to at this point?"

"Ah, that's the crux, of course. I had long since resigned this part of my life. I'd have left him in a minute, but I couldn't add any trauma to Alecia's life. That's our daughter's name."

"Was there any molestation?"

"Oh, no. Nothing like that. His offenses were psychological. He was overbearing, he was fanatically selfish. The sun rose and set on him and it was clear we only existed to serve him. Alecia would have a line in a school play and be all excited about performing for her daddy and he wouldn't show up. Some 'deal' was always more important."

"Did he make a living with these deals?"

She shook her head. "He did some real estate for a while," she said, "but it was too tedious for him. He made some small investments in property at the right time and we got by on it. I never bought a new dress or anything. I was still wearing my high-school clothes, but that didn't bother me. I never was possession oriented. *He* was the one."

"So what became of Alice?"

"Alice?"

"Your daughter." I thought that was pretty clever, getting her name wrong. But I was beginning to have queasy feelings about deceiving this perfectly guileless woman. And why was I doing it? In behalf of a guy I wouldn't let in my palm garden. And the more she told me, the guiltier I felt.

"Alecia," she said. "Her name is Alecia."

"Oh," I said. "Sorry."

"Alecia had a rough adolescence. It all culminated in anorexia, then bulimia."

"What's that?" I asked.

"You don't know what anorexia is?"

"Not eating?"

"Yeah, starving yourself because you are obsessed with your looks. Bulimia goes one better. You can eat all you want–you just make yourself throw it up afterwards."

"Not too pleasant," I said, superfluously. "What is she doing now?"

A frown clouded her face. "I don't know," she said softly. There I had it. All I was leading up to, hoping for, dashed. She didn't know, and there was no baloney there. I would wager she wasn't capable of any.

"You don't have any ideas?"

"None. Oh, believe me, I've thought of everything. And it's almost all possible. I just don't know where to turn." Now it was her turn to collapse, crying, her head on my chest.

I stroked her lustrous hair. "When did you see her last?"

"God, has it been almost a year? Michael put her in a

sanitarium. I didn't want to, but there was never any fighting Michael." A thought jolted her. "Oh, by the way, we were divorced by then."

"He had custody?"

She nodded. "He was, by now, filthy rich, with law firms dripping from every finger. Alecia was seventeen. She had less than a year until she was an adult, beyond our fighting over. So I walked out. Michael couldn't believe it. I couldn't believe his tantrum. But he had gotten a lot worse after he got out of jail."

"Jail? He was in jail, wasn't he?"

She nodded thoughtfully. "Selling arms to the enemy. Helicopters with cannons that could wipe out a town. And they did. Pretty gross stuff. But he made millions. Finally his dream of being really rich came true. It didn't seem to even occur to him that he had to break the law to do it. It got him four, five months in jail, is all, and when he got out he started spending like a drunken navy."

"Sailor," I corrected. I knew that one. "It's 'drunken sailor,'" I said.

"No. He spent like the whole navy. It disoriented Alecia. He wanted her to buy expensive dresses, and that only made her more self-conscious about how fat she thought she was. But she was one of his trophies. Anyway, her rebellion was too much for him. He went to court to get custody, I didn't fight it. Alecia has never forgiven me. She thinks I abandoned her. Even though I explained the impossibility of prevailing in court before she was eighteen, she thought I should have taken a symbolic stand. Of course, I had no money to fight with. He wouldn't let me go to work. And by then he seemed to own every lawyer as far as the eye could see, so I just left."

"He gave you no living allowance? Nothing?"

She shook her head and the bronze hair flared out above her shoulders in the most engaging fashion. "Oh, he tried to give me something. Wanted to do the honorable thing. I wouldn't take any of his tainted money. It drove him crazy."

"So," I said, the light bulb going dimly on in my head, "that's why I got beat up? If he can't have you, nobody can?"

She didn't look at me. There seemed something on a blank wall ahead that caught her fascination. Slowly, painfully, she responded. "I didn't think so."

"You have any other gentlemen callers since you left?"

She shook her head.

"Anybody parked outside? Any suspicious persons at the restaurant? Anywhere?"

She shook her head again. "Not that I noticed. That's the uncanny thing. How could he know about you?"

"Maybe it was a random mugging. Or a mistaken identity."

She looked at me. What a face. It overflowed with compassion, spilling all over me, washing my pain away–temporarily. "But they made no effort to rob you or to touch me. It's just so strange."

"Do you think your ex knows where Alecia is?"

"No, no. And it's driving him crazy. He's done all sorts of investigations, and his money can buy just about anybody."

"Not you," I reminded her.

"No."

"And not me either," I added. It was not so much the bald-faced lie it sounded. I had then and there decided I no longer wanted to work for him. I realized my heart was checkmating my reason, but there you have it.

"Or you either," Helen said, as though she believed it.

"Would you like me to help you find your daughter?"

She was back at the face-inspecting gambit again. Looking under the skin for the real skinny. "Why would you do that?"

"Because I like you."

"Just like that? What makes you think you could find

her when her mother and father, and all her father's mighty minions can't?"

I realized that made me a mighty minion. I was momentarily flattered. "Maybe because Alice would be glad to have *you* find her. Alecia, I mean, sorry. And maybe she wants no more of old Dad—just as you said: like mother, like daughter."

She just smiled.

I could see telling her story had drained her. She was getting drowsy. More than once her head jerked and she snapped back awake.

"That's a beautiful story," I murmured into her armpit.

"Beautiful? I think it's sad."

"Hm. But from you it's beautiful," I yawned.

"Oh, no," she said, "I'm out of autobiography."

"'S all right," I said, fading. "Helen?"

"Hm?"

"I don't think I have a concussion. I think we should go to sleep. Thanks for keeping me awake to make sure."

She gave me a gentle hug.

"Hey, how do you know if you have a concussion or not? Are you a doctor or something?"

"No, I think after all this time, I'd have blacked out, and I didn't."

"Too bored." She laughed.

"*Au contraire*," I said.

"Listen, I'd feel a lot better if we took you to a hospital or a clinic or something. You could be bleeding inside or have a couple broken bones—or even the concussion."

I didn't think going to the hospital was such a hot idea. Oh, health-wise—it was unarguable. But what did I say when they started asking questions? Report the crime? *They* might report it. Soon the cops would get wind I was playing detective without a license. Maybe I could bring it off, but I didn't want to take any chances. On the other hand, if some bone started sticking out of my chest, I might have no choice.

"I think I'm going to be all right," I told her with no foundation whatever. "I think I can sleep. Stay with me, will you?"

She grinned, "I only have one bed."

If she said anything after that, I didn't hear it.

12

It was the sound of someone clunking down a trash can at first morning light that awoke me.

I chalked it up to my pain that the sound of a trash can made me think of my partner in the rite of marriage. To call her and wake her? The bedside clock said six-thirty-seven. Better to get there as soon as possible. The tale to be spun in the car, en route.

I tried to get up, but fell back in the bed.

Helen opened her sleep-laden eyes to half-mast. "What's a matter?" Then closed them again.

"Nothing," I said soothingly. "Just tried to get up. May be premature."

I tried again, very slowly, and was able to flip my feet off the edge of the bed and onto the floor. Efforts to lift myself to the standing position were futile. Those bozos knew their trade.

I waited as long as I could before I spoke again. "Helen," I said gently, as I watched one eye pop open.

"Hm?"

"It might be to both our benefits if I could get to the bathroom fairly soon."

She hopped up and lifted me so I could lean on her shoulder, and disaster was averted.

She helped me back to the bed, where I sat painfully pondering my scant options.

"Maybe I ought to drive you to a hospital after all,"

she said, "just to make sure nothing is seriously out of whack."

I still didn't think that was such a hot idea, but I couldn't think of a really convincing argument.

"Come on," she said, "I'm taking you to the hospital." And she jumped up and snatched some clothes from her closet in less time than it took to look. She went into the bathroom, closed the door and took an eight-second shower.

I had managed to stand on my own feet, albeit unsteadily, but before I had time to flee she was back and dressed in a pale-blue sheath dress that made her look like a goddess.

I sat down again. No sense overdoing it.

"Ready?" she said, not so much a question as a reminder. As though we had made some deal and it was time for me to pay off.

"I can't go to any hospital."

"Why not?"

"I've got to get home."

"Home?" She seemed puzzled. Didn't she think I *had* a home? Just lived out of my car and ate in restaurants? "Why?"

"My wife will be worried." I really don't know what I was thinking to blurt that out so carelessly. But in an instant I knew what she was thinking.

The blood drained from her face as though someone had pulled a plug in her left ventricle. She glared at me with the most anguished twist of her lips. "You...didn't...tell...me...you...had...a......wife," she said like a zombie.

I tried to get up again, as though that would make everything all right. I couldn't move. I opened my mouth to speak, but nothing came out.

"You said...you...*used* to be married..."

We stared at each other for seven or eight years. The sinking inside of me was worse than my bruises.

She garnered the nerve to speak first. "Do you want

me to drive you home, or just put you in your car?" The warmth was gone.

Wow, I thought, I sure blew this investment. Though I seemed to have gotten all she had, there were always future possibilities. That's the price you pay for learning on the job. That's what I told myself in my hard-boiled persona. In reality, I was smitten with Helen. Lying any more to her would have been unthinkable. So I told her the whole truth. It didn't work.

"And you're working for my ex-snake besides! This is all too much."

"I'm not working for him anymore," I hastened to reassure her. "This is all too much," I repeated her words while pointing to my wounds. I thought it cleverly endearing. She didn't agree.

"You *lied* to me," she said, as though it were the first time that had happened to her. "I trusted you. The first man I've trusted since my divorce. You spit on me–working for that snake–and *married*!"

I don't know which she thought was worse. From the look on her face, they were both rock-bottom on her despicable meter.

Frantically afraid of losing all contact with her, I renewed my offer to help her find her daughter.

She sneered at the offer. But even her sneer was engaging–as though it were an expected reaction but she didn't really mean it.

I guess I said all kinds of foolish things then. But I couldn't swear to it. You'd have to check with her if you want any kind of accuracy. Trust what she says, she's true turquoise.

I said I cared for her, I loved her, the last thing in the world I wanted was to hurt her.

"Ah, but you did," she said. She was not letting me off easily. "How could you lead me on like that? To make me believe you were a legitimate suitor? All to pump me for info in behalf of that sterling ex of mine. What's he paying you?"

"Nothing," I said.

"Hah!"

"No, no, I told you, I'm quitting. I didn't get an advance. I was to get paid if I found Alecia."

"Ah, you *do* know her name. That 'Alice' stuff was just more of your tricks. Ah, you're a sly one, Gil Yates, and I'll bet that's not even your name."

"That's right. It's as phony as I am," I admitted. "Do you want to know my real name?"

"No," she said. "I want you out of here. I'm withdrawing my offer to drive you home. I'll put you in your car and you're on your own from there."

"I deserve it," I said with practiced humility. I learned something from my decades with Tyrannosaurus Rex. "But, please," I begged her, "take my phone number in case you want me to work for you. Gratis. No charge. I've started the thing and I've gotten hooked."

"No way," she said.

I took a pen from my pocket and scrawled my "business" number on the back of an envelope on the bedside table. "I hope you change your mind," I said. "I want to make this up to you."

Without another word, she lifted me to my feet, and, leaning on her for support, I made it to my car, where she deposited me in the driver's seat and retreated to the house, without looking back.

It must have been ten minutes before I psyched myself up to start the car. As I got to the spot where I could see Helen's window, I caught her looking out at me.

Home sweet home. Composition roof with gray rocks–beige paint on the stucco. Earth tones are very big in California, as though a coat of beige paint could make these monotonous stucco-box tract houses look like they were part of the earth. The earth can do better.

My earth did better. It gave sustenance and succor to

my palm trees, which by now were crowding the front of the mundane stucco box. Well, okay, the sides and back too.

The trees and house looked welcoming after my near-death experience. But now I wondered if that experience was my beating, or was it angering Helen?

I could have written my reception at home before it happened.

"What in the world happened to you? We were frantic." This from the Rex. She was often given to hyperbole when the sentiments were negative enough.

"I got mugged," I lied with the best of them.

"Oh, you poor, helpless boy," she said. It was neither in sympathy nor a compliment. She let it be known she would not have been as helpless. If someone had tried to mug *her*, she would have simply stomped on him.

"Sorry I don't have any time to fuss over you," she said, "I'm prepping for my show. I'm leaving this afternoon, remember?"

"I remember," I said, but I didn't. I just couldn't keep track of her myriad of movements. How *are* you gonna keep 'em down on the farm after they've seen Venice? Or Santa Monica, for that matter?

Boxes were spilling over from the family room into the living room and kitchen. She certainly was an optimist when it came to pushing her product. Hope springs eternal in the old girl's ticker. There the shiny figurines were, lined up as if ready to step off into a Halloween parade. The ballerinas, the jockeys, the dogs and horses, the little lasses with watering cans turned on a gnome, the little lads with the saturated kidneys.

Tyranny Rex was not in the habit of inquiring into my activities. It didn't seem to occur to her that I had to spend the night somewhere. She would give me blow by blow the details of her glass-blowing trade as though they were just the most fascinating things in the world. Yet if I happened to mention something legitimately fascinating about a palm or cycad, it was like I was talking to the wall-to-wall carpet.

Tyranny Rex was off on a gaggle of sales that would keep her hands happy for an indeterminate time. Oh, she knew how long she would be gone, and I'm sure she told me, I just have a great deal of trouble tuning into those details. It was even difficult for me to keep straight one sale's location and duration, and now she was gone on four or five, so there was no chance at all of my accounting for them.

I waited until she left, in her usual flurry of activity, before I called the phone company.

I had one message. It was not the half of the ex-marriage that I hoped. Well, I thought, catching myself sighing like Helen, I better get it over with. Call in your resignation to old Hadaad.

I did the job in a simple, businesslike manner. When Quasimodo put Hadaad on the phone, I simply said, "Mr. Hadaad. I hereby tender my resignation."

"What are you talking about?" he said, as if he didn't know.

"I'm simply too busy licking my wounds to spend any more time on your case. Sorry, it's been great fun. Especially the beating."

"Look–forget what I said. A guy with your tenacity is valuable to me."

"I'd like to forget what you said, but it hurts when I forget."

"Oh, yeah, well, that. What can I say? Sorry."

Just like that, I thought. How magnanimous. A lot easier to pass off pain if you are on the delivering end. "Sorry?" I said. "Not half as sorry as I. And I do realize that was only the tip of the icebox..."

"Berg," he said.

"What are you talking about?"

"'Tip of the ice*berg*' is how that saying goes."

"Oh, yeah? Thanks...sorry." I thought he had some nerve correcting my gaffes. "I guess you get the picture. Next time I could be killed."

"No one wants to kill you. I want my daughter."

"So you said. So you cripple the guy who is trying to

84

find her for you."

"I told you to stay away from my wife."

She referred to him as "ex"–he, in the present tense. Another possession he couldn't bear to part with. Like a specimen *Brahea pimo* palm.

"That you did," I said as slowly and as deliberately as I could. "Why is that so important to you?"

There was a dead silence. "You're talking about a woman who spends her working career giving options on salad dressing."

"Is that what she did when you married her?"

"That's different. We were students. I got rich; she's still grinding fresh pepper on salads."

I tried to ignore his snobbery. Was dispensing ground pepper worse than being in the slammer? I held my tongue. I always do.

"Last time we talked, I said there could be no conditions. I won't do anything that could land us in jail. Other than that, I don't take orders. If you want to find Alecia without the help of your ex-wife, be my pest."

"Guest," he said impatiently. "It's 'Be my guest.'"

"Okay. Just so you understand I'm no longer working for you. I won't be returning any more calls."

"You're a quitter."

"Not exactly. I'm not giving up. I'm just not working for you. We'll see if I turn anything up, I might call you."

"Well, you're crazy. But do call me–I'll stand by our deal. Bring her here, you'll be rewarded."

With more than a bash to the skull, I hoped, but I simply hung up the phone.

Free at last, thank God Almighty, I'm free of the past. Now I could function without interference as the hopeless amateur I was.

Each person makes his own escape from anguish. Things he finds to do to fill time until his hope becomes a reality or until he gets over the forlorn hope.

After another day of rest and recuperation, I putzed the palms, hoping Helen would call. As the days passed, my hopes faded and I found myself losing interest in palms. Something else would be needed to keep my sanity.

I tried to read a book, but the first page took about ten minutes and I realized I had no idea what I read.

I called the voice mail ten times a day. At least. Nothing. Tyranny Rex had left for her shows so I would have a few days of peace before she left for Scotland when I would achieve *world* peace. All the more reason to succumb to this insanity, so I picked working on the case. Maybe, if I found Alecia, I could win Helen back. Or at least her good opinion of me.

13

She called! Who said thirteen was unlucky? This is Chapter 13, isn't it?

My wounds, it turned out happily, were superficial enough, and in less than a week I wasn't even thinking about them for 10-20 minutes at a stretch. Of course my color had changed to blue-black with some yellowing, but no one was looking at me anyway.

"Gil," she said on the voice mail, "this is Helen. I've been thinking about what you said. Maybe. You can call if you want."

If I *want*!

I thought of all the reasons I might not reach her. Maybe she didn't have an answering machine. She would be at the store, changed shifts with someone at work, went for a walk–or, worst of all, would have changed her mind and be sitting in her two-room apartment listening to the phone ring.

And I was usually an optimist. And, besides, I was checking my voice mail every hour–sometimes oftener–and she couldn't have gone far since she called.

She answered on one ring. That used to be a no-no. Girls didn't want to appear too anxious. Usually got it on two, because some people would hang up after three rings.

"Hello."

"Oh, Helen," I enthused, "I'm so glad you called."

"Oh, is this...Gil–or whatever your real name is?" She

was less enthused.

"Malvin," I said. "My real name is Malvin." I just couldn't rein in my excitement.

There was a thought-provoking pause. "I think I like Gil better," she said. "Mind if I call you Gil?"

"Call me anything you want, just *call* me." I was playing hard to forget.

"I did."

"Yeah! When can I see you?"

"It's got to be strictly business," she said. "At your house," she added.

"Yeah, sure. Fine."

"I don't fool around with married men."

"Good for you," I said, wondering how long it would take to get a divorce. Of course, then I would be out of a job, and two of us living on Helen's tips could be tight. A penny saved is a penny spurned. Of course, if I could find the girl and still get a half a mil from Hadaad, I could run off with his ex-wife. Wouldn't that be the cat's nightgown? "So when can we meet?"

"I don't work till five today."

"I'll pick you up in an hour."

"How many buses would it take to get to your place?"

"About twenty-seven. And you'd be on the road a couple hours each way. If you left now, I could see you for three minutes."

"Okay. I'll be ready," she said. "Thanks...Gil."

"Wow. Geez." I called the office. "Tell the boss I'm still surveying," I said to our pert receptionist. When you pay minimum wage and you want someone fairly presentable out front, you don't always get a *Gigantus mentalus*. So half the messages went to the wrong people, and the other half were wrong. She was my kind of girl.

"Okey-dokey," she said. It was her favorite expression. I think she liked old movies.

Helen was not a girl who played dress-up. She wore simple clothes off the rack at JCPenney or a cheapo of that ilk, but she always looked smashing. *She* made the clothes, not the other way around.

She met me in a simple open-necked white blouse that could have been standard issue in a convent, and a pair of jeans that might have gotten her thrown out of the convent.

I pushed open the car door for her. As she swooped in, we both said, "Hi," simultaneously. Literally.

As we drove toward the San Diego Freeway, I started to apologize. She cut me off.

"I shouldn't have assumed," she said. "Maybe we'll do better in a safer environment. Now that we know the score."

"Yeah. Ninth inning. Nothing to nothing and the bases are drunk."

"The bases are drunk?" She frowned. "What does that mean?"

"The bases are drunk. Isn't that what you say? I don't know much about baseball. What do you say when the bases each have a player on them?"

"'The bases are loaded'?" she laughed.

"Well, it's the same thing, isn't it?"

"Not quite, but it is expressive."

Enough warm-up. I turned to business. "Why do you think Michael Hadaad wants to find his daughter so badly?"

"How badly do you think he wants to find her?" she asked.

"Well, he offered to give me a half-million dollars to find her. Said he loved her so much. Wants to be a better father."

"Oh, my," she said. We were going south on the 405, heading for the Crenshaw exit. "I don't know, but other than trying to control her life like he wants to control everything he touches, I never saw the slightest sign that he cared for her at all. I know she felt that way. That's why the anorexia bit. It was a bid for his affection and attention. He had told her her thighs were starting to look like fire hydrants. It cut through to her adolescent heart. She was at that so-vulnerable age when she wanted boys to notice her, and she was convinced since they were not, that it was a personal failing. You know boys at that age are usually crumbs anyway."

"You mean we *do* outgrow it?"

She wrinkled her nose. "Some," she conceded. She thought a moment in silence. "I don't know, I was only married to Michael seventeen years, but I would guess if he offered you a half-million dollars for Alecia, it must be worth ten million to him somehow."

"Well, he didn't exactly *offer* that sum," I admitted. "I set the price."

Helen's face broke out in a broad, admiring smile. "I'd have never guessed you had it in you," she said.

Me neither, I thought, but kept my mouth shut.

"I don't get it," she said. "Are you really a detective, or, what did you tell me, a property manager?"

I told her the story of starting the whole thing on a whim at the Palm Society meeting. She was much amused. "So what makes you think you can find Alecia? You don't seem to have any experience whatever."

I shrugged. "Earn while you learn. Or, in this case, just learn." We pulled off on Crenshaw and turned east on Carson. "Tell me something. If I did find her, would he really pay me that much?"

"Not if it was humanly possible to do you out of it. And the higher the stake, the easier that is."

We parked in front of my earth-tone tract stucco bungalow. The driveway had long since been sacrificed to a gaggle of smallish palms.

"Wow," Helen said. "You have a lot of palms."

We stepped out of the car. Helen had opened her door before I got around. "Will I get to meet your wife?" she asked as soon as her loafers hit the ground.

I shook my head. "She's at a sale. Somewhere."

She froze. "You didn't tell me."

"Did you ask?"

"Did I have to? I came all this way for a chaperone.

That was clear, wasn't it?"

"Oh, I was just so excited you called. Look, if you'd rather go to a restaurant or something..."

"Busman's holiday." She donated a smile to the cause.

"The library?"

"You're impossible, Gil. Let's see the palms."

I spent the next few minutes distracted by her use of "Gil" instead of "Malvin." Did it mean she was accepting my fantasy life?

I started my spiel on the palms and cycads as we walked around the side of the house and into the backyard.

"See this one? It's got a hairy trunk. It's a *Trithrinax.* Now look at this Chinese windmill palm, a *Trachycarpus fortunei.* See how similar they are?"

"Yeah. Look the same to me."

"The *Trithrinax* has a thicker trunk. See that?"

"Hmm."

"And it holds the leaf bases on the trunk. The *Trachycarpus* sheds the leaf bases."

"Leaf bases?"

"When you cut off the dead leaves, the part that comes from the trunk is called the leaf base."

"Oh, my. I'd go crazy."

"I've already gone crazy. It's part of the fun."

"Look at this," she said, pointing to the bygone swimming pool. "Was this a swimming pool?"

"Yeah. Nobody swam."

"So you filled it with dirt."

"And palms," I added.

We sat, side by side, on a bench next to some *Roystonea regias, Royal palms, and Rhopalostylis sapidas,* shaving-brush palms.

"Where do we go from here?" I asked her.

"Not to the bedroom," she said.

"Be fair," I said. "I'm talking about our mutual enterprise. You know, maybe it is more important to find out first *why* he wants her, before we go looking."

She looked at me out of the corner of her eye. "I'd rather find her," she said. "I don't care about him and what he wants. I care about Alecia. And I want to pay you. I don't have much, but I could give you a little every week."

I patted her hand. She withdrew it slowly.

"That really is charming. This is the same girl that refused a tip from a stranger because it was too big."

"Okay. We'll credit that to my account."

"Done," I said. "So what can you tell me about Mr. Hadaad? Where did he come from? What was his family like? Who are his friends? Any bad habits? As I see it, according to California law, you were entitled to half of everything he made during your marriage, and that is half of a nice piece of change."

"Phew," she said. "Slow down, will you? That's about a hundred questions already. Let's start with him. I told you where he's from. As far as I know he was an only child. It wasn't too long after he was born his father demanded his mother's family sweeten the dowry. In those countries, that is not unusual, I'm told. And failure to capitulate can result in thinly veiled 'accidental' death–like slipping on a butcher knife in the kitchen.

"Her family had some money, but they weren't keen on her husband. They thought not only was it a disappointing flop of a marriage, but the guy was a scumbag."

"Like father, like son."

She nodded. "He was always telling me how much better he was than his father. Anyway, I guess her family was fairly important in town, and they got word to her husband that if anything happened to their daughter, it would be the end of him. So her husband took the easy route, as one does in those cultures. He went to the steps of the town hall and said, 'I divorce thee,' three times, and that was the end of it."

"What became of him?"

"I understand he was gunned down in some dispute over a pack of cigarettes or something equally weighty."

"Quite a heritage," I contributed my two dollars. "So where is *Mama*?"

"In Santa Monica."

"Really?" I shot up. "You think there is anything there?"

"I think that's just the trouble," she said, biting her lower lip. "There's very little there. What little there once was is fading fast."

"Do you still see her?"

"Oh, no. Her son wouldn't permit it."

"Would you still want to?"

"I don't know. I used to be fond of the old girl. She's pushing seventy-five, but it is a real push. But even so, she's a pleasant, open woman in her way."

"What's her way?"

"Oh, ditzy might sum it up. In those desert climates not too much was expected of women. Raise the kids and stay out of the way. I expect Sheila was good at that."

"Do you have her address? Her phone?"

"She's in the book, I believe. S. Hadaad, no address. I have it somewhere though. I could take you there. It's a small cottage-like place near the ocean in Santa Monica. But I don't know what good it would do."

"Could it hurt?"

She looked me over. "Did it last time?" she asked. And we had a fair laugh. "I just mean I don't know what she could know or remember."

"She like her son?"

"Fair-haired boy."

"Mutual?"

"Yes, believe it or not, he was a fairly attentive son. Bought her that little house. Offered more; she wouldn't have it."

"Like mother-in-law, like daughter-in-law?" I asked.

She smiled. "Michael liked her a lot better."

"Why?"

"No sass," she laughed.

"What are her hobbies–her passions?"

"That's easy. Dogs–she loves dogs. I think she still has three or four of her own. She just dotes on them. Walks them every morning and evening."

"Ugh," I grunted. "I hate dogs."

"Oh? Why?"

"They bark," I said. "Say, can I offer you something to eat?"

"Thanks, I usually eat at the restaurant. It's part of the deal, and also how I can pay the rent."

"Take you out somewhere?"

"No, thanks. I get enough of restaurants six days a week."

"Get you an apple or something?"

"Okay, an apple would be nice."

"Stay there," I said, getting up.

"Don't worry," she said.

I was actually flattered that she seemed to fear me as a *roué*. When I returned, I saw the sun was casting the shadow of my tallest *Caryota urens* frond on her white shirt.

"I've been thinking," I said, handing her one of the two apples I brought back to the bench in the palm garden. "If you'll show me where she lives on our way back, I'll get a dog and walk it so I can bump into her. Who knows, she may know something."

I took a bite of my apple. Kind of flavorless and mealy. I apologized. "Rex isn't much of a shopper," I explained.

"Rex? You send your dog to the store?"

"No, sorry. Nickname for the glass blower."

"And you call her Rex?" She was looking at me as though she were having second thoughts about my sanity.

"Well, Tyrannosaurus Rex, actually. Tyranny Rex, for short."

"Well, that's a relief," she said without conviction.

"Say," I said, inspired, "what do you say I hire a killer dog to take a bite out of one of hers? How would she react to that?"

"I expect she'd go to pieces," Helen Hadaad, née MacDonald, said.

"Good!" I exclaimed.

94

14

I didn't try to kiss Helen or anything when I left her off in front of her Diner Diner. Not that I wouldn't have liked to. I just said, "I'll be in touch."

She had shown me Sheila Hadaad's house, a cute little bungalow a rock's throw from the Santa Monica beach.

Now here I was, the next morning, sitting in my Plymouth beside a growly dog which I had hired from one of those animal trainers who services movie accounts. I had spent the night before learning how to handle the pooch. Pit bull, I think he called it. Learning how to prevent him from handling *me* would have been more like it.

It was all a matter of pressure on the leash, whether he took a bite out of his enemy ("A little nip," was the way his charming trainer put it) or simply devoured him.

Killing Sheila Hadaad's dog, I decided, probably wouldn't win me any silver moons from the great Michael Hadaad's dog-loving mother.

I was a block and a half down the street, between Sheila and the ocean. I wanted to see her come out so I could take my dog for a walk without her suspecting I was laying for her–which she might have done, had I alighted in front of her house.

She came out a little after eight. She had three dogs in tow. Little poodley-looking things, but I don't know dogs from my Uncle Emory.

Rather than Sheila Hadaad walking the dogs, the

dogs seemed to be pulling her along.

Along with the dog, I borrowed the dog trainer's cap, which said, "Dog lover," across the front. I put it on. It was a little big for me, but my ears kept it from blinding me.

I stepped out of the car with my pit bull, who had slobbered all over my front seat. I don't understand what anyone would see in a pit bull, unless they took some kind of perverse pleasure in seeing people scared out of their wits, or bitten, or both.

As the poodley dogs pulled Sheila Hadaad closer, I did a quick take. She looked like she was stubbier than she would have liked, but it did have the advantage with the dogs–being so close to the ground made it harder for them to pull her over.

She looked fussy and a little ditzy: the kind of person who would call you at five-thirty in the morning and ask if she awakened you. She was wearing a wraparound skirt that looked like one of those tablecloths from an Italian bistro. Her blouse was some orangey thing that could only be worn with the red-and-white-checked skirt by someone eclectic or color-blind.

She got within spitting distance. I tipped my cap, hoping she would read that I was a dog lover–no dog lover could be all bad.

"Nice pups you have there," I sang out.

Sheila squinted into the sun. "Oh, dear, they aren't pups at all. No, sir, they're all old dogs."

"Really? They look so spry to me."

She beamed, as though I had paid her a personal compliment. "Why, thank you."

"How long have you had them?"

"Land sakes." She twisted her cheeks in deepest thought. "I don't know. Many years."

"Well, they certainly are adorable," I said, looking down at the ugliest dogs I ever saw. "What are their names?"

"Well, this is Nina," she said, pointing to the lead dog. "And this is Pinta, and over here is Santa Maria. I named them for Columbus' ships." She seemed to get a little taller. "The man who discovered America," she explained.

"Wonderful!" I exclaimed. "I was just headed for the ocean, how about you?"

"Why, yes. I walk my poochies twice a day."

"Well, good for you. I do too. Funny, I don't think I've seen you before. Mind if I tag along?"

She looked down at my snarling, slobbering pit bull. He was straining at his leash and I was holding him back, just as I had been taught. "Oh, I think I'd be afraid of your dog," she said. "He looks so ferocious."

"Oh, he's a lamb really," I assured her.

"Really? He looks like a dog to me."

"Well, yes–I mean he's a pussycat."

She frowned. That didn't seem right to her either.

"A cream puff," I explained. "Very gentle."

"Oh, I see." She wasn't convinced. And just to cap it off, my pit bull gave a snarling growl that said, "Lady, get those poodles outa here or you're going to be standing in three puddles."

"Well," she added, "I'm afraid I'd be uncomfortable for my pooches. No offense. So I hope you have a very nice day." And she trundled off. Seeing the parade from the rear was even more amusing. Of course, I had no thought of letting her slip out of my thumbs that easily. I noticed little Santa Maria was eying my Killer. I thought it looked like a taunt.

My Killer thought so too. He took a lunge at Santa Maria, who was lagging behind. Just as her mistress, in an effort to get the laggard dog to keep up, snapped, "Santa Maria!" Killer chomped his lethal teeth into Santa Maria's stern, causing the ugly little thing to yelp to the heavens. The parade of the three ships came to an abrupt halt.

"Killer!" I admonished my charge, giving him a good swift kick to his haunches. "Don't you *ever* do that again." I really don't have the slightest belief that dogs understand English, but I thought Sheila would not find the prospect unreasonable.

I started to turn on the ooze. "Oh, I'm so terribly

sorry. Do you think she's hurt?"

"Well, I certainly do," she huffed. "Wouldn't you be if that vicious animal took a bite out of you?"

"Oh, I'm so sorry. Look, my car is right here. Let me take her to the vet."

"That's not necessary," she said slowly enough to let me know she really thought that was a good idea.

"Look, I insist. At my expense, of course. If you can't come, I'll take her alone."

"Well..." she said, "that's good of you."

"Not at all. It's my fault. I can't understand what got into Killer. It's the least I can do."

"Well...if you're sure."

She piled in the back seat with her three ships, and as I started the car, I wondered how many weeks it would be until I got the dog smell out. Killer, as though he sensed he had done his duty, was sitting on the seat beside me, triumphantly. And speaking of smells, Shiela smelled peculiar but familiar, but I couldn't put my nose on it.

She directed me to the family veterinarian, a ruddy-faced chap, bursting with obsequious enthusiasm, by the name of Dr. Royce Tankersley.

The doc took one look at Santa Maria, tsk-tsked his pink tongue and pronounced, "Emergency," and swept the dog into the inner sanctum for surgery. Like it was a real emergency. Like he was doing us a tremendous favor. His waiting room was empty, and if he had a receptionist, she was on sabbatical.

Sheila fretted and Sheila worried. I tried to calm her down.

"Do you have a son or daughter you'd like me to notify?" I thought that sounded suitably concerned.

"Oh, my son is a very important man," she said, almost trembling at the thought. "I wouldn't dream of bothering him."

"A grandchild perhaps?"

She looked off in the distance, which in this small waiting room didn't take her beyond the far wall with cute pictures of puppies and a litter of kitties that looked like they had been cut out of magazines and framed.

"She's gone," she intoned as though she were in the chorus of a devil-worshiping cult.

"Gone where?" I asked. Wasn't I clever?

"I don't know," she said, maintaining her lugubrious singsong.

"Does anybody know?"

She shook her head.

"Is there anyone else I should call?" I asked solicitously. "You probably don't want to be alone."

She pursed her lips, then shook her head. "I'm all alooonnne," she said, drawing the syllables through her nasal passages.

"Doesn't your son visit you?"

"Oh, no more. Not since the business."

"What business?" I asked, forcing down my excitement.

She pinched her lips tight shut as if to show me that was a secret that wasn't passing her lips.

It hit me at that moment. What she smelled like. It was lemon-scented dishwasher soap. Either she had used it to wash her clothes, an understandable mistake, or she had used it to wash her person. Less understandable.

"Well, whatever it is," I said, "I hope you are still friends."

She didn't answer.

"Have you tried to find your grandchild?"

"Oh, he has. He has to find her. My business, you know. I thought I was doing a good thing. I really did. Michael didn't think so. I guess I got a little mixed up."

"How mixed up?"

"Oh, very," she said, but nothing more.

"So it's a granddaughter, is it?"

She nodded.

"Well, I'll bet she's the apple of your eye."

"Was..."

"And I bet she worships you."

"Well, I don't know. If she knew what I did, maybe. But I don't think so."

"You mean you did something nice for her?"

She nodded again.

"Was it nice for you too?"

"I'm afraid I'm in the doghouse with my son."

"Ahh," I pooh-poohed her notion, "I doubt that. Why, gosh, any guy'd be darn lucky to have a mom like you."

She sat staring at the puppies on the wall, as though she were searching my words for a grain of truth. She opened her mouth to speak, but nothing came out. At that moment, ruddy-faced Royce came out with the pooch under his arm.

"There she is, Mommy," he said, handing the homely but humble dog to Sheila. Santa Maria seemed to be scoping out the place for a sign of Killer, my rented pit bull. We had tied him outside, a respectable distance from Nina and Pinta, who seemed insulted. The puppy doc fixed me with a less ingratiating, more businesslike eye.

"Is this the gentleman I should settle up with?"

"Well, I don't know," Sheila began, but I cut in.

"Oh, yes, I insist. All my fault."

Three hundred and fifteen dollars! Could he have been back there with the mutt a half-hour? I doubt it—more like twenty minutes—and I'll bet in spite of the dramatic splint and bandaging, the doc probably rubbed a little antiseptic on a superficial wound. If it were mine, three bucks would have been my limit.

Try and collect this one from Hadaad. This lark was getting expensive. I'd think twice before I'd ever again tell anyone charging for expenses was for a small-timer.

15

Ten more minutes with a car full of pooches and I'd have gladly turned the job over to the Pinkerton Agency. I bit my tongue and drove Sheila and the dogs back to her home. She said she would have to set up a convalescent ward for Santa Maria, and she didn't much feel like walking the other two. "Though Lord knows they need their exercise."

"Mrs. Hadaad," I said, "I'd be honored to walk your dogs. After what's happened, I should think it's the least I could do."

"But what about your dog? I don't want another trip to the vet."

"Nor do I," I said. In fact, no one wanted another trip to that highway robber less than I. "I'll put my dog in the car."

"Oh, dear, will he like that?"

"Maybe not," I said, "but I think he'll understand."

"Wellll," she said, drawing it out so as to not be deemed a pushover.

"Good," I said. I took Killer to the car and considered leaving the windows closed in the hope he would fry. But humane instincts won the day.

Walking Nina and Pinta on the beach I plotted my strategy. First, I would take Sheila to a sedate restaurant. Romance her with attentive charm. As I walked along the sand, the two poodles wiggling ahead of me, the rest of it fell into place.

Back at her cottage I popped the question. "I do hope you'll let me take you to lunch?"

"Oh, my, that's very kind of you, but I'm afraid it would be an imposition."

"Not at all. It would be my pleasure."

"But, you know, I have nothing to wear, really. I go out so seldom."

"What's the matter with what you have on?" I asked. "Looks perfectly fine to me." (Gulp.)

She was persuaded. Actually, she was a pushover. Women's resistance to men diminished proportionally to their age. The Gil Yates theorem of sexual attraction.

I tied Killer the pit bull behind her house, while her three adorables were safe inside, and we trundled off to Westwood for lunch. Well, *she* trundled–I sort of sashayed.

I wanted to take her to a sedate restaurant for two reasons: One, to show her I was a sedate kind of guy, and, two, so her red-and- white-checked skirt wouldn't match the tablecloth.

Reynards was such a place. A little corner cottage that would have been at home in Carmel, Reynards was catering to the sedate set long before I can remember. Originally there may have been a Reynard in there some-where, but Jack Marsh was doing the honors currently, having bought the place from Ed Greenblat. It was a miracle it was still putting out tea and crumpets in the afternoons and cute little sandwiches whose crusts went into the stuffing for the evening roast goose.

You'd think anyone with red-blooded, all-American greed flowing in their veins would have leveled the place long ago and thrown up a high-rise where all the tenants would have poodles and arthritis.

As it was, I think one of the families got fat on air rights, but I wouldn't know; I've never gotten fat on anything but junk food.

Sheila and Reynards were made for each other. It was the kind of place where you wanted to stick your little finger out from the teacup.

She ordered the cucumber and dill on rye and I had the ham and cheese. The heartiest thing they offered at lunch.

Settled in with Sheila, I started the meaty conversation. "You say you don't go out much," I began. "You don't mean you don't see your children?"

"I only have one son."

"Are you close?"

"He used to live a lot closer. He's up the coast now–dear, about an hour and a half, I guess."

"Does he come down often?"

"Oh, no. Not since my faux pas."

"Faux pas," I said in mock shock. "I don't believe you would ever be capable of faux pas."

"Why, Mr. Yates, then I would say either you didn't know me, or you had very little notion of human nature."

Hmm, I thought. She doesn't sound quite as out of it as I was led to believe. My strategy could rather well become the fodder of her hidden intellect.

But I had nothing else. I would have to bank on human nature as I had experienced it.

"So what was this faux pas? "I asked as though I were simply making polite conversation.

"Oh, dear," she said, "I couldn't possibly bore you with all our family squabbles."

I reached out and laid my hand on hers across the white tablecloth. "Nothing you could say would bore me."

She patted my hand with her other one, bringing it up from her lap. "You're very sweet," she said. But she said nothing more.

"I'm sorry I forgot," I said, "did you say you had any grandchildren?"

"One. I have only one: Alecia. But I don't see her. I don't even know where she is."

"Oh, dear," I commiserated, "you seem to be pretty much alone. Your son has a wife, I suppose?"

"Divorced."

"Isn't it a shame all the divorces nowadays?"

"Oh, yes."

"Irreconcilable differences," I scoffed. "Who doesn't have irreconcilable differences? I certainly do, didn't you?"

"I don't know," she said, taking a dainty sip of water, "I usually went along with anything. I didn't want any conflict."

"There don't seem many like you today," I said.

"I suppose not."

The sandwiches came and we munched.

"Did you like your son's wife?"

"Oh, my, yes."

"So often mothers-in-law don't get on with daughters-in-law," I said. "So it must be a tribute to you if you could get along." I was throwing out the compliments, but I wasn't getting anywhere. "So do you know why they got divorced?"

"Well, I shouldn't wonder. My son can be difficult."

What was missing from Sheila Hadaad, I decided, was the elaboration gene. She was telling me things I already knew, without any elaboration.

"Are you sure you won't have a glass of wine?" I tried again. She had refused my earlier offer and she refused this one. All visions of her falling over drunk and laying out the whole story for me seemed to go up in the flames or down in smoke–or something very much like that.

"You know, I've got two kids of my own, and I know what a chore they can be."

She nodded solemnly.

"Sometimes it seems like all I'm needed for is to write checks," I chuckled. Her head was still bobbing. "I often said money may not be everything, but it keeps you in touch with your kids."

Her eyes opened wide, her head bobbed up and down, but her mouth stayed closed. I shot another arrow in the dark:

"Your faux pas had nothing to do with money, I suppose?"

"Why do you say that?" She seemed a little offended.

"Well, I just can't picture a sweet woman like you troubling your pretty head about...money," and I laid such a terrible inflection on the word "money." I said money was overrated, and anyone who would waste their time worrying about it wasn't fit to lick her boots.

"Well, you don't know my son," she corrected me, deliciously anxiously, I thought. "I think money is *all* he cares about."

"Is that so?" I prompted.

She nodded, pinching her eyes closed. "And so the only faux pas I could ever commit in his eyes..." She opened her eyes abruptly.

"Would be about money," I completed her thought. For an instant I thought I had something. Then I realized it was nothing. "Does he give you money?"

"Oh, yes. Plenty to live on. But this was different."

"More?"

"Much more."

"Millions?"

"Many, many millions."

"What did you do with it?"

"That was my faux pas."

I was hoping I could hold my temper while I was pulling her molars trying to get information. It was frustrating in the extreme.

"You didn't spend it?"

"Oh, no. It wasn't for me to spend. I was just supposed to hold it for a while."

"Did you hold it?"

"Well, Mr. Yates," she said, looking me in the eye like I was one naive puppy, "you don't *hold* that kind of money. You put it in a bank somewhere."

"And you didn't put it in a bank somewhere?"

"Well, yes I did."

"So then there's no problem."

"Yes there was. I was supposed to put it in my name."

I sat silently staring, realizing she had just, finally,

given me the mystery. She didn't have to tell me the rest. But once you loosen a woman's tongue, there is no tightening it.

"I thought, gracious, what does an old thing like me need with twenty million dollars? So I just put it in Alecia's name. I understand so little about banking. In the old country a woman's place did not include the bank. So Michael told me to put it in my name, in trust for him. So if anything happened to me, he would get the money automatically. So I just put it in Alecia's name–in trust for Michael, of course–it was perfectly innocent. I mean, how was I to know she would disappear and he would suddenly want the money?"

"Yes, how could you?" I said. "But why would he give you all that dough in the first place?"

She shook her head. "I don't know. Something to do with business or taxes or something. You know I'm just a stupid old woman."

I looked her square in the eye. "That," I said emphatically, "is one thing you are not."

She blushed. I'm sure no one ever hinted before she had any brains.

"Say," I said, "I don't know a lot about this high finance myself, but aren't you limited to a hundred thousand insurance per account?"

"Well, he wanted me to put it in more accounts–different banks–you know–but at the time, he seemed in such a rush to get rid of the money, I must have been distracted, because I didn't remember that part of it."

"Let's see, to insure twenty million you'd need two hundred banks, wouldn't you?"

"So you see, that's a lot to expect from an old woman," she said. "Besides, the bank we used is perfectly safe. Been around longer than Michael has. And he said it was only for a year." Then I had to strain to hear her murmur, "Now the year is up."

"So now Michael wants the money," I said, "and Alecia has disappeared?"

She nodded.

"Has he looked for her?"

"Oh, yes. But he can't find her."

"Did she love her father?"

She frowned. "I don't know if you could say that. I think he was pretty hard on her. And she had those food disorders..."

"Would she give him the money?"

"Good gracious, I never thought she wouldn't. Money didn't ever seem important to her. But you mean she might not do it to spite him?"

"Or she ran away so he couldn't get at the money."

"Why, I never thought of that," Sheila Hadaad said.

But I knew she had.

16

Back in the Plymouth, pointed west into a sinking sun, Sheila convinced me she had no idea where Alecia could have gone. She hadn't ever seen her that much.

She had gotten her to sign the bank card by saying it was just a favor for her grandmother. That seemed to satisfy any curiosity Alecia might have had.

I saw her to her door and we both checked Santa Maria, to find her in frisky spirits.

We exchanged phone numbers and a promise to "keep in touch."

I gathered Killer from the backyard and together we highfooted it back to his home base.

"Do all right for you?" his handler asked.

"Couldn't have been better," I said, and paid my tab without wincing. I got back in the car and headed to the Wemple office, where I used the phone.

Not being a guy given to jumbo savings accounts, I needed a little help understanding the ramifications of an "In trust for" savings account.

Esther Gonzales, at my friendly local bank, set me straight. It was a time I was glad I had decided not to bank where Daddybucks had all the business accounts. It's supposed to be a confidential thing, banking, but you know how people talk.

In case you aren't a big investor either, I'll give you the scoop. "In trust for" accounts are used by people who have many hundreds of thousands they want to put in the same bank. By changing what they call the "vestings" on each account, the U.S. government will happily insure the account holder against the nefarious acts of the savings and loan cons.

"In trust for" works this way: A person holds an account in trust for another person. As long as the account is in force, the person on the account, the trustor, has control of the account. If the trustor dies, the beneficiary automatically gets the money.

Which, of course, made me think if Hadaad was desperate for the twenty mil or so, if someone was pressing him for something, he might consider killing his estranged daughter. To say nothing of me, if I stood in the way.

There were a lot of arguments why Hadaad wasn't that kind of guy, but none of them convinced me.

I thought I'd better do something quickly. It wasn't going to be as easy to sneak out of the house to see Helen when Tyranny Rex came back from her trip.

I called for my voice mail to see if Helen had called. Instead, I had a message from Hadaad, my ex-employer. Just in case I still had a shot at the fee, I called him. After all, now I knew why he wanted Alecia. Dead or alive. She was probably better to him dead. Then she wouldn't have to be cajoled into signing the account over to him. He would get it automatically.

"I've sent you a contract to your office," he said. "Did you get it?"

"Contract?" I said. "I thought we understood I was no longer working for you."

"Yes, yes," he said, as though that little matter were of no consequence. "But I do intend to pay you if you do find her, so I thought it would be to your advantage to have something in writing."

I was stunned to silence. Hadaad was not a man to look out for the interests of others. So immediately I smelled a rodent.

"I'll look at it," I said noncommittally.

He was saying, "Good," as I hung up the phone.

On a hunch, I called Helen on my Realty office phone. I thought there might be a tap on my number that Hadaad had. Though they had followed me to work, tapping all those lines would have been a gargantuan task.

She didn't answer. On reflection, I was relieved. Why wouldn't they tap *her* phone? All my communication would have to be at her restaurant, Diner Diner.

I started to go to my "office," for the letter, when I got another hunch to stay clear of the place. Instead, I called Saul and asked him if he could check the door for me with the key he had kept.

I got to Diner Diner just as they were closing for the night. Helen was puttering around with salt shakers and sugar bowls, and I asked if she ever got them mixed up.

"Not yet," she said.

I told her what I learned. She didn't seem surprised. "Do you think he'd kill Alecia, if he had to, to get his hands on twenty million, give or take a few dollars?"

She looked me in the eye and spoke without emotion. "I don't think he'd hesitate for a minute."

I pressed her for people Alecia might have shared a confidence with.

She shook her head. "The police and the FBI, not to mention the other detectives, have been over that ground again and again. Nobody knew anything," she said.

"Okay, I'll just sit in a church somewhere and wait for a divine inspiration," I grumbled. "Look, the game is changed. If I found Alecia for him, he'd ask her to sign the account over to him. She might refuse. He might kill her. So what do you say you give me what you have? It's better than nothing. Maybe someone has had their memory jogged about some insignificant incident that might shed a light on something more germane. Maybe some of them are protecting her. Maybe there was no chemistry with the interrogator."

"Oh, okay. You want to hit your head against the wall, I'll give you some names. Some of these people aren't too pleasant. She seemed to run with freaks and Hell's Angels types."

"Why?"

She shrugged her pretty shoulders. "Maybe to get back at her dad–maybe me."

"You? Did you have a bad relationship with her?"

"Not till I didn't fight for custody."

"Were these people you are giving me acquainted with her before that time?"

"Yeah, I guess. I think she may have met one guy afterwards. He was a real brute. Butch was his name. Butch Bacon, believe it or not."

"Beat her?"

"Oh, I don't think so."

"Maybe I should start with him first."

"He may be the most likely to know anything, and the least likely to tell."

But he was the hardest to find. So I went methodically through the list, and a larger collection of duds you'd never hope to see. How they could all get through life with so little awareness and knowledge will mystify me for generations–should I live so long. Alecia was apparently not one for close friendships. Some of the names Helen gave me seemed to have trouble remembering who Alecia was.

I finally turned over a lead on Butch Bacon, and found him in the Straight Up Pool Hall and Beer Parlor.

It was one of those semi-dark places where you thought you would choke on the cigar smoke, where the smell of barley and hops fermented put you at ease about your body odor. And the look of the clientele made you count your blessings for the beer smell.

Butch, the barkeep told me, was the big guy hunched over the pool table in the far corner. This direction was followed by a friendly word of advice: "And if you know what's good for you, no jokes about Butch being a name for lesbians. Not if you want to get out of here straight up."

I went over to the corner. The closer I got, the bigger Butch Bacon became.

He was built like three ordinary fellows, back to back.

Butch was a walking tattoo. He looked dirtier than it was possible to be. He had a Yukon gold digger's face, as big as all outdoors and a vast beard of steel wool.

He was a person whose opinions were not likely to meet much opposition. If you had to choose sides, you could do a lot worse than throwing in with old Butch.

I can see Alecia introducing him to Michael Hadaad, her dad. "Dad, this is my friend Butch. Why don't you tell him what you said to me about guys with tattoos who hang out in pool halls?"

Butch was playing himself in a game of pool. He was winning. Boy, *was* he? One after the other the old balls were dropping in one pocket or the other.

"Hi," I said, sticking out my hand. "I'm Gil Yates."

Butch just looked at my hand, then at my face, as though he were trying to figure out why I would want to shake his hand when I could see he was busy.

I cleared my throat, but it didn't help give me more courage. "I'm looking for Alecia Hadaad. I understand you knew her."

"Yeah," he said, cuing up the balls. "I knew her. She was an okay broad."

"If I told you she was in danger–life-or-death danger–would you help me?"

He half-closed his bear eyes and with two fingers scratched the pile of hair on his face. "Anybody lay a hand on her, I'd kill 'em–no question."

"So you must feel..." I gave up the thought. It was gilding the garbage can. He'd said enough.

"Well, I have reason to believe her life is in danger. I want to get to her first."

He squinted at me, then laid the eight ball to rest in the corner pocket. He looked up without any special satisfaction showing on his face–as though he were telling me, for him it was an easy shot.

"How do I know you're for real?"

"Just by looking at me, I should imagine."

"Hm." He scratched his beard. "You do look sort of like a wimp," he said. "You play any pool?"

"Oh, geez," I said, "not like you."

"Here." He handed me a stick from the rack on the wall. "Give it a shot. You sink a ball before I sink 'em all, I'll play ball with you."

He set them up. I was perspiring. I had a fair idea how to hold the cue and some sense of the physics of the game, but I had played only in my teens and had little hope of meeting his challenge...

"Break?" he asked, "or shall I?"

Well, I thought, I have no hope in the world of sinking a ball on the break, but he easily could, and then run the whole pack in one turn. Yet if I broke them, he would be better set up to run the table. "You break," I said, swallowing it like the wimp he thought I was.

He broke and sunk the three ball while he was at it. The force of the blow, I thought, should have put all the balls in some pocket.

"So how did you meet Alecia?"

"She came in here," he said, lining up and sinking the six.

"Alone?"

"Yeah." The nine ball disappeared like a shot.

"She play pool?"

"I taught her."

"She good at it?"

He nodded, then sank the seven. "In a game with you I'd take her with odds." He wiped the table clean, leaving one ball, then obviously missing it on purpose, said, "Your turn."

It was an easy enough shot he left me. Not far from the corner. Just a little nick and it would be home.

I missed it. Fortunately the cue ball missed falling in the pocket by a hair. I had left him a tough shot. I didn't doubt he could sink it in the far corner if he tried. Instead he set me up with an even easier shot. "Now hit it square–don't follow the ball into the pocket."

My hands were sweating, my heart was pounding, then I realized how stupid I was being. He was giving me the shot. He *wanted* to help me. Being a wimp has its advantages. This Butch wouldn't talk to those macho dicks that came around. Now here was a guy he could blow away by sneezing. I sank the ball.

"Congratulations," he said. "You did it! I'd still put my dough on Alecia, but you *did* it."

"Thanks," I said. "Not for the flattery, but for letting me do it."

"So what do you want from me?"

"Help me find Alecia."

"I don't know where she is," he said, "and that's straight," he assured me, tapping my shoulder with the cue.

"Ever have any ideas?"

"No. Lot of thoughts–no ideas."

"What kind of thoughts?"

He looked through me again, as if to discern my legitimacy. "Come on over to the table there," he said, pointing. "Buy me a beer."

This I was glad to do. "You don't want one?" he asked when I brought a lone beer from the bar.

"Don't drink," I said.

He nodded, as though he had guessed as much and this only confirmed his suspicions about my wimphood.

"What can you tell me about Alecia?"

When his head surfaced from the beer and the white suds stood firm on his dark beard, Butch said, "She was an all right chick."

"Where would you look if you wanted to find her?"

The mountains on both sides of his head heaved. "I don't go looking for people don't want to be found."

"I appreciate that," I said, "but if we don't find her now and before her father does, we might not find her alive at all. So where could she be?"

"Where do kids go when they drop out? On the road. Some to communes in the belly of a city, some live on the streets. Prostitution. Cults–some join those crazy religious organizations. They change their names, their identities. You're asking *me* how to find them? I wouldn't know."

"If you had to pick one or two of those destinations you mentioned–for Alecia–which would it be?"

He took a sip of the beer, then threw his head back and downed the rest of it. "I don't see her whoring, or living on the streets. She could be floating–on the road, you know–but she wasn't that flaky type–she was pretty intense."

"The kind of girl who might go bonkers for some tan-skinned messiah with bedroom eyes?"

The corner of his mouth hitched back. "I can't picture it. She has judgment."

"Maybe a nun?"

"Maybe. But I don't think she was a Catholic," he said, studying his empty glass. "I don't think she was religious at all."

"What was she like?"

He gave a short snort, like the question was impossible to answer. "Like no one I ever met. She was kind, you know, she'd give you her right arm five minutes after she met you. She was kind of intense–you know, took things pretty seriously. You could joke her about a lot of things, and most of them she'd believe. Most of all she was bummed out at what she thought was her failure to please her father, that horse's ass."

Butch's language had been a bit saltier than I have portrayed it, because I am sensitive to profanity. Just because I let his one little example slip through, don't get the idea that was the extent of it.

"So, how well did you know her?"

"Not that well, I guess. She used to come in here after having some battle with her dad."

"Did she ever say anything about her mother?" I asked.

Butch hiked a mountain. "Another helpless victim." He looked me over again, trying to understand something.

"You know, I do appreciate your help. It's very good

of you. Do I dare ask why you are confiding in me, when you kissed off all the others?"

He stared at me as though that were the stupidest question. "You're the wimpiest looking guy I've ever seen," he said, as though that answered it. "That idiot Hadaad would never hire a guy like you." I bought him another beer. He said, as though I had pulled the last stopper, "Do you know her story?"

I shook my head.

"Her old man was a bit of a failure. He's tried a whole bunch of schemes and never did well in any of them. Until he started dealing arms. He began with these tin-pot dictators in banana republics, hit the Caribbean and Africa, and was finally bringing in a nice piece of change. Then suddenly we were in a war in the Mideast. The enemy needs guns and planes and stuff, and he supplies them. Tens of millions he makes killing our own boys. Listen, I am no fan of war but what he did is the lowest. Especially with him being from that part of the world and all. So they throw him in the slammer for four, five months and he hides the dough somewhere. He gets out, he's a rich man. Alecia wanted so badly to look up to him–to have him care for her. Instead, he was riding her all the time. On her about her weight, her hair, her makeup, her clothes. Man, she couldn't do anything right."

"Couldn't she turn to her mother?"

"Her mother couldn't do anything. These girls want daddies. Her mother was too weak to fight him for custody. She left the scene and Alecia felt totally abandoned. I guess she got more anorexic or something and old Dad commits her to a nut house or something. Alecia finally blows that scene, and no one has seen her since."

"Including you?"

"Yep."

"She ever talk to you about suicide?"

"Yeah. She considered it, she said. I never took it that seriously. She always seemed like a kid who could work things out."

"She ever run away from home before?"

"Well, she spent a couple nights at my place once."

I must have looked shocked, because he said, "Hey, nothing happened. I wouldn't take advantage of a vulnerable kid like that."

I started to say I understood, but he kept talking.

"I'll tell you this, Gil old buddy, no way did that girl deserve the shake she got." (You know he wasn't saying "shake," but you get the picture.) "I would have done *any*thing to help her out, and that includes putting her old man on a boxcar for Alaska. But she didn't think that way. You ever need any help, you call me here. They'll get the message to me."

"Thanks."

"You say there's any chance he'd harm a hair on her head again, I want to be there to stop him good."

17

Driving home that night, I speculated on Alecia's whereabouts. She wanted a father. Kids hooked on religion were often looking for a dad. Maybe she lost herself in one of those fringe religions–the Hare Krishnas, the Moonies, Scientology. There were a lot of them, and finding kids was like hens' feet–or something smaller on a hen. They changed their names, usually moved far from home, disguised themselves in any way possible to keep the kinfolk at bay–so they wouldn't show up with an army of lawyers and deprogrammers. Just what Michael Hadaad would do if he got wind of anything.

Before I plunged into the impossible task of checking out the cults, I thought I'd try my theory out on Helen–give me another excuse to see her.

When I got home I decided it was too late to call. In the morning, I decided it was too early to call, so I went to the office. There was Daddybucks, elevated like the King of Siam, reading his newspaper. "Hey, Malvin," he hailed me. "Boy, take a look at these unemployment statistics," Daddybucks said, slapping the open paper on his desk. "Up, up, up."

It was a tenet of Daddybucks' operation that, from time to time, he would make remarks for the purpose of eliciting from his charges a feeling of deep gratitude for having a job at all. The above-mentioned unemployment observation was designed for the wide-eyed response: "I *know*, Mr.

Wemple, we're all so lucky to have jobs, thanks to you."

I usually grunted, and thought, "If you could find someone to marry your daughter, you should give them the company." Once or twice I came close to putting those sentiments audibly. But Daddybucks was not a man given to self-deprecating humor or introspection.

He was, rather, what we called down at the nut house, self-absorbed.

Back at my desk, I checked for messages. Good and bad. Good from Helen.

"Been thinking about you. Hope you did well yesterday."

The other from Big Shot. "I have not heard your reaction to the contract. Did you get it?" His voice was its old imperial self. "By the way, I'm tired of never being able to reach you–leaving messages on machines is demeaning. I'm getting you a car phone and I want you to use it." He always talked to me like I was an indentured servant.

Wow, I thought, this guy bought me awful cheap (or awfully cheaply if grammar is your thing). The relationship was deteriorating so rapidly that I didn't have the strength or interest to argue. But now I knew why he was so anxious. Or I knew part of it. If someone was pressing him for money and he couldn't get to it without his daughter's signature. And the account was about to, as they say, "mature." In a few weeks it would be locked in for another year. Not good if the mob is breathing down your neck for a payoff.

I picked up the phone and called Helen. "Hi," she said cheerfully. I flattered myself that she knew it was I calling. "I knew it was you," she said.

I told her what transpired. "It's our first break," I said.

But we both knew, a break was a far cry from a solution.

I thought a car phone might be fun. In fact I had broached the subject to Daddybucks, who thought somewhat less of it than I did.

"Use the managers' phones," was how he put a cap on it.

Now I could have one, gratis. It didn't take long for my original excitement to dampen. Michael Hadaad was not the kind of guy to do anything gratis. Beware of geeks bearing gifts.

I called my buddy Saul for an assist.

"Malvin!?" It was my buddy Saul, putting his heart and soul into ridiculing my name.

"Hi, Saulie, what's down?"

"I did your errand. That is, I went to your, dare I say, *office?* Two bozos loitering in the hall, and not very subtly. So I didn't open your door. Asked if I could help them and they said, 'No.'

"Then I said, 'Are you looking for someone?' and the one guy looks at the other as though he were the answer department and he shrugs like he were a deaf-mute or something. The size of them tells me I don't want to rile them too much, so I mosey on out of there, waiting to see if they come out."

"Do they?"

"One comes out for lunch. Brings it in for the other. So what's your pleasure? Check back at five? Call the cops? Hassle them with our no-loitering policy?"

"Don't perspire it, Saulie. Next time you're there, check again. Don't touch the door, they're anywhere they can see you. If the Bobbsey twins are who I think, they pack a mean wallop and I wouldn't tangle with them."

"Roger," he said. Saul liked to make believe he was a pilot.

"Malvin, baby?" Saul seared the fiber optics. "The baboons were in their car out in a yellow zone. I slipped in the back door and picked up that cellular phone they left at your, you will excuse the expression, *office* door. I'm using it now."

"Using it?" I was startled. "So just don't say anything nasty."

"About the baboons? How could I? They're right on my tail."

"How did they find you?"

"Beats me. I took the phone down to the basement and out the back door. I parked on Holloway and soon as I got in the car I see them coming around the corner. I ducked down in the seat so they wouldn't see me and I'm damned if they didn't pull up behind me and park and wait. So I started driving and they're following me with all the subtle grace of an elephant tap-dancing."

"Can you lose them? Even for a couple minutes? Leave the car somewhere and call me from another phone. Leave the cellular phone in the car."

Twenty minutes later a breathless Saul was on the phone to me. "Malvin? Tell me something? Why the hell am I doing this jackass stunt for you? You want to diddle with these apes, that's your privilege. I'm bowing out."

"Yeah, well, I 'preciate it, Saulie. Just one more thing, if you will."

"Oh, brother."

"I take it the Barbie twins are not with you now?"

"Right."

"Go back, lose them again, dump the phone somewhere–anywhere–a garbage can, a gas station, anywhere. I think you'll be home free."

"Man, are you gonna owe me after this one."

"I'll give you a *Parajubaea cocoides* seedling."

"You're too kind," he said, and hung up with an uncanny verve.

That night, Saul reported in that it worked like a charm. "I pulled into a gas station on Melrose. Self-service. I pumped some gas. They were next in line. I put the phone in my pocket and when I went in to pay I surreptitiously let it fall in the trash can. Back in the car, I drove off and they looked at each other, trying to figure which end was up, but they didn't follow me."

"They're waiting there for me to pick up the phone." I laughed. "Let 'em follow it to the dump. They should be right at home there."

A couple days later I had an angry message on my voice mail. "Why didn't you pick up the car phone?"

It wasn't worth a response.

Guess who came home? I'll give you some hints: From a flurry of glass figurine sales. Second hint: This person was about to turn around and embark on another jaunt to Scotland, so naturally she wouldn't have time to tidy up the place or even put out of harm's way (*i.e.* the walking paths in the house) the myriad of boxes of unsold goods and display accouterments. Actually, most of the the stuff was piled up inside the front door because, naturally, that was closest to her unloading point. After that filled up, she moved on to hallways and the living room. I imagine by now, if your intelligence level is somewhere north of nine years old, you've figured it was Tyranny Rex who made it back, safe and sound enough.

"How did you do?" I asked her.

"Fabulous!" She said.

I looked at all the boxes all over the place. "So what's in all these boxes?" I asked.

"You know I have to take more than I can sell."

"Why?"

"Don't be ridiculous. You wouldn't want me to sell out, would you?"

"Sure."

"And not have merchandise for everyone?"

"Why not? Would make it look like demand for your stuff was so hot you couldn't make it fast enough to keep up. Should have them salivating for the little man who urinates."

"I sold him out right away," she said.

Go figure.

The next thing I know she is giving me sort of a kiss and saying, "I'm off," and I'm thinking, yes, but you don't know how *far* off.

And when I say, "sort of a kiss," I mean a peck with one lip somewhere in the vicinity of a cheek, and it isn't anything from which I will have to worry about drowning or anything.

I think she said she would be gone for fourteen days. Could I wrap this thing up in fourteen days? I wondered. It didn't seem likely for a novice, but I intended to give it the old university try. So it was full speed ahoy, and back to the office for me.

I was so awfully clever getting my first lead on Alecia Hadaad's whereabouts from Monica Watkins, a top producer for our own Elbert A. Wemple and Associates, Realtors. That's what Daddybucks called her, a top producer. The appellation always struck me as more characteristic of a milk cow, but I never actually sold real estate, so I have no idea how it feels.

Obviously, I couldn't flop down on her desk and say, "Monica, sweetie, I'm working this little gig as an unlicensed private eye, so how about giving me a hand? You know that guy who deprogrammed your kid? Where does he hang out?"

Nah. I was much more clever. Not that it was easy. Monica, being a top producer and all, didn't spend many of her waking hours sitting still. She wasn't a person you could chat up with ease.

Being a top producer, Monica never got any guff from the King of Siam for being at the water fount.

"How's Bunny getting along?" I asked.

"Fine," she said, pressing the water button.

"The deprogramming took?"

"So far, so good," she said, raising her hand and crossing her fingers.

"I guess that guy knows his business," I said.

"What guy?"

"The guy who does the deprogramming."

"Oh, Joe Evans," she said, the coveted morsel falling into my lap, "yeah."

"He's still at El Camino?" I asked, mentioning the local junior college.

"Harbor," she said, setting me straight. "Gotta run," she said, running on a pair of heels too high for running, setting in bouncy motion her derriere, like two bowling balls bouncing together down the alley.

Drawing on the freedom of my job, I drove over to Harbor College, in Harbor City, a strip of land between Wilmington ("Heart of the Harbor") and the Palos Verdes Peninsula.

I got directions to Joe Evans' office. As I made my way down one of those California specials, an exterior hallway, I saw a mother coming toward me with her zombie daughter. I knew without asking they had come from the deprogrammer himself.

Outside his office was his class schedule and office hours. He taught a course called Cults and Christianity. I knocked.

"Come on in," a husky voice responded. I entered the modest space that could easily have housed a couple mops and brooms before they turned it over to Joe Evans, lecturer in Cults and Christianity, but a guy whose forte was turning cult zombies into useful citizens.

He was sitting in his slat-back wooden chair on the back two legs, holding himself in that precarious pose with his blue-jeaned legs, reposing on the desk. Like the room, his desk was cluttered to a fair-thee-well and his legs were resting unselfconsciously on a spongy pile of papers. I was relieved he didn't try to get up. I realized he would have to, sooner or later, I just didn't want to be there to see it.

Joe was a young guy, in the vicinity of thirty years, who looked like he'd rather be surfing. Rumpled honey hair and seductive eyes that would, on their own, qualify him for gurudom. One glance at him and you lost your faith in the Catholic Church's ability to smoke out the unsuitables for the priesthood; for he had a movie-star quality, smooth skin, Steinway teeth and, as I said, boudoir eyes. More Sodom than Rome, more Gomorrah than Salt Lake City.

I introduced myself and said, "I think I passed a client of yours."

"How can you tell?"

"The glassy eyes?" I speculated.

He laughed. "My job is to get the glass out of there," he said. "What brings you here?"

"I'm looking for a lost girl. Thought she might be in a cult."

He frowned. "Any idea which one, or where?"

I shook my head.

"Over three thousand of them," he said. "You got your work cut out for you."

"Yeah," I admitted. "How tough is it to get into a cult to find someone?"

"Depends. Sometimes it's impossible," he said, "other times it's harder than that."

"Three thousand cults," I said. "How do you distinguish between a cult and a religion?"

"Frank Zappa used to say the difference was real estate. Not anymore. Nobody owns real estate like Manny (that's short for Emmanuel, get it?) Starr. His little candle sellers bring him hundreds of millions of dollars a year. He has a three thousand acre compound; a newspaper that lauds free-market capitalism, especially candles and flowers; a cruise ship displacing forty thousand tons; a 747 jet. He's got bedroom eyes like they all do–and gives his speeches behind a bulletproof shield."

"Give a good speech?"

"Nah. I never found any inspiration there. Rambles a lot. And rationalizes all their behavior. Lying for the sake of a greater good, a higher power. It's old stuff, but he's got new ears. The kids looking for a daddy."

"Yeah..."

"Look, I understand these kids. Wasn't long ago I was one of them. I thought things were worse than they were. Couldn't please my girlfriend, she ran away with a plumber, bore him a child, then another, without pausing in their passion for a marriage. Suicide seemed appropriate, but I didn't have the nerve. There I was, in the cruel world, without an inkling of what to do with my life. I thought I suffered so much, I would have to do something to alleviate suffering. But who would pay me for that? General Motors?"

"Guess not."

"But the mother church would. All I had to do was swear off women, and I had already done that, thanks to Jennifer. And they would take care of me for life. It's a womby feeling, you know? And everything seems to lend itself to this cozy security–the dark and dreary monastery, the black, somber clothes."

"So you went in?"

"I went in hook, line and sinker. I'd found my dad, God the Father–Father, Son, Holy Ghost, the whole bit. I thought I could pray away my memories of the worldly Jennifer." He stopped to reflect, shook his head and said, "Couldn't. The flesh had no resistance whatever, not only to sensuality but to hypocrisy, fleecing the poor, promising undeliverable promises. Building hopes and watching them dashed."

"So you got out?"

"Betsy got me out." He nodded. "The flesh again."

"You really made an about-face," I offered.

"Not really," he said. "I'm still at the alleviating suffering game."

"Only now you seem to be anti-church."

126

He smiled and you could have played *Clair de Lune* on those teeth. "Pro-people," he said. "Kids always need help. Betsy had a son who threw it all over for the Baghwan. He was my first case."

"Did you deprogram him?"

"Yep. My toughest."

I showed him a picture of Alecia Hadaad, told him the story and asked if he could show it around.

"Be glad to," he said. "Saving souls is my bag. If anyone recognizes her, I'll point you in the right direction and do anything I can to help."

Help, I thought as I left him. What a matter of definition that word was.

18

Deprogramming had become quite a little industry. Supply and demand, the American way. In the next few days, I visited eight more of them and flooded a dozen others throughout the land with photos of the striking Alecia Hadaad. One thing was in our favor: Alecia was so beautiful, one was not liable to forget her. But with over 3,000 known cults in the land, you were talking pins in haystacks.

I was still getting proprietary messages from the great Michael Hadaad, but I was ignoring them. I smiled when I considered the guys he had hired to find me. What could he tell them? Gil Yates? Not listed. An office in Hollywood, where he never goes?

Would he threaten his ex-wife Helen? Have the bozos beat it out of her? I banked on his desire to have nothing to do with her being overriding. What an embarrassment for Hadaad if Helen were the one responsible for finding Alecia.

But I was sure Michael H. was looking for me—with all he had. I never went anywhere anymore without looking over my shoulder. I never drove without constantly checking the rearview mirror.

And just to be safe, I called Helen. She assured me she would do nothing to help her ex get to his daughter. "I'm convinced he'd kill her for the twenty million—and I don't see her giving it to him any other way."

Still, how much torture could she take without

breaking–should the bozos decide to take that route?

My curiosity about what Mr. Hadaad was up to was slaked by a call from Saul.

"Malvin?" he said, with notably less bluster than was customary.

"Saul? You all right?" I asked.

"No," he said. "The same two baboons showed up at my office, asking for your address. I said I wasn't at liberty to give out anyone's address, and, besides, I never heard of anyone named Gil Yates."

"Good for you," I said.

"Yeah, but save it. They said, 'Well, you manage that building, we got your name from the elevator permit. Gil Yates has an office there. Somebody had to rent it to him. We want to know who.' When I said that was confidential, he should see you in your office or call the phone company, he said you never went there and you weren't listed. I figure if they get real hot, I'll give them your office number, okay?"

"Sure. They have it anyway. It's Hadaad's goons. Don't let them shake you up."

"Yeah, well, it's too late for that advice. I'm all shook up. Wasn't any doubt they want to work me over, I don't give them your address on a silver platter. Shall I call the cops?"

"Let me think about it," I said. "How much time they give you?"

"Tomorrow."

"I'll call you back," I said, but I had no idea what I'd say when I called.

You ever get to a point where everything looks bleak, and hopelessness just sort of settles in? It had happened to me.

What did I have to show for my lark? I got my pal Saul in a real mess. I jeopardized Helen's well-being. I found myself wishing my wife would stay away longer, and wishing I could spend more time with Helen. I had come to realize this private-detective stuff was not a game, but I was playing it as if it were, and playing it rather badly.

Perhaps the most outrageous conceit was that I could play this game better than the pros. The cops, the FBI, the experienced dicks. Surely they had all circulated pictures of Alecia Hadaad to the four corners of the earth. Yet here I was, jackassing around as though I were inventing the wheel.

All that might have been all right, except that a young girl's life was at stake. And I was dead certain that by now her old dad, Hadaad, had loosed another bunch of bloodhounds on her trail. He was not the sort, as he proved in the beginning, to let me go it alone.

So I felt I was in a trap of my own making. In a way, I was responsible for Alecia's jeopardy, therefore I was responsible for saving her. But I really had not the least idea of how to go about it. It was so depressing.

Then, as so often happens in life, when things look their blackest you suddenly get a break in the gloom and you begin to smell the peonies.

Joe Evans, the deprogramming ex-priest, called to tell me one of his subjects recognized Alecia from the picture.

Alecia was, he said, an Oakland Starr Child, plying her trade on the Berkeley-Oakland axis.

I was so excited by the lead, I didn't even consider it might be false. I congratulated myself on my timing–as though I had something to do with it. The cops, FBI and all my predecessors had not hit pay dust because there was no one at the time being deprogrammed who could, or would, identify her.

In my euphoria and eagerness to get on the road, I almost forgot Saul and his plight.

Just like bad news, good news sometimes comes in bundles, and I had a sudden inspiration of a scenario that might help Saul.

It meant sacrificing any chance of snookering Hadaad into a fee, but I wasn't willing to throw Saul to those wolves, not even for a half-million. Oh, it wasn't all altruism. By now I was realistic enough to realize Michael

Hadaad was not your garden variety good sport, and any chance I had of ever getting a nickel from him went up in smog the minute I met his ex-wife.

"Saulie."

"Yeah, Malvin–good to hear from you. I got, what, forty minutes left to live?"

"Saulie, Saulie, don't be so melodramatic."

"Easy for you to say." He was still sounding morose.

"Here's my suggestion," I said. "When they come back, act confused. Say you looked up your records and can't find any Gil Yates–would they mind telling you exactly where the office is. When they do, look dumbfounded. No, second floor you got so-and-so, and so-and-so, nobody else."

"That's when they reach out and punch me out."

"Not if you play it right."

"Thanks for the inspiration, coach."

"Pull out your records, show them the floor plan."

"You expect them to buy that?" His skepticism seeped through the phone line.

"Probably not. So they are leaning on you. You are indignant. Say, 'Okay, show me the office.'"

"So I've got to get in a car with them?"

"No you don't. You have an appointment. You'll stop off on the way. So when you get there and they show you the office, you are more confused. Tell them you thought they meant someone in one of the other offices. Then you can start to laugh, and tell them that office (mine) was just a joke. Some guy you never saw before or since gave you a couple grand to let him do it. It was just a lark as far as you were concerned. 'Here, let me show you,' tell them. Then open it, and chuckle. Then turn serious. 'Say, he's not some kind of criminal, is he? I better get this thing plastered up before the police come around.' Then look real stupid–shouldn't cause you much strain..."

"Hey, not funny under *these* circumstances, Malvin."

"Yeah, guess not. Sorry. But that's your exit line. 'I'd better call the cops if you guys expect anything shady.' Ask for their names and addresses for witnesses. Watch 'em turn green."

"Sounds good," he said skeptically. "But what if they don't buy it?"

"So call the cops. Maybe you can get one to go with you to meet the goons at the building."

"Fat chance."

"Yeah. How about a rent-a-cop? Have him stationed on the second floor. Don't you have a couple security guards on the staff?"

"Yeah–maybe. I got to make a couple calls, see if I can arrange it..."

"Keep me posted," I said.

He snorted, "Don't worry–if I live that long."

19

I shifted the phone to my other ear and called Helen. I couldn't wait to share the good news. Then I hung it up again. I had forgotten her phone had to be bugged.

I would drive to her restaurant. But then I thought better of it. Why put her in that spot? Suppose they did go after her and she had something to tell? How long could she hold out? And what if it were a false alarm? Mistaken identity? Or there were some other surprise in store?

Better not get her hopes up. Deliver the goods first.

I pointed the Plymouth in the direction of the promised land. My first thought was I had to fly to save time—but I looked in my bank account and divined what a strain a last-minute plane ticket would put on it, and decided driving would give me time to think. And when you figure the time getting to the airport and all, driving only adds about four hours. If you don't go to sleep at the wheel or lose a transmission.

I had plenty of time to think; I just didn't know *what* to think. Joe Evans had given me a potful of pointers. But it all cooked down to one thing: Cultists didn't want to be saved from what we thought was an oppressive, demeaning life. They thrived on it. It was their identity, even if we thought of it as dehumanizing, it served them some purpose, and purpose was usually what they lacked before joining their cult.

Everybody has their favorite things about San

Francisco: the hills, the cable cars, the bay views, the bridges, the skyline, Union Square, Union Street.

I like the bookstores, the restaurants, the bronze fountain just off Union Square, with details of the city, and the little white lights that light up the outline of the Oakland Bay Bridge. Now I was adding to my favorite things the northern climate, which enabled me to wear my trench coat, even with the lining.

The lights were on when I crossed the bridge. Fortunately, the earthquake and the repair crews had left me enough road to make the trip possible.

Oakland is a beautiful town. Radiating from the serene and picturesque Lake Merritt are a delightful concrete-bunker museum, the Piedmont Hills, Mills College and the *Oakland Tribune*. Across the boundary line is the vaunted University of California at Berkeley.

This Oakland-Berkeley axis was once the bastion of the Free Huey Newton Committee, and the Students for Democratic Action Committee, which at the time was worked up about saving People's Park from the hoary builders, for, well, the people. They were also hep on freeing Huey Newton.

Huey, as I recall, was incarcerated for killing a policeman. It was considered a "political" crime by the faithful.

I was part of the Free Alecia Hadaad movement. The only problem was, as Joe Evans said, she didn't want to be freed.

Always on the cutting edge of social revolution, the Oakland-Berkeley axis now played host to the paper-cup brigade. The hippies have made way for the homeless. It is difficult to move anywhere in the Bay Area without encountering a card-carrying member of this beggars' corps, sometimes jiggling the coins in the cup. It is reminiscent of the Salvation Army tambourines, but not as seasonal. Sometimes these hobos sat sleepily beside their paper cups, smoking a cigarette.

They have franchises, these modern-day beggars: exclusive locations, hours of operation, just like McDonald's.

134

I drove over to the UC campus and noticed they had thrown up even more concrete buildings since my last visit. Shouldn't be surprising–with forty thousand or so hot-shot students, you had to put them somewhere. A concrete vault seemed as good a place as any.

Concrete seemed to be the building material of choice of state-subsidized architects. It was also favored by that other consumer of state-sponsored construction: prisons. And for a lot of the same reasons.

Perhaps I should mention that I was not a Berkeley graduate. They were, as I recall, rather snotty about my high-school grades and SAT scores.

Alecia's "home" was not far from the Berkeley campus–across the line in Oakland. What better place to lose yourself if you are student age than in a town with a student-body population of forty thousand?

You couldn't tell by looking at the old brick apartment hotel that it housed a bunch of religious zealots. That's the way the Starrs wanted it.

Everything about the place bespoke the desire to blend into the surroundings. The landscape in the brief area in front was neglected only as much as the buildings on either side. The maintenance was probably a sideline of some guy zonked out after sixteen hours hustling flowers or candles.

Some cults send their acolytes all over the world–spread the word–missionary action. Win souls for Jesus or whoever their star attraction was. With the Starrs it was strictly business. Sixteen hours of selling, and the indoctrination came after. Bone-tired is bone-susceptible seemed to be the *modus operandi*. And if the balance sheet was any indication, it worked.

Parking in the Bay Area is not a plastic-pipe cinch. I needed a view of the brick apartment, but there were no spaces anywhere. And none of these kids had cars. Manny Starr had cars up the kazoo, but the kids took the poverty schtick.

I double-parked down the block, hoping for a miracle. I didn't want to get close. Joe Evans had preached how suspicious the Starrs were of anybody that even looked like an outsider.

So why was I here? It was a little late for soul-searching after schlepping over four hundred miles in search of the Holy Grail... But really, any objective observer would have to pronounce me nutso.

I started, under false pretenses, working for a man anyone would despise. I had a verbal agreement about an unrealistic, astronomical fee with a man whose word wasn't worth a farthing.

Then I got smitten with his ex-wife and almost got killed talking to her. So I told myself I would find her daughter for her, gratis. Like I was a millionaire and could spend all I wanted.

Then I decided Michael Hadaad wanted to kill his daughter and I put on my shining armor. So now I am a knight in you-know-what, blowing money I don't have, to save a girl I don't know, and if I do save her, she might be killed.

NUTSO.

I was ready to turn around and head back where I came from–putz with my palms. I was a reasonably content guy in the context of contemporary reality. I should be a hero to Helen Hadaad? To what end? So I could leave the glass blower and live on a waitress' tips? Where would I put my palms?

Suddenly a parking place opened up across from the Starr house and I glided the Plymouth into it. I took it as an omen.

Then my mind turned to sleaze and I began to formulate plans for getting my fee from Hadaad, while saving the girl's life and making her mom think I am Superman.

Nothing to it.

I felt the break before I saw it.

An army of women came down the handful of front steps. To the woman, they looked young, guileless, innocent, like a Sunday School class after a particularly mesmerizing lesson.

I strained to find Alecia, but there were so many of them. And it could have been a class in women's studies coming from a deadly lecture.

Then I spotted her–about two thirds of the way into the pack. She moved like all her mechanisms were on automatic pilot. It was a dehumanizing life, but that was her bag. If their father wished it so, it was so. He was, in that regard, an attentive father. You wouldn't find him ambiguous. He said, "Sell your flowers," and you sold your flowers. It was clear enough what was wanted to win his love.

If she were from a large family, you'd say she was the one who got the good bones. But those blank eyes, telltale Starr Children–blanking out hypocrisy, blanking out all but the service of the father.

At a rally, Manny Starr asked how many of his children wanted to increase their sixteen-hours-a-day flower-selling stint, and a cheer rocked the auditorium, but the eyes never blinked.

"You are the enemy," Joe Evans told me.

"Even if I buy flowers?"

"Even if you buy *all* the flowers."

I nosed my car down the street, staying far enough behind to not arouse suspicion, and close enough so a sudden move wouldn't cause me to lose her.

At the next corner, a van stopped and picked up eight of the girls. Then another van pulled up. Alecia went with the third van. I followed it.

They disembarked the van, each with an armload of flowers, each at a different stop. Like the homeless, they seemed to have their own territory.

Alecia got off at Shattuck, and headed for a Thai restaurant, climbing a good flight of stairs to get there.

I waited for her to come out. I wanted to make sure the van was out of sight and nobody from the club was watching us.

She came floating down the stairs perhaps ten minutes later. I didn't check the time, it just seemed long. I speculated she was probably a good flower seller. She was so astonishingly beautiful. So unthreatening looking, and when she reached the bottom of the steps, her load of flowers noticeably lighter, I stepped into her vision, assuming those were real eyes and not the glass marbles they looked like.

"Alecia," I said. "I'm Gil Yates. I'm a friend of your mother."

She was startled. As though I were the cat that caught the robin. She turned her head with a sudden jerk. "My name is not Alecia. I am Sister Esther."

"That's nice," I said, "they change your names. Biblical. Nice." Other than saying nice twice, I wasn't doing much. Charming her I was not. She looked up and down the street, as if for someone to help her make an emergency escape. I knew I didn't have much time. I thought she would call the cops any minute. I talked fast.

I laid out the story about the twenty million bucks in her name. I gave her her options. "You can ignore it. Tell him to jump in a lake. You can go down to Santa Helena and sign over the account to him. I can bring the papers for you to sign without telling him where you are. You sign the papers, I doubt he'll hassle you."

"Over my dead body."

"Yeah," I said with a stout heart, "good for you. Just remember, if you don't sign, the only way for him to get his money is to prove you are dead. So the transaction could well take place over your dead body."

She glared at me. The stare said, "Stay where you are. You can't penetrate this protective shell, lovingly placed on me by our Father Starr." I wondered when the last time was that those eyes recognized sunshine.

"Look at it this way. It isn't *your* money. You probably wouldn't take it if he offered to give it to you."

"Blood money," she muttered.

"Yeah, so the sooner you get away from it, the better. Nobody disagrees with you about your father. We're all on your side."

"Who's 'we'?"

"Me, your mother, your grandmother..." Then I

added, "Your grandmother's dogs," and hoped for a smile. I think her smiler was out of commission.

Cars were whizzing by, then slamming on their brakes at the corner stop sign. Alecia headed for her next stop. I kept the pace. I was afraid she would climb into one of those cars and vanish.

"Just so you know," I said, panting at her pace, "if I found you, your father can find you. You got a god here, and you don't want anything to come between you. Your father's god is money, and everyone who knows him says he will unhesitatingly kill for that god. And I think–it's just a hunch–that someone frightening is leaning on him for some of that money." I reached in my pocket for the slip of paper I'd written my "office" phone number on. I handed it to her.

"It's just a matter of time until he finds you. Then it may be too late for help. Please, I want to help you."

"Why?"

Here it was, out on the table. "Because I'm nuts about your mother."

The blank eyes came almost alive.

"And she's nuts about you," I said.

I put the slip of paper with my phone number in the pocket where she held the money from the flowers. "I'm going to stay the night somewhere. I'll be back tomorrow. Think about it. I could bring him up here. That way we'd have some control."

"He'll want to get me out."

"No he won't–all he cares about is his money."

"My mother then. She'll want me out."

"I think your mother will be so delighted you're alive. She didn't interfere before, what makes you think she will now? You can keep hiding if you want. I'm going to tell her I've found you. If you want me to give her a message, I will.

"I do," she said, staring that eerie gaze. "Tell her I don't want to see her. I have a new life. I have burned the old. Jesus said, 'Leave your family for dead'." She stared like her heart had been pâtéd by a meat grinder.

"Really?" I said. "He said a lot better stuff too, didn't He? Like, 'Honor thy father and thy mother'."

She turned into the next restaurant and I let her be. Who knows, if I didn't aggravate her, she might give it some thought and come around. And I knew where she was–at least for the time being.

20

I found a motel that didn't cost as much for the night as a month's mortgage payment and settled in.

I couldn't restrain myself any longer from calling Helen. She would be home from work. She had a right to know. It was her daughter, after all, and she had a right to know she was alive. I wouldn't reveal anything else just yet. I put in the call. She didn't answer. Perhaps she wasn't home yet. It was only ten after eleven. I tried again at eleven-thirty. Eleven-forty-five. Twelve.

I called the restaurant. No answer. I left no messages; I didn't want to be traced through a phone number.

A little after one, I was getting drowsy and a little angry, so I left this message on her machine:

"Found her. She is fine. Please tell no one. Sleep tight, wherever you are." Then I decided I should have said, "Sleep well," it would have been less flip, but by then I heard the beep signaling my precious time was up.

I was just about to nod off to sleep when it hit me. I shot bolt upright. Her phone had to be bugged. I had been so tired, it slipped my mind. This blunder was brought to you by a rank amateur, wet behind the ear lobes. It was a mistake I wouldn't make again, but it was too late to reverse this one. Oh, man. I was miserable. I just tipped our hand to the last person in the world I wanted to. I was immediately in jeopardy, I could accept that, it was my fault, but Helen–she was an innocent, but her ex wouldn't believe it.

Probably try to torture it out of her.

Then my mind turned in a different direction. Maybe it was good to tip him off that way. Maybe I could earn that fee. Sure, there were a lot of arguments why I should turn my back on that half-million. It was blood money, Michael Hadaad was a monster and no reasonable person would help him to his ill-gotten gains. And yet, I had trouble thinking of anyone more deserving of the dough than Helen and me. Oh, she probably wouldn't touch a penny of it, but I was finding I would be hard-pressed to turn it down. I could go into cycads big-time. I could try to pass some of it on to Helen without her knowing where it came from.

Fat chance.

Now, instead of being drowsy, as I was before the call, I was wide-awake, wondering where she was. Out on a date? Not impossible, I guess, but she did tell me she had no dates. Kidnapped and held hostage by macho ex? I called my voice mail. Two messages, both from Helen. The first, a cheerful "Call me when you can." The second, a frightened voice, hushed, as though someone were standing over her shoulder, someone who meant her no good. "Gil, where *are* you? I need to talk to you." There was a sudden click, ending the message. So sudden, I thought someone might have disconnected us or she did it herself under fear of discovery.

Whenever I have a restless night, I think I didn't sleep at all. But I'm sure I dozed off now and then, and by morning I was ready to go. But go where?

Just for the heck of it I called for my messages. What I hoped for was one from Helen saying she stayed at work for inventory, or some other perfectly understandable, unromantic explanation; a second from Alecia that said, "I thought it over. Let's get him out of our hair. Bring the papers, I'll sign."

What I got was nothing. No messages. Not even from Hotshot himself. I had not talked to him after the unpleasantness with Saul and the car phone. At first I was relieved. Now I began to feel ignored. After all, I had just about earned a half-million bucks, fair and square. I know what I said about not wanting a penny from him, but I was softening that stance, somewhat. Wouldn't you?

I made one more try to call Helen. It was six-thirty in the morning. Any other time I would have been afraid of waking her. This time I was desperate.

There was only the machine message: "Hi, I'm not here. Please leave a message." It used to sound so cheerful to me. Now, after repeated exposure, it sounded morose. And it was the same message.

I left the motel and headed back to the Starr hotel. Before I parked the car I saw a trio of girls come out for the early shift.

They waited only a few minutes on the corner until the van picked them up. The first one got out with her flowers and headed for a breakfast hangout near the Claremont Hotel. I followed. Parked my car at a meter and entered as she was leaving. I followed her next-door, ducking in a side door and helping myself to a table so I could observe her operation.

She took a lot of rejection, turning automatically to the next prospect. It was a case of ask and ye shall receive, more than it was of the hard sell. I decided the prettiest among Starr's sheep were given this table-hopping duty. When she came to my table, she turned on a tired smile and the glassy eyes seemed suddenly demure and engaging.

She looked shy of twenty years, had a bundle of dirty blonde hair, the regulation thin body. (They were not overfed. Though Manny Starr sported a paunch, his children were on the no-fat regimen. "So much healthier," he said. He didn't say it was a lot cheaper.)

She just stood in front of me as I looked into her eyes. Then I eyed the blooms: roses. Each stuck in a test tube with water, to give the illusion of prolonging its life.

Truly the softest sell, I thought. She didn't even ask me if I wanted a flower. I hadn't said no, avoided her eyes or waved her off, so I suppose she was encouraged.

"Whatya got?" I asked, more or less gauche.

"Flowers," she said. "Roses."

"Nice."

Still she didn't ask if I wanted to buy one. Then it struck me that it was the rule of the game. Just walking around with her arms around a bunch of roses was a free expression of her religion. If she asked for the sale, it was probably a secular infringement on the property owner's rights.

"How much?" I asked, and felt like I was soliciting prostitution.

"Three-fifty," she said.

"For the bunch?" I was buying time.

"Each," she said without levity. Just doing her job.

"Who do you work for?"

Her eyes turned glassy and wary. "Joe," she said.

"Joe who?" I was patting my pockets as though looking for money.

"I don't know."

"Good business?"

"I guess."

"How many can you sell in a day?"

"Depends."

I had found my wallet and was laying it on the table. "Depends on what?"

She shrugged. "Lots of things."

"What's the most you ever sold in a day?"

"I don't remember."

"A hundred?" I opened the wallet and started rifling the bills.

"Maybe."

"You connected with one of those religious organizations?"

"Three-fifty," she said.

"No kidding," I said, counting out the bills. "I hear young girls in those organizations work sixteen hours a day selling flowers for Manny Starr and people like that. Make hundreds of millions of dollars a year for the boss." I shook my head at the wonder of it all.

She said nothing, but pulled a flower from the bunch and waited for me to proffer her the dough. I took one more stab before I completed the transaction. "You work for Manny Starr?"

She shook her head. The zombie eyes took over. "I work for Joe," she said. I bought the rose, she gave me change, I didn't ask her to keep it. I watched as she plied her trade on the remaining tables. I had probably taken too much of her time buying one lousy flower. It's a volume business that depends on a fast in and out. She didn't sell any more in there, so she floated out of the place, no doubt on her faith.

A waitress came to take my order. My size thirty-six belt was in the last rung and the leather tip did not quite reach the loop, so it stood straight out. I figure I had a couple choices: One, lose some weight, or, two, buy some new belts. I ordered the pancakes, hash brown potatoes and sausage. I could shop for the belt later.

When the waitress brought my grilled sausage, I grilled her on the flower girls.

"It's a real nuisance," she said. "They give me the creeps. They're zombies, I swear."

"Do they sell a lot?"

"I see you bought one," she said with a forty-seven-percent smile.

"Yeah." I blushed.

"They must do all right, they're in here morning, noon and night. I never see a lot of sales, but they just keep coming back."

"The same one every time?"

"Oh, no. Always different."

I took out of my pocket my picture of Alecia. "Ever see this one?"

She frowned at the picture. "Looks familiar, but I don't pay that much attention to them."

"You know where they're from?"

"They're Starr girls," she said. "It's a weirdo religious cult."

"You know anybody in it?"

"Nah."

"Can you put yourself in their place–ever consider joining something like that?"

She sighed. The place was thinning out and I was her last customer, so I didn't feel I was taking her from work. "Yeah," she said, "I can dig it. Sometimes you get so low, you'd go with anyone who smiled at you. A dung-dipped Hell's Angel or one of those seductive messiahs."

"But you never did?"

"Never did."

"What held you back?"

"Ah," she said. "Easy. Freedom. It sometimes seems it would be cool to have a dad to provide for you–tell you what to do. But everything has its price, and their price is too high. Freedom is precious. They don't have it."

I thanked her for her time and left her a hundred-percent tip. I was spending like I had already collected the impossible fee from Hadaad.

I drove back to the Starr hotel, parked the car a block away and got out to stretch my legs. I looked across the street at the brick building and saw a mountainous black man come out and head straight for me. Oh-oh, I thought, here comes the enforcer.

I turned and started up the street. He came running.

"Hey, you," he yelled, "Yates!"

I was much impressed he knew my name, but wasn't up to risking stopping to praise him. He looked like he might have played linebacker for the 49ers, but he was too big. I could feel my bones breaking and I broke into a run to save my life.

How could a sucker that big run so fast? I asked myself as he grabbed the back of my shirt collar.

"Hey, Yates," he said, whirling me around to face him, "I got a message for you from my wife."

"You got the wrong guy." I shivered.

"Huh-uh," he assured me.

"I don't know your wife," I said. Okay, maybe I

wasn't as racially sensitive as I should be, I just could not see the two of them together. Then I remembered that Starr loved to arrange marriages with disparate parties, often not speaking the same language. This hulk spoke English, after a fashion. I couldn't place the accent. Maybe the Caribbean somewhere.

"My wife," he brought me down to earth, "leave her alone, you know what's good for you. I see you anywhere around here again, I make you a bongo drum." He smiled the most menacing smile of pride at his funny.

I was in no condition to argue.

"Now git!" he spit.

I got. But I did manage to call over my shoulder, "I'm on her side. Tell her to keep my number. I want to help her." Then I added my prize-winning redundancy: "And be careful."

It took me only seconds to realize in a confrontation with an army of Hadaad's bozos, this guy would prevail, no perspiration. But, if they got to Alecia alone, as I did...?

I drove back to the motel to check out and head back down the coast.

First I called for my messages–none. Then I called Helen–no answer. Then I called Diner Diner. She worked last night until midnight and wasn't due in today until four.

It was a little after ten. Maybe I'd catch her at work. I could probably do it in six hours or so if I kept an eye on the rearview mirror.

21

It took me almost seven hours. I called Helen's house twice more on the way. Nothing. It was the end of the month and the Highway Patrol was filling its quota for the month–that quota they always deny exists. On the way up I had seen about two CHP cars. On the way back I counted fourteen stopped, giving tickets, three in my rearview mirror and another five cruising the freeway.

Counting cop cars is one way to pass the time on a long trip. You got any better ideas, I'm willing to listen.

I got to Diner Diner around five-thirty. Helen wasn't there yet. She was due in at four. She had never missed a shift or been late without calling, the manager told me.

I found a phone booth across the street in a hotel lobby. I called Hadaad.

"Ah, Mr. Yates," Quasimodo said, "he's been expecting you."

"Where is she?" I asked him, but he switched me right to the big boy.

"Ah, Mr. Yates," he said, as though he and Quasimodo were joined at the hip.

"Where is she?" I asked, finessing the niceties.

"I understand I should be asking you that very question."

"You want to go to jail for kidnapping?"

"Oh, I don't think I need worry about that. Helen is not here..." he said, then added, "against her will."

148

So he did have her. Though it was impossible for me to believe she wanted to be there. Why wouldn't she have called her work?

"So," he went on, "do we meet and iron this out? Or are you continuing to be pigheaded?"

"No, I don't think we'll meet. We might negotiate on the phone–*after* you release Helen."

"I told you, she is not held against her will," he said. "She realizes my protection is best for her under the circumstances."

"What circumstances? I don't believe it. Put her on the phone."

"Oh, I don't think so."

"Maybe we'll let the police decide," I said.

"Oh, I don't think you want to bother the police," he said calmly. "There is the matter of you soliciting my business without a license."

"I didn't solicit."

"Well, that may be your view. I have a witness to it."

"A witness?"

"Certainly. Stan." It took me a moment to realize he was talking about Quasimodo.

"He wasn't with us."

"He will tell it differently," Hadaad said. "So why don't you just tell me where my daughter is, and you can have your Helen–though, frankly, I can't imagine what she sees in a wimp like you."

"The wimp who found your daughter?" I asked smugly.

"Touché," he said. "Found, but can you produce?"

"She wants nothing to do with you," I said.

"Ah," he purred, "so, as I recall, the ransom shifts into high."

"Ransom?"

"What would you call it?"

I was so startled, I hung up the phone. It took me slightly longer than it should have to realize he was going to accuse me of kidnapping his daughter for ransom. He was one of the world's weight shifters–used to throwing his weight around–and used to manufacturing his own reality.

But now what? I had to face my own reality: I didn't have the slightest idea what to do next. I slogged back to my empty nest and had another fitful night. Early in the morning, I made my way to my place of employ–the Elbert A. Wemple and Associates, Realtors empire.

I was one of the first of the flunkies on board, but I didn't beat old Elbert himself. No, it was the rare bird who beat that early worm.

Daddybucks was already at his platform desk, busy grinding the poor–a task for which no man is better suited.

I told some elaborate lies about where I had been. Daddybucks said with this tight-teeth, FDR smile, "When the cat's away, the mice will play."

Oh, man, I thought, give me a break. First of all, nobody alive but her own father would refer to the Tyrannosaurus Rex as a cat. A cheetah would be more like it. Second of all, his smutty speculation was more of an insult than on its face. What he meant, between those tightly-clenched teeth, was that the idea of my having anyone to "play" with was so patently absurd, it would double the laugh value of his hysterical joke.

He dumped some stuff on me. A boiler shot here, a kitchen fire there. I had them all taken care of the quickest and, ergo, the most expensive way. Then I called for my messages:

Number one: "Don't be a horse's ass, Yates. You keep your end of the bargain, I'll keep mine."

What a clever jackass, I thought, remembering his view of the end of the bargain may be at odds with the "bargain" I remember.

It was the second message that sent the electric shock through my brain. Now I know what it feels like to be lobotomized. Hurts.

"Mr. Yates," an excited female began. I didn't recognize the voice at first. "I need you. My husband has disappeared. Can you help? I can't get calls here, but I'll call back at five. Believe me, I wouldn't call you, but I'm desperate." There was a pause. "Oh," she said, sounding embarrassed at the omission, "this is Sister Esther... Alecia Hadaad calling."

Oh, wow. Was it really coming together? Could I balance this religious kook on one arm and her megalomaniacal father on the other? Please them both and get my mitts on a cool half-mil? Okay, okay, I know. But still...

The bummer was I didn't have a telephone to answer that line. And I had only that jack behind the dummy door in Hollywood. At three-thirty I went home, called the phone company, then got back in the Plymouth and pointed it toward the office of Gil Yates, private detective. I was pretty confident the bozos would not be on hand.

I had called the phone company to ask how I might check for a bug on my line. They gave me several options. I knew it couldn't be in the telephone instrument, because I had brought that from home. I called Saul, the building manager, who went so far out on a limb for me, and he told me where the telephone box was.

Yep. There was the little device that sent the call to wherever Hadaad's goons were receiving it. I took it off and went upstairs.

I tried my best to look like a telephone man, sitting on the floor in the hall, with my door open to the blank drywall with the little telephone plug near the floor.

Five o'clock was probably not the best time she could have picked. Lot of people going home at five. But I didn't dare miss the call; she might not call again.

The phone rang at five sharp. I picked it up on the first. "Gil Yates," I said, sounding more professional than I felt.

"Mr. Yates, this is..."

"Say no more," I cut her off, "we may have company on the line. If you still need help, I'll be there."

"I do." There was a sickening desperation in her voice.

"Okay. Let me do the talking." I was nothing if not careful. I thought I removed the bug–and yet, could there be another one? "Can we meet tomorrow morning at seven? Where we talked before?"

"Couldn't we do it before?"

I calculated if I left right then, and the Highway Patrol quotas were filled, I might see her at eleven-thirty–but there could be hitches–and I wanted to make a call first.

"One a.m.?" I said.

"I don't think I could. Wait. Yes, I'll do it."

"I could be late. Don't worry, I'm coming. I've taken the bug off the phone, but I expect they will replace it. So if you call, don't leave any addresses, cities, phone numbers or names. Just say when you'll call back."

Immediately on hanging up, I dialed Hadaad. When he came on the line, I said, "This is a yes-or-no question. Do you want to give me something for Alecia to sign? We can have it notarized. I'll have to have it in ninety minutes."

He paused for a moment. "Gil?" he asked, as though he didn't know my voice. "Where are you?"

"Yes or no?"

Another pause. "Certainly. No problem."

"Good, we'll talk fee later."

I heard him grunt. But I knew the twenty million would be worth the two-point-five-percent commission. He had earned more than that in interest. I also knew he would be plotting, nonstop, how to do me out of it. I did not put wiping me off the face of the universe past him.

So be it. I would be counterplotting on my trip. "One more thing," I said. "If I have the slightest inkling anyone is following me, the deal is off."

"No problem."

"I will drive up to the door; I won't get out of the car. No one is to touch the car. The papers can be handed through the window."

"Where are you going, Gil?"

Did he think I was that stupid?

"Just thought if there were any last-minute amendments, I have lawyers all over the state."

"See that there won't be any need to change any-

152

thing," I said. I learned already that tough talk could not only make you sound tough, you might actually feel tough.

But not tough enough to suit me. "And while you are at it, give me a signed, notarized statement from you saying on receipt of these signed documents I will have earned my five hundred thou fee."

"Surely, under the circumstances that is negotiable," he said without a lot of steam behind it.

"Surely not," I said. "Oh, and one other thing. Send Helen out with the papers."

"Sorry, pal," he said. "Not possible."

"Have her at a window then. Somewhere I can see her."

"We'll see," he said.

"Minimum. Don't horse me around. Time is more precious to you than to me, *or* Alecia. Ninety minutes," I said, and hung up.

His spread wasn't that far out of the way. I realized I did risk his trying to grab me, torture the info out of me, but I think he realized how obstinate Alecia could be, and he might as well take his chances on this easy way first.

I drove up the coast, contemplating all the pitfalls and what my reaction should be.

I carefully checked Hadaad's neighborhood for signs of hidden cars ready to pounce, but saw none.

The address was out front. I considered that a cheery good sign. I drove slowly up the driveway–that reminded me of the 17-Mile Drive, between Carmel and Monterey–watching carefully for signs of ambush. I got to the front door unscathed.

I fought the impulse to get out of the car for a quick look at his palms and cycads. I blew the horn. It didn't take long for the great Michael Hadaad to appear alone on the scene.

His stride was surprisingly jaunty. "Gil!" he hailed me as though I were an old army buddy who'd saved his life. "Thanks so much for coming," he said like you might thank the milkman for bringing the milk.

He was standing by the front window which I had lowered two inches. Enough to hear him and take the papers, but not enough for him to pull me through.

"Won't you come in, Gil?" he was still using the voice of Southern hospitality.

"No, thanks," I said. "No time. You got the papers?"

"They're being worked on this very minute," he said. I had the motor running and the car in the drive gear, the hand brake off.

"Sorry," I said, "can't wait." I started to pull away.

"Stop!" he shouted. "Gil! Come back! They're here. The papers..." and he took from his blue blazer breast pocket an envelope and waved it at me. I didn't back up, so he came running.

When he had handed the envelope through the space in the window, I shook my head and said, "Lying again, huh?"

He shrugged, as though he had made the most insignificant mistake. "Can't blame me for trying," he said. "I want to talk to you."

"No time," I repeated. "Where's Helen?"

He gestured toward the middle upstairs window. There I saw a ghostly back-lit figure. She waved slowly. I waved back.

"Anything happens to her–I mean, you muss a hair on her head and the deal is off."

"She's fine."

"Kidnapping's a crime. They could put you away."

He shrugged and shook his head. "Not kidnapping at all. She's my wife."

"Ex," I corrected.

He corrected *me*. "I never signed any divorce papers," he said.

I didn't have time to argue. "Don't mess me up with any tails, captain," I said, hoping to demean him in his yachting outfit. It didn't work.

He shook his head. "You do your part, I'm satisfied."

"I'll call you if I need anything else." And I left him in a cloud of hydrocarbons.

22

I drove south on 101, then pulled off on Padaro, a fairly sparse street where a couple Hollywood swells rented a pad for our president.

At the end of the street I turned around. No sign of anyone following. Maybe Hadaad *was* satisfied. Before heading north again, I took out the papers Hadaad had given me. They seemed in order. Alecia's letter was a simple statement authorizing the bank to release her account to her dad, Michael Hadaad.

Back on 101, I headed north, checking the old rearview for signs of tails and cops.

You may get the idea from all my schlepping up and down the coast that I am some kind of terrific driver. Don't. Reasonably careful I have become with age, but still erratic and inconsistent, and too easily distracted. I still manage to bang up the car every 5,000 miles or so.

That's one thing you can say about freeways–you don't find too many girls in bikinis or tight jeans to put you off course.

L.A. to San Francisco was a long hike. But now I seemed to be commuting, and my detour to Hadaad set me back an hour plus.

I crossed the Oakland Bay Bridge at about forty minutes after midnight. Not bad, I thought, congratulating myself on what would pass in any country in the world as mediocre driving. The bridge lights were sparkling, like diamonds in the rain.

Just to be safe, I pulled off the Oakland side of the bridge on Cypress Street, local traffic only. No one followed. I got back on and headed for my rendezvous with Alecia, or Sister Esther, as the case may be.

I found her standing on the corner with an armload of flowers. She squinted in the car when I stopped, and then, when she recognized me, she got in. The squinting seemed to relieve her of the zombie stare.

"Didn't sell many flowers," I said, looking at her bundle.

"Didn't try," she said. "We can stay out until the flowers are gone," she explained. She laid the flowers in my tiny back seat.

"Don't you ever get tired of selling flowers?" I asked her.

"If you think about it, I suppose you would. Most of us don't question, we just do."

"Your husband too?"

She nodded.

"Well, someone apparently wanted him for something. Why don't you tell me what you know and what you guess. Start with when you met him."

"Can we go somewhere out of the area?" she asked with a shudder.

"Give you trouble staying out so late?"

"I haven't sold my flowers."

I glanced back at the bunch lying harmlessly on the back seat. "I'm afraid you have too many for me to buy."

"I'll sell them," she said with quiet confidence, based, no doubt, on solid experience.

We drove up Ashby and turned to Claremont Avenue, then went over to 13. She checking behind us all the way. "If you see anyone looks like they're following, tell me, will you?"

I nodded. "You can't go out on your own?"

She shook her head. She was pensive and a little jittery.

156

"What are they afraid of?"

"Afraid we'll leave," she said.

"Would you?"

"No."

"But your husband did."

"No." She checked the back window. "Turn off here," she said, and I turned. She checked again. Satisfied, she gave me directions and we wound up in a pleasant all-night joint that featured greasy fries, brown walls, gas-station coffee and a staff that should have been asleep. We ordered innocuously and they left us alone at a table around the corner, where we could not be easily seen.

"Patrice didn't leave," she began when we settled in. "Not by choice."

"Could they have moved him, without your knowledge?"

She shook her head. "They wouldn't do that. We're married," she said as though that were that. I wasn't so sure.

"How did you meet him—Patrice, is it?"

"Yes."

"His Starr name is Brother Bemand. In Santo Oro he is Patrice La Bec."

"How did you meet him?"

She frowned, as though she were contemplating trusting me.

I spread my hands. "Alecia," I said quietly. "If you want me to help you..."

She nodded. "Manny Starr arranged it. We met on our wedding day. I was apprehensive. So was he. Neither of us fit the other's fantasy imagination as someone we thought we would marry. Father Starr is noted for that," she said without a smile. Not a judgment, just a fact.

"Of course the Starrs are looking for him—but they won't tell me anything. They think he's defected. They put me through a lot of questioning and surveillance. I can't believe there isn't someone here watching me—maybe the waitress."

"Is that a good way to live, Alecia?"

She shrugged. "Has its advantages," she said. I didn't notice a lot of conviction.

"Do you know where your husband is from?"

"Certainly. Santo Oro. It's in the Caribbean–a small island. His father used to be El Presidente."

"Why did he join the Starrs?"

She bounced a shoulder again. "Same reason we all do. Looking for more meaning than we found in our other worlds."

"Do you find it selling flowers?"

She glared at me. "Cheap shot," she said.

I agreed, apologized and shut up.

"Look," she said, "here I am, telling you my life story and I don't even know you. For all I know, you are with *them*."

"Who is 'them'?"

"The people who took Patrice."

I thought she had meant the Starrs. If it's us against them, it's nice to know who's who. She didn't seem ready to jump ship yet, though I was ambivalent about what I wanted her to do.

"So why *are* you confiding in me?" I asked.

"I have nowhere else to turn. You just came by at the right time." She frowned. "That's why I think you might be with them."

"I'm not with any *them*."

"My father?" she asked cautiously.

"No, you could never put me with *him*."

"But you want me to sign over the account."

"Wouldn't you, for a fat fee? And for your sake you can get him off your back. A lot worse than I could come looking for you."

She listened, absorbed, and didn't argue.

"So what's your guess?" I asked. "You have any idea what happened?"

"I think I *know* what happened. That's the scary part. I think he's back home."

"Is that bad? Would you consider joining him?"

She shook her head. "If he's back home, he's in jail or dead."

"What? Why?"

"His father was El Presidente. The insurgents deposed him. They put in some tin-pot dictator. I think they were afraid Patrice and his dad wanted to take back the government. I'm afraid they might have shot them both."

"Do you think Patrice ever considered going back and trying to take over?"

She shook her head. "He was happy here," she said, then seemed to correct herself: "content." She considered the larger question a moment longer. "He couldn't abide politics."

"Could he have deceived you in that?"

"No." She seemed sure.

"Misled you, perhaps?"

"No."

"But how well can you know someone in the working conditions you live under? How much time did you spend together?"

"Believe me, I know."

"Okay, then how did they find him? Look at the trouble your father had finding you, and you're in the same state."

"Well, he stands out a lot more than I do," she said. "Any number of people could have tipped them off."

"Or they could have known where he was all along," I said. "You sure his father or somebody didn't know where he was?"

She stared at me, the eyes seemed to glaze over again and she was back to the zombie. Then she seemed to pull out of it. "I guess I don't know what I'm sure of anymore."

"What do you want me to do?"

"Find him," she said, as though I had asked a self-evident question.

"What makes you think I can?"

"You found me, didn't you? With a lot less to go on."

She had the arguments all right. "Did you tell this to

the Starrs who interrogated you?"

She looked away and said, "No." I thought it interesting she couldn't look at me.

"Why didn't you tell them? They have a lot more resources than I. They might get him back for you."

She turned back and looked in my eyes. She was sharing a painful confidence with me. "Because I'm afraid they'll kill him."

"Who, the Starrs or his captors?"

"Both."

"Why would the Starrs kill him?"

She stared at me again before she answered. "By accident, because they are too anxious and paranoid about people leaving; because they won't understand the natives and the crackpots who are running the government."

"Don't they speak English?"

"Everybody will be speaking English, they just won't be talking the same language."

"So assume a miracle happens. I get through to them and they admit they have him in jail as an enemy of the state. How do I talk them into releasing him?"

"I thought that was your specialty. Look how you talked me into doing what you wanted."

"You haven't done it yet."

"So get it out. I'll sign."

"We need a notary," I said. "So any ideas how I could entice these tin-pot politicos?"

Her cheeks lifted in consideration. "They're poor people. Money might help."

"I don't have any money, unless twenty bucks in the hand of the police chief will do the job."

She shook her head, dolefully. "I guess they're not *that* poor."

"But I am. I couldn't even scrape together the air fare to go down there and see if he's there."

"Why don't you call?"

"Really? The telephone?"

She nodded.

"You think they'd tell me?"

"Might."

"Then I should find out what's the price on his head?"

"Good idea."

"Well, if you don't have a nice chunk of American dollars stashed somewhere, I'm afraid we're out of luck."

"Didn't you say Daddy was desperate for my signature?"

"Oh, no, you want my fee?" I muttered, seeing my well-laid plans slip through the dirt.

"No, not your fee. Not all of it anyway. Just tell Daddy that's my price–Patrice's ransom. *Your* price is something else."

"Is it ever," I sighed. But I agreed to make the call to Santo Oro in the morning. "How can I get in touch with you?" I asked.

"It's never easy," she said. "I'll have to meet you again on the street. But when they see how late I'm getting back, they're going to be suspicious. I may be kept in for a while or put under heavy surveillance."

"Why not come with me, tonight anyway? I'll get you a room in my fleabag."

She shook her head. "No, if he did come back and I wasn't there, I'm afraid we'd never meet up again. No. Thank you." She shook her head as if convincing herself. "No, I can't."

"Do you have any money–to buy personal things?"

"No," she shook her head. "It's all provided. We have nothing."

"I better give you some," I said. "Could you hide it, or do they have room checks?"

"I'd rather not have any money."

"Me too, and no one has been closer to achieving that goal than me. But you are going to have expenses and you'll need money. Is there anyone around who you could trust to hold it for you?"

"No," she said. "We don't mix with outside people."

"Could you put it in your shoe or something?"

"If they find money, they will assume I have stolen it from my receipts, or took personal tips that I didn't turn in."

"Which is worse?"

"Both about the same. I'd be under house arrest. It's too risky."

"Then think about some place we can hide it. Maybe on your route?"

"They change it all the time."

I was beginning to lose patience. "So maybe we should just let it go."

"No," she said.

"All right," I grumbled, "you make a suggestion."

"When I need money, I'll shake a cup," she said. "That way I won't have to keep it around. When I get enough in my paper cup, I'll make the call, or whatever I have to do."

"Is that reliable?"

"Very," she said.

"Here, I almost forgot," I said, taking the bank letter Hadaad typed for her to sign out of my pocket and pushing it across the table. "This is for you to sign—when we get that far. Hang onto it. I'll let you know when your father's completed his end."

I drove her back to the corner, where she offered her flowers to a couple sitting on the bus bench. He bought one. It must have been another good omen.

We agreed I would be in my motel room at nine, twelve and three in case she called, or I would cruise the corner, where we met tonight, at five, seven and nine.

The rest would be up to me. But was I up to it? I didn't feel optimistic. Even if I located him, I'd have to go there, and how I would get to a remote, unknown Caribbean spot in the ocean, without any *dinero*, was a big mystery to me.

23

I awoke at first light, about six-fifteen, and put in my call to Santo Oro. I started with the jail. I asked for the head honcho.

"Who?" the voice on the line insisted. He sounded both sleepy and macho.

"The big enchilada," I said.

"Listen, friend," he said, "this is not a beaner republic. We speak English, here."

"Pity," I said.

"What?"

"You got Patrice La Bec in your slammer?"

"Oh, ho, ho," he chortled, "I get it. Slammer is Yankee word for jail."

"You have him or no?"

"Who wants to know?"

"I do, obviously. I'm asking."

"Who are you?"

"A friend of his wife's," I said.

"Oh, ho, ho," he said, "want to know if the coast is clear so you can get *real* friendly..."

"Listen, amigo," I thought I'd needle him with a little more Spanish, he had it coming, "that may be funny where it's a hundred and ten in the shade, but it doesn't melt any ice in these parts. Who should I talk to? Obviously you are small tomatoes down there. Let me talk to El Presidente."

"With pleasure," he said, surprising me. In a minute another voice came on the phone.

"This is the President," he said in suave English. Obviously it was a prank. But I couldn't be sure.

"Your office must be very close to the jail."

"We are in capitol, not in jail. My police chief is right next door to me. He is my trusted aide. We have police all over. In these volatile times one cannot be too careful."

I had to say this for the guy. He was well-spoken. Probably went to Harvard or somewhere hot like that.

"Are you holding Patrice La Bec in your jail?"

There was a pause. "What if I am?"

"You should release him." Easy to talk tough on the phone.

"That is your opinion."

"What's yours?"

"If we had him," he said, "I would easily justify his detention. His father was an enemy of the republic. We had to, for the sake of peace and harmony on our little island, eliminate him. We do not wish any repercussions from his son."

"So you *do* have him," I played along. "I would ask you to consider where you got him and why he was there. He was in a religious sect. He was attempting to hide from his father. How could you think he cared about politics in your country?"

"Could be a ruse?"

"A ruse?"

"A wonderful, almost suspicion-free place to bide his time for an insurgent takeover. Many have done it before him. All over the world."

"If you had him," I asked, "what would it take to release him?"

"If we had him, we would count on our system of justice to mete out his punishment or release, whichever direction the evidence took us."

"How much money exactly would it take?"

"My dear sir, you are not offering to bribe the

President of the Republic of Santo Oro, are you?"

"Certainly not. You didn't let me finish. How much to get him a competent defense?"

"Oh, that is much different. You must understand that lawyers here are not a dime a dozen as they are in El Norte. Consequently, with the demand being greater than the supply, competent legal representation does not come cheap."

"Naturally," I said. There was something warm and scuzzy about being extorted by an expert president. "Would you think perhaps twenty-five thousand would buy some savvy?"

"My dear sir, that would depend."

"On what?"

"If you wanted to *win* the case."

"But of course."

"I am afraid then, sir, the ante would have to be somewhat higher."

"Thirty thousand?"

"Oh, my dear sir. I am the President. Do you think I am a man who would quibble over a measly five thousand?" He sounded genuinely hurt.

"I'm so sorry," I said, "but I'm afraid I need something from you–some indication of what you are thinking."

"I am thinking you are trying to bribe me, and you are thinking I am asking for a bribe."

"Oh, no!" I said. Horrors, I tried to put in my voice, perish the very thought! But I didn't succeed in convincing him of that which I was not convinced of myself.

"Listen, if you wish further discussion on this matter, I would recommend you visit Santo Oro. I will personally make you feel very welcome here, and we can at that time interface over this matter."

"That's a long schlepp from here."

"But it is paradise. The weather is delightful this time of year and we are small and the pace is leisurely. *And* there are no tourists."

Because they are scared of being caught in the crossfire of one of your stupid civil insurrections, I thought, but didn't say. "I would need several guarantees," I said, "to come that far."

It is a tribute to the insignificance of the island that its president would respond to such a demeaning demand. "Yes, what are they?" I suspected he smelled money.

"I have to know that Patrice is there," I said. "I have to know he will be alive when I get there, and that his release is negotiable."

"You may have my guarantees," he said, "with one guarantee of my own requirement."

"What is that?"

"That you bring along your checkbook."

Oh, my, I thought. He doesn't want *my* checkbook.

"Our lawyers," he said again, "are expensive."

"Suppose I brought my own?" I didn't have one, of course, I just thought I'd bug him.

"Oh," he said with a foreboding tone, "we have found it to be much more expensive with outside lawyers. They are not familiar with our laws and systems, and arranging matters, when they can be arranged at all, takes much more time."

"I'll be there as soon as I can," I said, then added, as if an unimportant afterthought, "I trust I will be safe?"

"But of course," the hearty voice came back, "you will be an honored guest."

While I was hanging up, I wondered what that meant.

I also wondered how I was going to get there. When you worked for Daddybucks, you were not bogged down with excess funds for discretionary spending.

My options seemed to come down to working another deal, and I didn't have the stomach for watering my stock with Hadaad by asking him for a plane ticket. Besides, the less he knew about my whereabouts, the better.

Alecia called me at noon. I related my conversation with El Presidente to her. She was relieved to be given that much hope her husband was alive.

166

She spoke in hushed tones. "I don't have long. I may be being watched. But is there not a danger they will hold *you* for ransom? Then who would pay it?"

"Good question," I said, wondering about my chances, both of being locked up and of being ransomed. Not that I might not be better off away from Daddybucks and the glass blower.

But how could I depend on Hadaad to cheerfully fork over *this* ransom? I could see my fat fee trickling down and out.

"Do you think we could get your group to blow me to a ticket to the Republic of Santo Oro? Round trip, of course. And the return for Patrice?"

"I must see you," she whispered, and we set the time and place.

I arrived early to check for suspicious cultists, who, Alecia told me, were watching her like a hawk.

In ten minutes she came around the corner with her arms loaded with the unsold luncheon flowers. She jumped in the car and I whisked her away.

"How much do you know about the government in Santo Oro?"

"Not much," she said. "Patrice had very little interest in politics. He was not close to his father, and mother is no longer living."

It was my opening. "I'm afraid neither is his father."

She exhaled, as though exhausted at the news–not for the father whom she didn't know, but what it portended for her husband.

"They killed him," she said, as though she had expected it.

"Now we must see they don't do the same to his son out of some bizarre paranoid fear," I said. "What do you think about getting me a ticket from the club?" As soon as the words tumbled over my lips I realized they may have sounded a little flip to her.

She frowned. "I don't know how we could do that."

"Let me talk to the guy in charge."

She frowned again–or maybe it was the same frown. "They are not big on dealing with outsiders."

"Why?"

She shrugged. "It's the old fear that you are trying to take him away."

"But he is away," I protested. "I'm trying to bring him back."

"They'll think you're trying to take him yourself–to deprogram him."

"Could you go for him?"

She shook her head. "They'd never allow it."

"Why not?"

"They'd think I was going to stay there with him–then they would lose us both and we would become enemies."

"Why are they so afraid of enemies? We all have them."

"I don't know. That's something you don't know from the inside. I'm afraid they won't go for it. They'd have to know all the particulars, and they would send someone themselves."

"That's okay with me," I said. "Let them try to get him out. Who knows, they might succeed."

"I don't think so," she said. "I don't think their methods are very subtle. What that tin-pot government wants is cash. Big American bucks. The Starrs won't pay it."

"So let me talk to someone. I'll try to convince them this is their best bet. For the price of an airline ticket, I will bring him back."

"And where will you get the ransom money?"

"Your dad," I said.

You could see if she weren't restrained by her religion and afraid of attracting attention, she would have laughed out loud. Her body quaked slightly and she had an open smile on her mouth. I stopped the car on the asphalt apron of one of those outskirt coffee shops and waited for someone to follow us there. No one did, so we went in and had a couple teas. "I can just see it," Alecia said. "You tell him you want a hundred-thousand dollars ransom to return my black husband to me so we can live happily ever after in a religious order."

"You're forgetting one thing."

"What's that?"

"He wants your signature."

"That badly?"

I wondered if such an intelligent-seeming girl could be that naive. "Twenty million dollars tied up, Alecia." I used her given name. I wasn't comfy with that Sister Esther stuff. Maybe if she wore a black habit, but not with an armful of roses and zombie eyes. "Your father puts on a good front. But maybe arms dealing is a little touchy for him just now. Forbidden, even, by the requirements of his parole. And maybe he has a couple creditors at his heels. They might be the kind of guys who aren't noted for their patience. Maybe a little violence in their backgrounds. You know, they start pulling out his fingernails one by one, he might be more amenable to a little ransom money. Like a commission to complete the transaction."

Alecia shuddered.

"So the question is, how do we get the price of the ticket without tipping our cards to the wrong people?" I asked her.

"If you think my father will kick in a hundred-thou ransom, he should be good for a couple hundred for a plane ticket."

I shook my head as if to clear it. It didn't clear. We seemed to be going around in circles. "I'd rather try the Starrs first. I don't want to show our hand to your father. It can only weaken our effort."

"So don't tell him what it's for."

"He won't go for it. He'll think it's a little extortion at a time. And the last thing I want is for him to know where we are. He'll send his goons to kidnap you. Can't I talk to someone up the ladder in the Starrs?"

"Waste of time," she said. "They would be just too suspicious." She bit her lip, pondering the scant options. "Let me try to talk to them first," she said. "I'll call you on the same schedule, or see you tonight on the corner." She frowned at her second thoughts. "Trouble is, once I tell them this I'm liable to be locked in for good."

"Do you see another choice?"

"We could rob a bank," she said.

I laughed. Then it hit me. "You know what, Alecia," I chortled, "we're being stupid. Your grandmother gave *you* control of that twenty million. You could simply ask for a check made out to you for the full amount. We'd have all we need. If you want to, you could give the rest to your father–or the Starrs, if you prefer."

The mention of the Starrs seemed to put the glaze back in Alecia's eyes. She looked out the window and said nothing.

I said nothing. Years ago I asked a friend who had an accomplished daughter what he did to raise such a fine specimen of womanhood. He said, "Just get out of the way." I tried it with my daughter and met with only sporadic success. Sometimes it was good to get out of the way, but sometimes you had to be there. I thought this was a good time to get out of the way.

My patience was rewarded. Alecia finally turned to me and said, "I don't care about the money. I would be most uncomfortable having it. I'm sure Father Starr would be grateful for it, but I think I'll stick to selling flowers. All I want is my husband back. Maybe we could get the money, but could we do it without my father tracing us?"

"Not very easily," I allowed. "And not very quickly." There was, I realized, Daddybucks. But I was away from the office so much lately I didn't think he would blithely advance me a couple grand without asking a boatload of questions.

But there didn't seem any other option. I did have a

credit card, but Tyranny Rex put it over the limit with her trip to Scotland–like she always did. We always got a letter from the folks at the bank-card company, asking that we please refrain from further charges until we could pay down our balance.

I left Alecia staring into her teacup and went to the pay phone on the back wall by the rest rooms. So named, because it is where you go when you are tired of controlling your bladder, I guess.

I dialed my work place.

"Is the beloved founder and patron saint of property management in harness?" I asked Franny, the pretty receptionist.

"You better believe it," she said ominously.

"Would you be kind enough to put him on?"

He must have been already on, he picked it up so fast. "Malvin? Where the hell are you?"

"I got called out of town."

"You did? Well, get your fanny right back here, we got a ball of snakes over on Artesia! Want you to unravel them." He went on to tell me an elaborate tale of a tenant-manager conflict. A story I'd heard countless times. Daddybucks was a mountain maker. And he did most of his work using molehills as his raw materials. One phone call would usually solve what he thought would require a face-to-face arbitration by the Supreme Court.

"I'll take care of it," I said. "In the meantime, could you throw a couple thousand in our bank account? Dorcas has sent me to the bindery with her Scotland trip."

"What's this?" he boomed. "You are not the master of your own house? Who is wearing the pants over there anyway?" And he rattled on in this fashion ad nauseam. It was old potatoes. Then he stopped to chuckle, and until you've heard Daddybucks chuckle you don't have a real appreciation of the word. Sort of like a Sherman tank grinding its gears.

When he came up for air, he changed the sound of his voice to the purring of a kitten. "Well, Malvin, tell me something. Is your sudden need for filthy lucre in any way connected to the female of the species?"

"Damn right," I said with uncharacteristic force. "If that female I'm married to didn't continually strip my account for those glass trinkets she makes and sells at a fraction of their cost to us; if she wouldn't jackass all over the world on my meager pittance, we wouldn't always be in the hole."

"Hey, hey, Malvin, is that you? Calm down, will you? My question has to do with unrelated females." And he relished asking it.

"Yes, it does have to do with a young, beautiful female," I said in anger, realizing I was blowing my chances for good. "And her mother," I couldn't resist adding. I was about to tell about the man in the family, when old Daddybucks surprised me with another stripping of gears. "Why, you old reprobate. I never thought you had it in you!" He chuckled again and it was starting to grate on me. I was already forced to search for nonexistent alternatives, when I heard him say, "Two thousand, did you say, Killer? I'll make it three for good measure—hey, hey, hey. You old Don Juan, you! Just understand it's coming out of your paychecks and you can do the explaining to Dorcas."

When I hung up, I was stunned. Was he pulling my leg? He had to be. But a check with my bank, an hour later, proved me wrong. The money was there.

I went back to the table and arranged with Alecia for her to be at a telephone at 5:00 each evening. If she couldn't make it I would call every hour until 10:00.

24

I put Alecia back on the street to hawk her flowers. In less than a minute she had melted into the crowd in Berkeley.

I went to the first travel agency I came to. In spite of some unfriendly doubt about my check, being so far out of town and all ("Call the bank," I said, and she did), I got my tickie. My flight left just after midnight. Malvin saves: on the motel *and* the cheaper flight.

People are growing taller by the minute. The average height of a soldier in the War of 1812 was five-foot-three. Now I'd guess we were pushing five-foot-nine to five-foot-ten as an average. I was five-foot-ten and three-eighths so I was above average. But the airlines seem unaware and/or unconcerned about it. The legroom keeps shrinking.

As soon as we took off and the friendly "boing" sounded, the guy in front of me laid his seat in my lap. I grunted, but he was impervious. I have never had the nerve to drop my seat in someone's lap, so I spent the journey to Miami in that discomfort.

In Miami I got a plane for St. John's–where I changed for the short hop to Santo Oro.

I telephoned ahead and El Presidente's secretary, who sounded an awful lot like the police chief, said they would with pleasure pick me up at the airport.

Two things astonished me when I landed. The first was what a tiny dump it was. The airport building was a

Quonset hut the size of a couple contiguous outhouses. There was a main street, but the only thing "main" about it was the building which looked like a bus station in a fair-sized banana republic.

The second was the visiting-dignitary reception I got from them. Six chaps marching a goose step, with rifles over their shoulders and black leather boots on their feet, followed what I guessed (correctly) was the police chief. He was dressed to the sevens, with gold epaulets and a tangle of medals over both breasts that would have weighted to the earth a lesser man.

He saluted when he saw me. Did I salute back? or did you need one of those gold-braided caps with the shiny black visor scrambled with more gold braids? I sort of made a gesture between a salute and a wave to protect me from a major faux pas, protocol-wise.

In Santo Oro the sun got right to you. There was no grace period. And the humidity saw to it you were wringing wet as soon as you took a few steps.

The chief seemed to be sniffing the stifling moisture in the air. I decided they could smell money, and that's why I was getting this rifle-brigade reception.

"Welcome to our humble Santo Oro," he said, extending his hand. I shook it. Humble was an overstatement.

"Where's the capital?" I asked. I thought we were in the outskirts.

"This is the capital," he said.

I looked around. I wasn't convinced. "May I talk to the prisoner?" I asked.

The chief's face fell. Crestfallen I believe they call it. "Oh, but, sir, the President is waiting for you. He would be so disappointed..." He spread his hands to show it was out of those hands.

"Then will I see Patrice?"

"But of course." He looked at me, perplexed. "Ah, sir, you have no baggage?"

"No, ah. I only can stay the day."

Disappointment drowned him. "Oh," he groaned, as though the economy of the island depended on my presence.

I soon learned that was nearly the case. He and the goose-steppers led me to the bus station, which turned out to be the capitol. The walls were thick and rough plastered, covered with whitewash. The floor was free of any artificial substance to mar the dirt.

The President greeted me with open arms, then crushed me in an overly familiar hug. He was a short man with powerful shoulders and a world-class squeeze.

He waved me onto the plank bench in front of his desk, which consisted of a slab of unpainted plywood held up by two sawhorses. Either this was a low-overhead operation or they were putting on a poverty show for my benefit. It seemed to me the latter, for surely they could have melted down the rifles and gotten enough from the scrap metal alone to furnish the President's office.

"I trust you had a pleasant journey," he said warmly.

"Sure, the joy is in the journey, not the arrival," I said, but he didn't get it.

"We are honored to have you in Santo Oro," said the President.

"I'm honored to be here," I said. Then I realized if I had had more experience with tin pots, I wouldn't be so banal. "I hope I will get to see Patrice," I said.

The President looked as crestfallen as the police chief had earlier. "But of course. I would only hope you would give me the opportunity to tell you of the hopes and dreams of my administration," he said.

I turned around and saw the six rifle-bearing goose-steppers at present arms. I decided I would listen to the chamber of commerce pitch first. "But of course," I said.

"Good," he said, beaming, "very good. Yes."

I decided the President had a star quality about him. Errol Flynn with darker skin. A pencil moustache, oily skin, and one of those ingratiating Uriah Heep manners.

He laid it all out for me, sparing me nothing, from

the new deep-water harbor that would attract "millions of tourists," to the humanitarian hospital where countless lives would be saved.

"Ah, but you have come to see your friend Mr. Patrice, and we must not detain you."

"I appreciate that," I said. I stood up. Too soon.

"If I could have a moment more, Mr. Yates," he said with his buttery smile. I sat again.

"We are hopeful that our story has reached out and touched your heart."

"Oh, yes..."

"And that you will be in a position to consider a sizable donation to help us get started on our most ambitious plans."

"What size donation did you have in mind?"

He put both hands on his chest and sank back into his chair, as though my blow to his dignity had sent him there. "But, sir, I wouldn't presume to restrict your generosity."

Restrict down, or restrict up? I thought, but I didn't wonder which he meant. "Well, I will certainly give it serious thought," I said.

"Certainly," he said with that fiendish grin that said, "if you want to get out of here alive."

"Pardon me, Mr. President—but where is Patrice?" I realized that I was sitting here with the head of state and I had never gotten a real commitment that he was alive—or here. Maybe this was a simple extortion racket and I was the next victim.

His face grew long. "We will show you Mr. Patrice," he said, "in good time. First I must prepare you. He is alive and well, but he is a very bitter young man. He has put his own interests above those of the state. As did his father."

"Where is his father?" I asked.

"Ah," the President's face fell somber, "for the good of our country, as well as his own good, we had to put him out of the way of harm."

"By killing him?"

176

"Is a very harsh word. If you put 'mercy' before it, all right. It was as much for his own good. His ideas are very unpopular here. We were afraid he would be slowly tortured to death by the people he tortured." He spread his hands on the plywood table. "Naturally, Patrice sees it another way. He, too, is an enemy of the people. It was just your phone call which spared his life. We are of two minds about him, are we not, Chief?"

"Yes, Excellency." The chief clicked his heels and proffered a snappy salute.

"On the one hand, we fear him. If he was angry before his father's death, he is furious now. He is young," he spread out those active hands to show me the impossibility of reckoning with youth, "and he is, I daresay, impetuous. Frankly, we fear for our lives, do we not, Chief?"

"Yes, Excellency." The click and salute were part of his windup-toy mechanism. I couldn't understand why the President was consulting the chief all of a sudden. The chief had sat silently behind me throughout.

"We were about to take him down the same path as his father. Surely you understand the grave risk to us–letting insurgents roam free?"

"Isn't that what they called you?" I asked.

He showed me his teeth. They were a gold mine. "Very astute, sir. But we are now incumbents. That is simply the difference. But as I was saying, you saved his life with your intriguing proposition."

"Proposition?"

"To make a donation to Santo Oro, in exchange for this young man–of course you would have to personally take responsibility for his neutrality in the affairs of our country."

"Patrice has a wife in the United States. He is not the least interested in politics."

The President frowned. "He may have changed his mind." His eyes were downcast, then they bounced back up. "Chief," he said, "we detain Mr. Yates no longer. Show him to the prisoner."

"Yes, Excellency," with the requisite handshaking

and small, insincere-sounding expressions of gratitude.

The chief and his troops with the boots led me to a warehouse further along the main, and only, road.

I marched with the troops about a block up the main dirt path. I didn't goose-step. I don't do it very well. There was a rather long building, two to three times the size of the capitol building. Naturally, I thought, the largest building in town is a jail.

But it was a banana warehouse as well, with only a corner devoted to cells. I imagined cells were superfluous here. Enemies of the state were simply shot. It was quicker and cheaper. As if to validate my opinion, I noticed Patrice was the only prisoner.

He didn't look as menacing as he did on the street in Berkeley, when he was Mr. Macho, warning me to leave his wife alone.

When he saw me, he shook his head. "You?" he said, as though I were the last person he'd expect to see.

He looked like he was wearing the same clothes he had been kidnapped in: a pair of khaki pants and a tee shirt that must have been made by a tentmaker.

"Hello, Patrice," I said. The troops were so close at hand I could smell pâté from the goose step. "Say, Chief," I said. "Could I talk to him alone for a while?"

"Sure, you talk, we don't listen."

They had very sophisticated bugging systems in Santo Oro. They stood by your side and pretended not to listen.

"No," I said, putting my foot down. "I want to make sure Patrice is no danger to you. He can't speak freely if you are..." I was interrupted by a spitting sound. I turned back, to see Patrice spitting again.

"Murderers," he said. "Let me out of here–I'll strangle the lot of you."

I frowned at Patrice. He wasn't going to make it easy. "Not very tactful, is he?" I said with a stupid smile. "He doesn't mean anything by it."

The chief rolled his eyes. I went to his side and whispered in his ear. "Hey, you want a donation, I'm going to have to straighten this guy out. I can only do it alone. Step outside. I can't dig a tunnel or bring down these bars."

"Sorry, sir, but I have my orders."

I haggled with him some more and got a big concession from the chief: He would watch us from across the warehouse, where he would surely be unable to hear.

But half the time, the outraged, ornery Patrice spoke in such a booming voice, they must have heard every word. One thing was certain, there was no mistaking his feelings.

"*These people are bloody murderers!*" he shouted at the top of his voice. "*They killed my father in cold blood!* They killed dozens of others. They have modern weapons for sophisticated killing. I've seen them do it; they've all been in here. I'm the last one left. Any day now there won't be *any*one left!"

I tried to calm him down. "Patrice," I whispered. If I had anything to say about it, the chief and his geese wouldn't hear more than half the conversation. "Listen, pal, don't be crazy. You have any desire to get out alive, calm down and listen to me."

"*Murderers!*" he belted out again.

"Okay–get it out of your system. Nobody needs to be told what's going on here. Now, if you want to see Alecia again..."

"Who?"

"Your wife. Sister Esther, is it?"

He seemed to melt at the mention of her name. But was it possible he didn't know she was Alecia?

I thought about the cult and Manny Starr and decided Patrice wasn't acting. All that real-world stuff Starr put behind them.

"Okay. I'm going to tell it as fast as I can. Please, no more theatrics. I want to get you out of here."

"Why?"

"Excellent question. Long story. No time. I got a job. It's turned out contingent on getting you out and back to Alecia."

"Sister Esther."

"Sorry. At any rate, the geese were about to cook your goose. I stalled them with a hint of filthy lucre."

He frowned. Just in case, I spelled it out, "Money. I don't know how much yet or if I'll be able to get it, but I'm going to try. If you see them coming in here with the boot brigade, you'll know I failed."

He gave me the strangest look. "Do I have to get deprogrammed?" he asked like a child.

"No strings," I said.

I joined the troops and marched back to the President for final negotiations. As we went out the door we heard the bleating of a shackled sheep.

"*Murderers!*"

25

"A million dollars!" I almost fainted. It was twice my most optimistic fee. "This is not the President of the United States you got locked up here," I complained.

"For him we would take less," the President said through a Fort Knox smile.

"But it's madness."

"No," he insisted, "it's for a good cause."

I wasn't much of a salesman; that's why I was in the property management arm of Elbert A. Wemple and Associates, Realtors instead of being a top producer in Sales.

"But I can't get you a million," I said.

He looked startled. "You are an American," he said, as though that explained everything.

"Hey," I said, "all Americans are not millionaires. I myself am a paltry salaried individual."

"So how did you propose to, ah, donate anything to the welfare of Santo Oro?"

"I had a source. But I could never raise a million."

"How much did *you* have in mind?"

"Gee, I don't know," I said. "I must be frank, I don't know if I can get anything."

The police chief looked dismayed. He gestured to the President by drawing his forefinger across his neck. The President put up his hand to forestall the hasty decision. "If you could get anything, what would it be?"

I was on the spot. I thought about my fee. What

chance did I have of getting the half-million? I wondered. Less than one percent. After paying off these ghouls, maybe I could get something, but what? Fifty thou? A hundred? How much of it would I graciously hand over? All of it? Half? I frowned, as though in the deepest distress.

"I will be frank with you. I was not counting on this in my work. It is not related except in the most oblique way. I am not sure I will get any fee at all, but I would be glad to split what I get with you."

"How much?" The President spoke to his interest. He had a way of getting to the hub of the matter.

"I hope to get at least a hundred thousand," I gulped.

The President rolled his eyes in the direction of his chief of police.

The chief spoke. "You dare to insult my President with an offer of fifty thousand paltry dollars?" He was in a huff. "In nineteen twenty that might buy us a modest bridge. Now, it is nothing!"

I nodded sympathetically. "On the other hand, if you execute Patrice, what will you get? Can you sell his body to a hospital?"

"We have no hospital. This you were going to provide," the chief said.

The President fixed me with his dejected, long-faced gaze. "We will have the satisfaction of having liquidated one more enemy of our country. This will be a great good. Not something we would ever exchange for a paltry fifty thousand."

"How about a paltry one hundred thousand?"

"Mr. Yates!" the chief reprimanded me, "you insult His Excellency our President with your penny-ante bargaining. This is not a two-bit banana republic where you can shake the nation for a hundred grand. You realize how plentiful Americans with a hundred grand are? You think we serve the interests of our revolution for a paltry sum?"

"Patrice has no interest in revolution."

"How can you say that after you heard him call us murderers?"

"I suppose if you did kill his father he might be a little upset."

The chief waved my thought away. "We killed him in self-defense."

"Kill or be killed," the President said, expecting me to understand.

"Patrice has no interest in governing your island. He left here voluntarily and wholeheartedly. *You* brought him back. He had no desire to return. Release him and tell him if he returns you will shoot him. You'll never see him again."

"Ah, how many times have we heard that?" the President asked the chief.

"More than I can count," he nodded. To me he said, "These revolutionaries hide many places in the world. There they organize the dissidents, and one day, pow!" He slammed his fist into his other palm.

The President stood up. "We must not detain Mr. Yates any longer. I do not think we can do any business. But as a courtesy for his visit, we will give a stay of execution for one week. The chief will give you instructions for wiring the million dollars to our bank. Please do not insult our countrymen with a lesser offer. Do not nickel and dime our dignity."

"Well said, Excellency," the chief added his three cents. "We are becoming more proficient with our executions. This last one will make us rest easier at night."

A million bucks for an insomnia cure, I thought as I was escorted back to the airport, without the rifle guard. Either they no longer feared me as a threat to the nation, or they decided I wasn't worth the honor.

I had only an eighteen-hour wait for the next plane, and I was requested to spend it in the airport.

Miami, I decided, was the ideal place to telephone Michael Hadaad. I would check into some minimal motel and telephone him from a phone booth. Let him trace the call. I was ready for his stalling tactics. But it wasn't as easy to send the goons to Florida as it was to go a couple miles in California.

The one great thing about Hadaad was he was always by the phone, as though he had nothing to do in this world but field my calls (and, no doubt, the calls of sundry nefarious schemers and connivers).

"Where *are* you?" It was one of his favorite greetings.

"I am where I have to be to solve your problem," I said, "but it won't be cheap."

"I thought we had an agreement," he snapped.

"That we did. It is still good. However, some complications have developed. I found your daughter. She refuses to see you. Since I am assuming you will be satisfied with her signature, I approached my assignment from that perspective."

"Don't ever assume anything," he said. His lectures were beginning to sound like Daddybucks'.

"Well, I'm telling you what the possibilities are. As you know, you are not obliged to take any of them," I got a little stern myself. "One, I will not force her to meet you. Two, she has agreed to sign over the account. In addition to my five-hundred-thousand-dollar fee, however, she will require the payment of an additional million."

It was as though someone had dropped an atomic bomb at the other end of the phone. Ranting, raving, screaming. There is nothing so dear to a man who has a lot of money, than money. "Extortion," was one of the first coherent words I heard, followed by, "I know a blackmail scheme when I see one. Next it will be two million, then twenty! I'll call the police!"

I let him run down. "Mr. Hadaad, we both know you won't call the cops. If the money you want to free from Alecia's big bank account were that legit, you wouldn't have hidden it in the first place."

Another explosion: light artillery. "Listen, you little wimp–I don't want you telling me my business. I'm damned if I'll give you a million and a half when the outside limit of the deal was originally a half-million–and that was only if you brought her to me against her will. Now I've sweetened the deal and it still isn't enough for you."

"You are not obligated to take my offer. All it is is an offer."

"But a million and a half!"

"You didn't let me finish," I said. "The million is not for me. You make the check out to someone else. Cashier's check," I added, knowing what went through his mind. Stop payment.

"Who, someone else?"

"You go for the deal, I'll tell you."

"Oh, a tough guy. Is it...a relative?"

"No. But speaking of relatives, how's Helen?"

"I'll worry about Helen," he snapped.

"Up to you, Mr. Hadaad. I'll call again tomorrow. Unfortunately, the offer is not open-ended."

"Ransom!" he spat into the phone, and I almost felt his saliva.

"Yes," I admitted, "in a convoluted way. We would ransom someone very important to your daughter."

"Who?"

"I'll call you in a day or so."

"No, wait," he said as he had that first day we met. He had expressed the opinion my *low* fee was ridiculous. I walked out. Now he wanted more time to trace the call.

"Surely you've had enough time to trace the call. For all the good it will do you. I'm on the move. My next call will be from somewhere else. And it will be a lot shorter. Just yes or no is all you have to say. If it's no, I'll hang up and give up. If it's yes, I'll give you your instructions for the money."

"Hey, you don't expect the money without the signature? What guarantees...?"

"Say yes on the next call–I'll give you your guarantees." And I hung up.

I went back to the motel and conked out for ten

185

hours–I hadn't gotten a lot of sleep in the Santo Oro airport.

My next stop was Chicago. You can fly direct from Miami to L.A., but if you go Chinese, it costs less. So I booked a flight from Miami to Chicago to Houston to Denver to Los Angeles and saved a bundle. You might think I would soon have a nice chunk of cash and could even buy a first-class ticket, but you would be forgetting I had not seen a nickel of the fee and I was dealing with Michael Hadaad, not Mother Teresa.

I had almost two hours between planes and went straight to a bank of telephones. Hadaad was a cool customer all right, but I knew he had a little pressure of his own.

He hit me with a barrage of questions. I knew he would. There was no yes or no with the big cheese.

"I'm not putting out a million to some tooth fairy. I've got to know who and why," he said, "and your fee is out of proportion."

"I knew you'd welch," I said. "Well, I guess it's no then."

"Wait," he said.

I smiled. "Yes?"

"I pegged you for a man of your word," he said.

"Thanks for the compliment."

"But you are not producing the girl against her will. You are not producing her at all. Dead was originally one hundred grand."

"She's alive," I said. "Are you forgetting our written agreement?"

"That has been considerably compromised by your request for an extra million."

"Not for me."

He exhaled some fire into the phone. "Technically,"

186

he said, "that's correct." I knew his saying, "Technically," was meant to convey he did not want to appear hard-hearted. He just wanted to lower the fee.

Unhappily, he had a point. "Two hundred was, before our written agreement, I believe, the price if she was willing to see you. Let's just suppose, for argument, she comes to see you surrounded by bodyguards. You see she's alive, you ask her to sign the account withdrawal slip–she refuses. I whisk her away. I have earned two hundred grand. You have nothing. How much extra would you pay for the signature?"

"Listen, Yates, be reasonable..."

"Sorry, Hadaad, got to run catch a plane. Call you from my next stop."

In Houston the phones were full and we didn't have enough time on the ground for me to scout for an available phone. Okay with me. Let him wait.

I found a phone in Denver.

"Look here, Yates," he said when he graced me with his voice on the line. "This is most unsatisfactory. I can't negotiate on the phone–tell me where you are, I'll come to you–or you come here."

"And have my fingernails pulled out? No, thanks. Tell you what, put Helen on the phone, then I'll give you my bottom line."

"Can't do it."

"She still alive?"

"Certainly."

"Still there?"

"Yes."

"Prove it. Put her on the phone. You can stand beside her."

"No."

"Listen in, then."

"Wait a minute."

In what seemed like an hour, but was more like three or four minutes, a voice came on the phone that reminded me of the vibrant Helen I had known, but now seemed morose.

"Helen?"

"Yessss?" It was a question–like they hadn't told her who she was talking to.

"This is Gil, Helen. You know I found Alecia?"

"Yessss." She slurred her monosyllables like she was drugged.

"Are you all right?"

"Yesss."

"Could you speak a sentence to me please?"

"I am all right, Gil," she said, and Hadaad grabbed the phone.

"I'll give you two fifty, Gil, final offer," he said.

"And the million?"

"I'm not writing any blank checks. You haven't told me who it's for."

"Yes–I will. But one more thing–Helen must be released."

"Who is the million for?"

"We have an agreement? Two hundred fifty thou for me, Helen's release and a million dollars to ransom your daughter's husband, who has been kidnapped and will be executed without your ransom."

"Husband! Kidnapped?" he said. "Sounds like a setup."

"It isn't," I said.

"How can I be sure it isn't?"

"The cashier's check will not be made to me, but to a government."

"Which government?"

"A small island in the Caribbean..."

"Don't tell me...is it...?"

I cut him off. "I won't tell you until I have your agreement."

"You want it in writing, where shall I send it?"

188

"No, I'll take it verbally."

"Which government?"

"It's called Santo Oro."

"Oh, no!" he exclaimed. "No, no, never! Impossible!" he said. "You'll have to find another gimmick." Now it was his turn to hang up the phone.

26

When the hoods are after you the pressure builds. I didn't have long to wait. There was a message for me when I got home.

"We have to talk," it said. Guys as important as Michael Hadaad didn't have to leave their names. You knew who they were. He probably realized not too many people had my phone number. Even so, it irked me.

I called. With a noticeable drop in cordiality, Quasimodo put the hotshot on.

"I may have been hasty," he said. "Unduly so. Do you have any knowledge of my connection with those fruitcakes in Santo Oro?"

"No."

"They didn't mention me?"

"Why would they?" I asked. "Are you connected with Patrice, their hostage?"

"We have to meet."

"Sorry."

"When and where?" he said. "At your convenience."

"No meetings," I said, but he must have caught the wavering in my voice.

"You don't expect me to leave a million and a quarter at that cute office you have?"

I heard myself swallow. He was baiting me with the money. "You know, if I felt I could trust you..."

"Trust *me*!?" he yelled into the phone. "I'm the one

required to pony up the million and a quarter. What do you have to lose?"

"Oh, nothing much. Only my life, maybe."

"Man, let me tell you, if I wanted you dead, you'd be long dead."

"Ah," I said, almost relieved at his frank display of power–"you see?"

"See what?"

"Obviously, you want me alive when you think I can do something for you. But when you are in a position to get what you want *and* save a million and a quarter, I expect my life will be very cheap to you."

"Listen, you pipsqueak, I am a man who makes hundred-million-dollar deals on a handshake. This deal is small potatoes to me."

"Only one thing smaller," I agreed. "Me."

"Fine. What reassurances do you want?"

"Here's the deal Mr. Hadaad," I said, and I could hear him grumbling on the other end of the phone line. He was not a guy who could get used to having anyone as insignificant as I was tell him what the deal was. "Are you listening?" I rubbed it in.

"I'm listening," he grumbled.

"Two things," I said. "You come alone except you bring the money and Helen. And it must be done the day after tomorrow. The day after that, Alecia's husband will be dead and you will not get your signature even if you give her *all* the money." Okay, so I exageratered a bit. I didn't think it would hurt to have extra time. *Carpé diem* they say, and boy did I *carpé diem*. "And, by the way, I would counsel against going to Santo Oro yourself to try and track down Alecia's husband. The natives there are not that friendly, and the regime has a way of justifying their homicides."

"Don't worry," he muttered. "Those bastards reneged on our deal. That's why I'm in a bind for money now. If I could get my hands on an atomic bomb, I'd drop it on them."

His unusual candor was melting me. I was a

pushover. "When can you have the money?"

"You said it had to be the day after tomorrow."

"Only if you want Alecia's signature."

"Very funny. Just fax me Alecia's signature on the instructions to the bank. Then I'll see you. Do you want to come here?"

"No, thanks."

"Then name your place."

"Get the money," I said.

"You're a hard man," he said.

"That's the nicest thing anyone's ever said to me," I said.

At five sharp I called Alecia. It was some restaurant office. The man who answered turned the phone right over to her.

"Hello!" she said with a heartbreaking eagerness.

I told her where we were. I could tell she was down about the news of Patrice.

"Listen," I tried to encourage her. "He's alive. Where there's life, there's hope."

"But I know my father. He'll never give a million dollars to free him. He doesn't even know him. But, by now he knows he's black, and I'm sure it's just too tempting to have someone kill my black husband. He'll try to work me over afterwards. Maybe even offer me the million."

She knew her father all right. I only wished I'd had an argument for her.

"I'm going to see him," I said.

"Be careful."

"Yes. But first he has to fax to me copies of his checks–a million for Santo Oro. Do you know why your father is so upset about that?"

"No."

"He sold arms to the new regime and they stiffed

him. He feels he should get a credit, not have to pay them more. It's insult to injury as far as he's concerned."

"So you'll see a fax of the checks before you go to meet him?"

"Yes, but I must fax to him your signed letter."

"Can't he use that–forge it or something?"

"Well, I expect if he wants to take a chance on forgery, he's got a lot of samples of your signature."

"But couldn't he make a case that this was the real thing, since he had a fax?"

"Copies and faxes don't hold up in court. Too easy to doctor them," I said.

"How do you know?"

An excellent question. "I read a lot," I said. "So I'm going to a fax shop to receive his. I'd like to be able to call you to send yours at the same time. Will that be possible?"

She hesitated.

"If you're worried about his doing something with the signature, I'm going to scramble it on the fax–I'll make some copies first, then cut the signature and send him part of it. But I have to have the original to trade him for the check. If you have a hesitation about trusting me, I can understand that. I'd be happy to have you come yourself. Could you get away?"

There was a long pause. "No...I..." was what she finally said.

I was trying to be forbearing. "Do you have any suggestions?"

Another pause. "Could you all come here?" she asked. "Getting away from here is not easy."

"Yes, I'm sure I could get him to come there. Of course you realize your father will know where you are then."

"Not necessarily. I could have flown in from anywhere."

"But why you didn't come to where I am or where he is might be harder to explain. Up to you. We could go to Frisco and you could stay out of sight. Watch from somewhere. Could you get to San Francisco for a couple hours?"

"I don't know. Be easier than L.A."

"Okay, let's plan on it. Then you don't have to mail the bank letter, just fax it to me."

"May I mess up the signature?"

"Good for you," I said. "There really is no good reason you should trust me. Sure you can do it–just leave enough so he knows the document exists, signed."

"Where shall I send it?"

"I'll call you at this number. If you aren't there, I'll leave the fax number and the time," I said. "How will you get to town?"

"I'll take BART."

"Rattle the cup?"

"Yeah. Gil?"

"Yes?"

"Do you think it will work?" There was a heartrending catch in her voice. "Will I get Patrice back?"

"If your father comes through."

"Do you think he will?"

"I expect he'll try everything he can to double-cross us, so we just have to be ready for him. I know this. He wants that twenty million in the worst way, and you could be holding him up for a lot more to sign it over to him."

"I don't want his money," she said.

I do, I thought.

While I was waiting for word from Hadaad that he had the dough, I took a quick trip to the poolroom.

The man mountain was chalking his cue. It looked like Butch Bacon had lined up a patsy for a hustle. He greeted me like he was truly glad to see me.

"I've been waiting," he said.

After he sent his patsy to the bar for drinks, I told the big guy what I had in mind.

"At least four guys," I said. "Big ones.... Can you get...?"

"No problem," Butch said.

I told him I would get him the airline tickets and come back the next day with the specific details.

It took three calls to reach Alecia. We arranged alternate fax times for early the next day. Then I laid out my plans for her approval.

27

Early the next morning, I called Santo Oro to inquire into the health and well-being of Patrice La Bec. The chief of police trotted out his oleaginous personality to assure me, "We are men of honor. Here in Santo Oro our word is our bond."

"So why didn't you pay Hadaad for your armaments, you big turkey?" I could have said, but didn't. Instead, I assured him we were close to getting the cash and I would, as they say in Santo Oro, keep in touch.

My next call was to the phone company's answering mechanics.

"Call me." Click.

I went to the neighborhood fax shop to receive Alecia's fax, then went to the corner gas station to call Hadaad. He was gruff but ready. I laid out my plan.

"Frisco!" he balked. "Why so damn far?"

"Mr. Hadaad, it is a great deal farther for me–and I don't have a private plane."

"Why don't you just come here? We'll make the exchange here."

"I'm afraid Alecia wants to be close by. Frisco is her choice. Easy flight, I guess, from where she is."

"Where is she?"

"Gee, Mr. Hadaad, I wouldn't know."

"Don't get cute with me!"

"Sorry."

"So bring Alecia here. I'm doing the paying in this deal, I should have something to say."

"I agree with you, Mr. Hadaad. But I guess the *reason* you are paying is your daughter has something worth paying for, and she seems determined to call the tune."

Hadaad grumbled. I gave him the detailed instructions I had worked out. And the ground rules. "No rough stuff. Leave the goons at home. If you don't feel this is an acceptable deal for you, let's let it go."

"I never travel without a bodyguard," he said.

Well, I thought, fair enough. If I were as crooked as Hadaad, I'd want a bodyguard too. "Only one–and not in the meeting. The meeting is one on one, or there will be no meeting," I said. "Of course, there will be no deal if you don't bring Helen, in good health and undrugged, and release her to me."

"I gotta tell you something," he moaned, exasperated, into the phone. "I've never felt like I was dealing with such amateurs before. It makes me nervous."

Good! I thought. True enough, I *was* an amateur. But, tomorrow, with a quarter-million in my pocket, I hoped to turn professional.

"Are you ready to fax the checks?"

"Just give me the number."

"I'm at a fax shop," I said, and gave him the number. "I will wait here five minutes, then I'm leaving. I'll call you from another shop–so don't bother tracing me."

"Do you have the document to fax to me?"

"Yes. As soon as I get yours."

I hung up and went back to the shop. There was a guy using the fax. I watched the clock. It was four minutes before he was finished. I was watching the door all the time. Four minutes seemed like an eternity. Not much time to find the shop and send the goons, but I'm sure nobody ever increased their life span by underestimating Michael Hadaad.

The sweetest music I ever heard was the unique sound of the fax machine grinding out the fax. True to his conservative (cheap) nature, Hadaad had put both checks on one page. The first was a cashier's check for a million dollars, made out to Santo Oro. The second was for two hundred and fifty thousand dollars. It was made out to cash.

I didn't fax Alecia's bank letter to Hadaad. I got, instead, into the Plymouth and drove to another fax shop–then found a telephone at a gas station a half-mile away.

"Cute," I said when he took the phone from Quasimodo.

Hadaad didn't waste any time being coy. "It's for your own protection," he said.

"You bring your bodyguard. I'll look out for protecting myself."

"But you are liable to criminal prosecution if they find you have been practicing private investigation without a license. This way they can't trace it."

"Baloney. It's not criminal. It's a one-grand fine, which I will gladly pay. The only problem with your check is it is just like cash, so if I happen to get hit over the head on my way to the bank, I am left with zilch–while you can just slip it back in your bank account."

"You have not faxed Alecia's letter."

"No, and I'm not going to until you perform your part. Now how much time will it take you to get my name on that check?"

"But you have given me a fictitious name. Do you think someone will honor a check with a phony name?" he asked. "A check that size?"

My stunned silence showed he had me. I had simply neglected to consider that hurdle. Amateur indeed. Slowly, I recovered. "So you go to the cops and say I stole the check," I mumbled. "If it's not made out to me, it's..."

"Don't be silly. I could just as well claim you extorted a check out of me by unlawful means–blackmail–I could make a hundred claims, each of which would get the money returned to me."

Sounded easy. I was sure with my name on the check it would be tougher.

"Of course, if you want to give me your real name..."
He wasn't rich because he was stupid.

"Okay. Here's what I will accept. Send me by fax a signed letter from you. Refer to the check by bank, date and number–and amount. Say this is in payment to a man known to you as Gil Yates as an irrecoverable fee for services rendered to you. Sign, date and bring it along tomorrow."

It was not perfect, but given all the circumstances, it was the best I could do. The last thing I wanted was for him to get my real name and hunt me down. I'm sure with the working over his goons would give me, I'd be delighted to give him his money back, as well as my house and wife.

Speaking of wife, she was due back from Scotland tomorrow. Two weeks had flown by. Her return was another good reason to get my case over with.

"Send me Alecia's letter while I'm having your note typed out," he said.

"Better not."

"Why not? You've seen the checks. It's your turn."

"Yes, except then I lose my leverage for the letter," I said.

"Oh, all right." You could tell he was mighty tired of being pushed around by a pipsqueak, but I sort of enjoyed aggravating him. "What's the fax number?"

"How long will it take you to type the letter?"

"Five minutes."

"I'll call you in five minutes," I said, and hung up.

To save time, I went to the new fax shop, got the number and called him. "You have it typed?"

"Yeah." He sounded weary of the whole thing.

I gave him the number.

"Now you're going to fax me Alecia's?"

"Right away."

"It's signed, isn't it? Her signature?"

"Yes, but for safety we have garbled it a little. You'll be able to tell it's hers. The original is not garbled. You'll see it tomorrow before you hand over the checks."

In a minute, Hadaad's letter arrived on the fax. It

was perfect, which made me wonder what else he had up his sleeve.

I returned the favor with Alecia's note to the bank. Then I called him back to verify our meeting and to reiterate the ground rules.

Then I made contact with Alecia and told her we were all set.

She sounded exhausted, and I could just see the zombie glaze take over her eyes.

"Do you want me to handle it alone?" I asked.

"No...I...it's just so hard to get away. They are watching me."

"Your husband's life is depending on this. We can't fool around. It has to all work tomorrow like clockwork or they will execute him. If I were you, I'd just skip out of there. When they find out you have saved another soul for the fold, all will be forgiven."

"I'm not so sure," she mumbled so I barely heard it. But, finally, she promised to come and meet me by noon at The Donatello hotel, on Post Street, just up from Union Square.

28

I knew there were a thousand things that could go wrong with my plan. Even though I had gone over and over everything in my head, facing the real people could spawn a thousand more pitfalls I had never considered.

I got on the plane in L.A. with the four huskies that looked like a classic Notre Dame backfield. Butch, Hank, Steve and Rock were their names. Rock was the midget in the outfit, weighing in at 225 and standing an even six foot. As I fretted my plans to them, Butch, the big boss, kept nodding and saying, "Don't worry, we'll handle it," and he didn't look worried.

Handle what? Hadaad was the arms king. We were liable to be hit with a sophisticated laser rocket from a helicopter.

We checked into The Donatello hotel and garnered a potful of looks from all the staff. Five guys. One room.

"No luggage, sir?" the bellman asked, trying to keep his eyebrows under control.

"Just here for the day," I said.

He showed us to our room, facing the Portman Hotel, across the street. The room had a nice view of the hotel entry and the glass elevator.

Hadaad had his instructions to check in at the Portman between eleven and noon with Helen and one bodyguard. I told him I would leave word at his desk at five of one where the one o'clock meeting would be.

Hadaad checked in and we saw the three in his party go up the elevator.

I sent Rock across the street, to hang out in the lobby and call if he saw hefty-looking bruisers. Probably a pair.

Alecia had not yet arrived. I called our telephone contact. He had not seen her. I told her to meet us by noon and it was twenty after. No sign. No call.

At half past I started to fidget. At quarter of one I began to think she had changed her mind. What could keep her? Could the zealots physically restrain her? Maybe shaking the cup wasn't cutting the horseradish. Hadaad was here, so that should rule out the possibility that he might have found her and forced the agreement from her.

I scrawled a message for Hank, the linebacker, to take across the street to the desk:

Here and ready. Alecia's plane late.
Will keep you posted every half-hour.
Gil

I thought that fiction would keep him guessing. Might even check the airport to see which planes were late.

When Hank returned, he told me he saw two suspicious-looking guys hovering around the parking entrance, out of our sight line. I told Rock to keep an eye on them.

In ten minutes Rock called to tell me Hadaad had come down for the note, read it, crumpled it in disgust and had gone outside to tell the two goons on the sidewalk something. Hadaad went back into the hotel and the two guys got in a car in the garage and drove off.

Hadaad's movements, he said, were shifty. Always looking around to see if he was being followed. The fullback thought Hadaad paid no attention to him, but that's doubtful.

I sent Hank down to the street with a picture of Alecia to roam around to see if he could see a lost girl–to see if the goons were nearby–I expected they were.

Two notes to Hadaad later, Hank came up to the room with Alecia. She looked bedraggled. Shell-shocked from her experience. With a trembling hand she passed the signed letter to me.

Butch threw his arm around her. "Hi baby, how're ya doin'?"

Alecia looked startled, then she realized who he was. "Butch!" she screamed. "Oh, wow, Butch–it's great to see you. What are you doing here?"

"Came to help you out, baby."

Tears clouded her eyes.

"May I order you something before your dad comes?" I asked Alecia.

She shook her head but gratefully drank a glass of water.

"Are you okay?"

"I'm okay," she said. "Let's get it over with."

"All right." I checked my watch, it was ten minutes after two. "Twenty more minutes? Your father checks every half-hour for notes. I'm going to write him one telling him to come immediately, without returning to his room. That should shake him up."

"You think he'll do it?"

"No. He's got to coordinate his goons. And he has to bring your mother."

"So what's the scam?" Butch asked.

"I'm going to write in the note that a man will be standing on the corner in front of his hotel. He and his wife, Helen, must present themselves and follow immediately. No one else can be told where they are going."

"Won't he balk?"

"Maybe. He could fear he would disappear and never be heard from again. I don't think he'd think twice about wasting *any*one for twenty million. I'm afraid that includes you, Alecia."

She closed her eyes and nodded.

"But we won't be putting him to that test. We are giving him what he wants, in exchange for what *we* want."

I wrote the note:

Mr. Hadaad:

> *Please take Helen and go directly
> to the corner in front of your hotel. There
> you will find a man who will identify himself
> by saying, "Michael Hadaad and Helen."
> You will show him the checks and if that is
> in order, he will lead you to me. The signed
> letter is in my possession. Alecia will not be
> here, but the letter will be. Do not contact
> anyone or try to set up any ambushes or you
> will not be brought to me.*
>
> *Your every move is being watched. The
> man will be on the corner only until 2:40. If
> you are not there with Helen, we will leave you
> other instructions at 3:00 p.m.*

I gave Butch the note to deliver to the desk. Then he was to station himself on the corner to await the Hadaads' arrival. Rock would keep an eye on the Portman lobby, then follow Hadaad out and come directly to our lobby to verify it was free of goons. My main interest was in separating Hadaad from the bozos. I thought in a free-for-all melee I'd gladly stack my four against his three, but why take chances?

"Where do you want to be, Alecia?"

"Can I hide in the bathroom?"

"Sure, but he is liable to go in there. Might insist on checking the closets, under the bed. It's up to you."

"I don't want to see him."

"The boys are going to sit out the meeting in the stairwell at the end of the hall."

"Good. I'll go there."

At two-forty sharp we saw Hadaad come out of the hotel with Helen and make contact with Butch. Helen, from my vantage point, looked drained of life. Her purse hung lifelessly from her hand. Our man, Butch, examined the checks, which didn't leave Hadaad's hands. Hadaad put them back in his jacket inside pocket, and then Butch patted him down for a weapon. Satisfied he was clean, Butch led them into our building.

Steve and Hank took Alecia to the stairwell. Rock had instructions to call us if he spotted Hadaad's goons in the street or in the lobby of our hotel.

My heart was going bonkers as I awaited the knock on the door. When it came, I thought the pounding in my heart was louder than that on the door.

"Who is it?" I croaked–as if I didn't know.

"It's Butch with the Hadaads." He was announcing it as much for the benefit of the troops in the stairwell as for me. As soon as they were inside, one of them would come into the hallway while the other would watch over Alecia, hidden in the stairwell.

When I opened the door, I saw that Hadaad was a most unhappy camper. His feathers were ruffled. He was a man who *gave* orders. It had been years since he had taken any, and he announced, "I resent being treated as a child."

"I'm sorry. I'm new at this," I explained.

"That's obvious," he snorted.

I looked at Helen. She returned my gaze, but said nothing. She looked tired, but aware of what was going on.

"May I see the checks?"

"I showed them to this man. It's my turn to see the letter." He looked me straight in the eye and his message was of the don't-mess-with-me variety. "And the meeting was to be with us alone," he said, looking distastefully at Butch.

"He's seen the checks," I said, "what is the point of excusing him?"

"It was the agreement," he said.

"No. The agreement was *you* would not bring any-one but Helen. Nothing was said about me."

"Well, it was certainly implied," he said, peevishly. "'One on one' you said."

"Certainly you don't plan any funny business, Mr. Hadaad. So what difference does it make? Give me the checks, I'll give you the letter."

Hadaad pursed his lips and shook his head.

"No?"

"I'm through being treated as a child. I'm sick of your petty games. I'm alone–you be alone or I walk out of here and I'll get my twenty million with a court order."

Nice bluff, I thought. But no way would he be delivering a million and a quarter if he thought he had a Mongolian's chance of getting it free.

"Okay," I said, "Butch can wait outside the door." I motioned to him with my head and he went out.

"Much better," Hadaad said, and his whole self seemed to sift into a happy relaxation. "Show me the letter."

I took it from my jacket pocket, opened it and held it up for him to see. "Now, the checks, please."

"Helen has them," he said.

Helen frowned. It was clear that was news to her. He took her purse and opened it in the same motion, deftly lifting out a tiny derringer. If I read Helen's expression correctly, she didn't know it was in there.

Amateurs, I thought, shouldn't play these high-stakes games.

"All right," he said, pointing the gun at my nose, making me think, with a ridiculous twist of logic, it would probably clear up my sinuses. "Let's have the letter."

"Let's have the checks," I said without thinking. If he wanted to give me the checks, he wouldn't have brought the gun.

"You won't be getting any checks," he said evenly. With the firearm, he was once again the man of the house.

"I guess you have a permit for that," I said jovially. "Guess you sell a lot of them."

"Yes, and I sold a lot of them to Santo Oro and they didn't make their final payment. I'm not giving them a dime. I don't care if they burn that black monkey alive."

I nodded. I understood him. How could you not? He was as transparent as cellophane. "Man of your word? Didn't you tell me that?"

206

"My word was forced out of me. I was defrauded. I've been the victim of extortion, blackmail and God knows what all else."

"You plan to shoot us?"

"Us?" He smiled. "The gun is pointed at you. Helen brought it."

She shook her head. It was all the encouragement I needed. Too bad I didn't have the nerve or expertise to disarm him.

"Just give me the letter," he said, holding out his free hand.

Dilemma. Heretofore if there was one prize I would have the inside track on, it was the coward's prize. I startled myself when these foolish words came out of my mouth: "Not without the checks."

"Don't be a fool," he said.

"It's too late for that advice," I said.

"All I have to do is give you a third eye–between the other two–and I'll get the letter."

"I have a responsibility to your daughter," I said. "No check, no letter."

"Where is she?"

"Close by."

"Get her. I'll talk to her."

"She doesn't want to."

"Let me speak to her. I'll change her mind."

"With that?" I said, nodding to the derringer, which was uncomfortably close to my nose.

"I love her. I have to tell her."

"You always did have a peculiar way of showing it," I said, looking over to Helen, who was frozen in place. I saw her face twitch at that. It was one of the few gestures she'd allowed herself to show she was conscious.

"Alecia can't throw her life away on a black savage. I *know* those people. They're savages. How did she hook up with him anyway?" he asked, his eyes pinched in personal pain. "I'll bet those idiots in Santo Oro set her up."

"But how would they find her if you couldn't?"

"Well, they did."

"I think it was more innocent," I said, desperately trying to buy more time which was doing nothing to help me, one, get the gun away from him and, two, get the checks.

His hand came out again. "The letter," he said.

"The checks."

"You don't think I'd shoot you?"

"What I think is if you want to shoot me, you will, whether or not I give you the letter. Just as easy to kill me after I hand it over. Probably save you the nagging urge to fulfill your agreement."

He stared at me—his eyes frightened me more than the gun. They flashed as though fired and he suddenly turned the gun on Helen.

She closed her eyes as he got behind her and put a choke hold on her neck and pointed the gun at her temple.

"The letter," he said.

I hesitated—but he was making headway and he knew it.

"Come on, you think Alecia would sacrifice her mother over some lousy piece of paper?"

"Okay—you win. I don't have the stomach to watch a man with a gun at his—wife's head." I almost said, "Ex-wife," but I didn't want to rile him. "But before I go to utter defeat, show me the checks."

"Why?"

"I want the satisfaction of knowing I accomplished *some*thing."

He actually smiled. He let go of Helen's neck, but kept the gun pointed at her head. Oh, how many movies had I seen where the hero lunged at a time like this? And, magically, the gun didn't go off, blowing the hostage to kingdom come. I wasn't trying it.

He reached into his pocket and produced the checks. As I looked at them, I drooled. I gave him the letter. I was counting on the Notre Dame backfield to retrieve the checks. Of course if Hadaad started shooting...my boys were

208

not armed. How would they react to the gun at Helen's head? I didn't want her killed over this silly money.

Hadaad replaced the checks and letter in his inside pocket. "And so, I say goodbye," he said. "It was a great pleasure to meet you. Have a safe journey home—wherever that might be." I didn't like the way he said that. It smelled of a threat.

He opened the door to face three of my huskies blocking the doorway. The gun was still at Helen's head. They glared at him. "Get out of my way!" he commanded them. They didn't move.

Hadaad's nervous eyes turned frantic.

"Get out of my way or I kill the woman!"

The boys just stared. Butch spoke: "So kill her."

Hadaad broke out in a cold sweat, and I wasn't feeling so hot either. It was immediately apparent they had out-bluffed him. Suddenly he pulled Helen back in the room, slammed the door and threw on the chain. He dragged Helen over to the window, opened it just a few inches, reached into his pocket and threw the checks out the window.

Believe it or not, I had an instant urge to jump out after them. I stood, mouth agape, watching them float down toward a homeless beggar shaking his paper cup of coins at the passersby.

I decided to talk tough-guy. "You better jump out after them. You just threw out the paychecks of my friends."

A wry smile crossed Tough Guy's face.

"I notice you didn't throw out the letter."

"That I keep."

"How do you plan to get it by our friends?"

"I have two hostages," he said, as though that were the answer. But he wasn't making another move toward the door.

So I did. I unhooked the chain and opened the door.

"Hey! Get away from there!" The three mountains closed in on him.

"Stop right there, or I'll shoot."

Butch, a man more adept at smelling out a bluff than I, kept coming.

"I'll shoot!" Hadaad repeated, sweating profusely. He moved the gun jerkily, pointing first at Helen, then at me. I must admit, I did not share Butch's confidence that Hadaad wouldn't shoot me or Helen or Butch or all of us.

"Put the gun down," Butch commanded. But Hadaad was not used to following orders.

So Butch, in the most amazing sudden motion, chopped the gun out of Hadaad's hand and it went scurrying across the floor like a surprised rat.

Disarmed, Hadaad sank into a chair like a Nerf ball stopped by a wall. He was deflated into simpering insignificance.

Butch threw his forearm across Hadaad's neck and reached into the pocket where he had seen Hadaad place the checks after he had shown them to Butch in the street outside. He was surprised to find only Alecia's letter. He looked at me.

I pointed to the window. "He threw them out there. Probably going to report them stolen and stop payment. Probably already did."

Hadaad wasn't talking, but he wasn't arguing either.

Butch said, "Hank!" and Hank made a flyline to the street below.

Fat chance, I thought. A quarter-of-a-million-dollar check made out to cash is just going to be lying unclaimed in the street.

And even the Santo Oro check. How long would it take someone to get a fictitious name for a haberdashery or pie shop named Santo Oro and open an account? Okay, that might be tougher.

"Give me the letter," Hadaad pleaded pathetically to Butch. "They'll kill me," he said.

"Who?" I asked.

"I have a debt. A big one. I have the money–but I can't get at it. These boys don't play games. Santo Oro stiffed me, but that doesn't cut ice with them. They don't get their money, they'll kill me."

"Well, get us our money, and we'll fulfill our part of the bargain."

Hank came back to the room. He was smiling.

I hugged Helen. She hugged back. "Keep an eye on Mr. Hadaad, will you, Butch and Steve? If we find those checks and they are still good, we'll give you the letter, Mr. H."

Hadaad said nothing.

I said, "It was a rare pleasure meeting you. I hope you have a safe journey home."

Helen and I took the stairway down with Hank. There on the landing there was a shrieking, embracing, tearful reunion with Helen and Alecia. I hope they didn't hear it in the room. But I guessed Mr. Hadaad wasn't leaving for a while.

We opened the door on the lobby floor, to see Hadaad's goons coming toward us. Since there were four of us in a public place, they didn't make a fuss. I saw Rock at the door keeping his eye on the goons and the street.

"Where's Mr. Hadaad?" asked the goon who had a handle on the English language.

"Up in the room," I said.

"Which room?"

"I forgot the number. He said if we saw you, he'd meet you in the lobby."

They looked at each other. They were obviously not guys who liked to be put on. But the last we saw, they were taking their seats in the lobby.

On the way out I said to the doorman, "See those two guys on the couch in the lobby?"

"Yes, sir."

"Have Security check them out. They got quite a bad rep–organized crime."

"Yes, sir–I will, sir," he said.

29

We were on the sidewalk before Rock handed me the checks. He had been watching for Hadaad's goons when he saw those beautiful pieces of paper float out of the window. He had then dashed over to snatch them out of the hands of the homeless man with the paper cup.

The boys were standing by, consulting some kind of electronic gear that they seemed to have trouble figuring out, Rock said. He thought it was a homing device that homed them to the hotel, but not to the right room.

"First thing we do is get the checks to the bank. See if they are good."

"How will we get Patrice out?" Alecia asked. "We can't just send them the money on faith," she said. She was so forlorn looking I realized even if she were up to going, the troops in Santo Oro would devour her. So I heard myself volunteer for the mission, then instantly think I needed a quick and thorough examination of my head.

We went into the first bank we came to. The checks were good. I couldn't believe it. I guess he thought we would check from the faxes (I hadn't) and decided that with the gun he was clever enough to put in his innocent ex-wife's purse, he would easily be able to walk out with them.

When he saw he couldn't, he decided to dump them and stop payment. So now all we had to do was deposit them in an account before Hadaad left the room.

Without any Gil Yates identification, I put the check

in my own name, requesting no statements be sent. It was a branch of a bank we had in L.A., so it worked out nicely. I got a pack of temporary checks to make some generous payments to my co-workers, and I even forced a few bucks on Helen.

Of course, I bought Alecia's flowers for the week. The suggestion met with only mild protests.

Helen agreed to accompany me to Santo Oro. I called the regime and told them I had the money and was on my way. I wanted them to meet me at the Miami airport to make the exchange. I didn't want to chance a meeting in Santo Oro. Too easy to ambush. Not that Patrice was that dangerous to them, but when you are talking about paranoia, you can never be sure.

I asked to speak to Patrice. "That would be impossible," the chief told me. "Prisoners are not allowed to use the phone."

"Then kiss the million goodbye," I said, "because I'm not schlepping to Miami on faith."

There was harrumphing and aheming and ahawing, but after a consultation with Mr. President, it was arranged. Patrice did not seem overly friendly or grateful or even hopeful, until I put Alecia on the phone. Then I could hear his booming exuberance come right through the phone. And Alecia squealed like a schoolgirl. When she gave me the phone back–after they had torn Patrice from the instrument–she hugged me and kissed me on the cheek. It was better than the quarter of a million.

Well–maybe not. After I made the arrangements with the chief, I didn't have any trouble talking Alecia into going with us. She frowned at first, considering, I suppose, the consequences from the holy of holies, but her love for Patrice won out.

"Shall we get the tickets here?" Helen asked.

"We'll get them at the airport. Won't make any difference," I said, "we're flying first class."

I called the hotel room. Butch answered the phone.

"Butch," I said, "you're the best. When I complete

this transaction, I'm sending you and the boys an honorarium."

"No need," he said. "Glad to help out in our modest fashion."

"If you call saving our lives modest, I don't want to hear the big stuff. Watch the mail. You can give Hadaad the letter and go now–Let me talk to Hadaad again, will you?"

I heard a grunt on the phone I took to be the famous entrepreneur, Michael Hadaad, a shadow of the pompous ogre.

"Mr. Hadaad, Gil Yates here."

Another grunt.

"I just wanted you to know how much I appreciate your patronage. I'm sorry for the unpleasantness at the end, but Butch will give you your letter and everything worked out like we all hoped it would. You got your money and I got me fee."

Now the sound was more extraterrestrial and I wondered if Butch had him gagged.

"Well, pal," I said with a disconcerting swagger, "I hope you'll tell your friends about me, about what a swell job I do–and how I don't take any guff from anyone."

"You'll get yours, Yates, or whatever your name is," he spoke at last. "I'll see to it personally."

I ignored his petty threats. "Come see my palm trees sometime," I said. "They aren't as big as yours but I have more species."

"Aggh."

"Now that I have some real dough I might be in the market for some of yours."

"Drop dead, Yates. Before I sold you a palm or cycad I'd burn them all."

"Really?" I said. "How would you know what they looked like?"

"Go to hell," he hissed and there was the explosive sound of the phone crashing down.

Geez, I thought, I've never talked like that to anyone in my life before. Felt kind of good.

We left San Francisco at 10:15 p.m. We were scheduled into Miami at 6:30 a.m. Eastern Time, which dovetailed with the Santo Oro flight which landed in Miami at 7:00 a.m. On the flight Alecia *was* a schoolgirl. Her personality had blossomed out of the cocoon of the Starrs. She giggled with her mother (I had let them sit together), and worried that Helen wouldn't like, or understand Patrice.

"Oh, don't worry," Helen said. "If you like him, I'll like him."

"Oh, Mother," Alecia said, "I *love* him!" and they both giggled.

In the Miami airport I took the precaution of leaving the ladies in a different waiting area while I stood off to the side to see that the chief was alone with Patrice. I didn't want to be overcome with the goose-steppers.

They came off alone all right, but Patrice was in chains. I was glad Alecia couldn't see it, because, innocent as he was, it was bound to be a traumatic picture for her memory book.

The chief made a great show of examining the check, front and back. They had originally asked for a wire, but the chief did not seem disposed to argue. When he was finally satisfied of its goodness, he handed me the key to Patrice's chains and said, "The people of Santo Oro are most grateful to you for your most generous donation to our humanitarian cause." He saluted as Patrice shouted, "Murderers!"

Hastily, I unlocked the chains, and, as hastily, the chief beat his retreat. Briefly, I wondered if that was the last Santo Oro would see of their police chief and their check.

We dumped the chains, the lock and key into the first trash can we came to and made our way to the area where Patrice's wife and mother-in-law were waiting. There was a joyous, eye-drenching reunion.

On the way back to L.A. I got to sit with Helen. As the young lovers discussed their future, so did we. I was spinning all kinds of dream sequences, when Helen brought me back to earth.

"You *do* have a wife after all. And I'm just so happy

my Alecia is well. So much has happened, I just want to get my feet back on the ground and try to help out my daughter anyway I can. I'm still a little ruffled from it all. Michael kidnapping me like that–keeping me prisoner."

"Why *did* he do that?"

"Was supposed to punish us, I guess, for what he called 'being unfaithful' to him. And he thought he could use me as a bargaining chip with you."

"Did he drug you?"

She nodded. "Nothing habit forming, I hope. I was just drowsy all the time."

"He's some guy." We declared our mutual love and, to make a five-hour story shorter, our mutual conviction that I was to return, for better or worse, to Tyranny Rex, but Helen and I would continue our friendship.

"Impossible," I can hear the cynics sneering. We'll see.

I overheard the kids discussing their future in the cult, and I could sense copious cracks in the facade. Time would tell. It always did.

Helen and I saw Alecia and Patrice on to their plane to San Francisco; the matriarch was still swallowing tears. I took Helen home in a taxi. While the driver waited I saw her to her door, and gave her a chaste kiss.

Well, not *that* chaste.

I arrived home, a richer and wiser man, two hours and twenty minutes before the Rex.

She made her entrance as she always did: dragged out from a killing trip across the globe, but bubbling to tell me all the news.

Surprisingly, I was able to absorb most of it. Maybe because I was independently wealthy and realized I didn't have to take any more guff from any of them. It put the most peculiar providential slant on the relationship.

I think Tyrannosaurus Rex noticed it too, for suddenly she stopped mid-sentence in one of her monologues and asked, "So what's new around here?"

"Same old stuff," I said.

TEQUILA

A GUIDE TO Types, Flights, Cocktails, AND Bites

by JOANNE WEIR

Food Photography by LARA HATA

Location Photography by Jenn Farrington

TEN SPEED PRESS
Berkeley | Toronto

To the agave growers who for centuries have tilled
the soil to unearth the spirit of a country.

Ten Speed Press
PO Box 7123
Berkeley, California 94707
www.tenspeed.com

Distributed in Australia by Simon and
Schuster Australia, in Canada by Ten Speed
Press Canada, in New Zealand by Southern
Publishers Group, in South Africa by Real
Books, and in the United Kingdom and
Europe by Publishers Group UK.

Cover and text design by Betsy Stromberg
Food and prop styling by Pouké
Styling assistance by Anne-Christina Milne
Photography assistance by Ha Huynh

Riedel Ouverture Tequila glasses photo-
graphed in the book (page 90) provided by
Riedel Glass Company.

Library of Congress Cataloging-in-
Publication Data

Weir, Joanne.
  Tequila : a guide to cocktails, types,
flights, and bites / by Joanne Weir.
       p. cm.
  Includes bibliographical references and
index.
  Summary: "A connoisseur's guide to
understanding and enjoying top-shelf
tequila, with sixty recipes for drinks and
tequila-infused foods" — Provided by
publisher.
  ISBN 978-1-58008-949-4 (alk. paper)
  1. Cocktails. 2. Tequila. I. Title.
  TX951.W4134 2009
  641.2'5—dc22

2008037776

Printed in China
First printing, 2009

1 2 3 4 5 6 7 8 9 10 — 13 12 11 10 09

Contents

Food

Acknowledgments

WHEN I STARTED this project, I had no idea there were so many people so in love with tequila! It is with the help of all of you fantastic bartenders, tequila experts and aficionados, and tequila-loving friends that this book was a pure joy to write.

To all the Agave Girls, especially Mariangela Sassi, Carolyn Alburger, and Shannon Smith!

To Dorothy Kinne, for your help with recipe testing, tasting, and coordinating, I thank you.

For your friendship, knowledge, and encouragement every step of the way, my heartfelt thanks go to Eric Rubin. And to everyone at Tres Agaves, thanks for everything you've done for me and this book—and for opening up the restaurant for our atmospheric photo shoot that produced the lovely lime slices photograph that you see opposite this page, and the Riedel tequila glasses photo on page ii! To the best bartenders who gave their time and recipes—Joel Baker, Ronaldo Colli, Duggan McDonnell, Jacques Bezuidenhout, Philip Brady, James Meehan, Julio Bermejo, Steve Olson, Andy Seymour, Tommy Schlesinger-Guidelli, Dominic Venegas, Ashley Miller, H. Joseph Ehrmann, Kacy Fitch, Lucy Brennan, Liz Baron, Audrey Saunders, Jennifer Gordon, and Enrique Sanchez.

To the people who so enthusiastically helped me along the way—Kern McNutt and Lance Cutler for your stamps of approval. And to Juan Fernando González de Anda, Carlos Camarena, Gary Shansby, Sofia Partida, David Partida, Gino Colangelo, Dave Signh, Valerie Villalta, Santiago Castillo Loza, José Valdez, JP De Loera, David Yan, Nicole Hajek, Ruben Aceves Vidrio, David Ravandi, Dale DeGroff, German Gonzalez Gorrochotegui, Paola Gutierrez, Eric Appleby, Alex Moreno, Koa Duncan, Kimberley Charles, Colleen Jezersek, Samantha Shuman, Liz Mitchell, Kirsten Mireault, Kyle Khasigian, Tina Gherzi, Claudia Tong, Erik Kokkonen, Emily Ehrlich, Abigail Ehrlich, Jeffrey Lloyd, Barbara Fenzl, Michela Larson, Scott Beattie, Linda Read, and Carole Kotkin.

A special thanks to Lara Hata for your lovely photos of food and drink and to Jenn Farrington for your beautiful Jalisco location shots.

Cheers to Doe Coover, my fabulous agent, who shares my love of tequila. A kiss, a hug, and a big thanks to Lisa Westmoreland, my editor par excellence. And thanks to the rest of the Ten Speed team: Betsy Stromberg for her gorgeous design, Susan Pi for her unending enthusiasm, and Debra Matsumoto for her fabulous ideas.

Last but not least, thanks to Joe, who's shared many a tequila cocktail and always looks in my eyes when we toast.

Preface

IT ALL STARTED several years ago, when I was invited to the launch of a spiffy new tequila in a sexy square bottle at the well-known tequila hotspot, Tommy's Mexican Restaurant, in San Francisco. Julio Bermejo, owner and acclaimed Ambassador of Tequila, was behind the bar pouring the most delicious 100 percent blue agave tequila. I noticed that the event was mostly attended by men. The few women who were there, however, seemed to be just as enthusiastic, sniffing, swirling, and sipping from their glasses.

I was curious about the other tequila lovers, so I worked the room, talking with everyone about their own particular interest in tequila. I discovered that night that, yes, men love tequila, but that women are also incredibly passionate about it and eager to learn more about its complexities. That evening was a revelation, and I was delighted to learn that, like me, many women don't just like tequila—they love it. They savor it with meals, drink it slowly from a snifter, and enjoy it mixed into innovative seasonal cocktails. I was thrilled to discover a sense of camaraderie among these women, and pleased to learn that I wasn't the only one out there who liked a beverage that had long been considered the domain of men.

I recognized that tequila had an alter ego, a more sophisticated, complex side, and that I wasn't the only one who appreciated it. That knowledge encouraged me to create a group called Agave Girls, to help women share their enthusiasm for fine tequila and to dispel the myth that a night of drinking it inevitably leads to a morning of regret and popping aspirin. We'd grown up and, just like tequila, we wanted to be taken seriously.

What started as a few women getting together to sip *añejo* and discuss its virtues has grown into a group of several hundred dedicated aficionados. Among this group's members is Elizabeth Falkner, a Food Network Iron Chef contender who was so excited about Agave Girls that she dropped everything at her wildly successful restaurants Citizen Cake and Orson to join; Traci Des Jardins, a James Beard Rising Star and chef of the award-winning restaurant Jardinière, who has offered her more casual Mexican restaurant, Mijita, to use for events; Renel Brooks-Moon, host of Bay Area radio show "Renel in the Morning"; Lynne Char Bennett, staff writer and wine coordinator for the *San Francisco Chronicle*; Tori Ritchie, host of the Food Network's *Ultimate Kitchens*; Amy Sherman, award-winning blogger extraordinaire; Stacey Reid, marketing specialist; and Renee Behnke, owner and president emeritus of Sur La Table.

It didn't take much work to put together a group of women excited about tequila. All I had to do was ask any woman I met the simple question, "Do you like tequila?" and the list of recruits kept growing. Pretty soon these women told their friends who liked tequila—or just wanted to know more about it—about Agave Girls, and the momentum grew.

Agave Girls, which grew out of an idea jotted down on a bar napkin, now hosts a wide range of events, from tequila seminars to tequila-and-food-pairing events to excursions to Mexico that support the group's mission: bringing professional women together in a non-competitive atmosphere to learn about this oft-misunderstood spirit and give back to the beautiful country that produces it. Agave Girls has already garnered interest among many local and international partners, including the tequila companies Partida Tequila, Tequila Tapatio, and Don Julio. There is also interest in forming sister chapters in New York, Los Angeles, Dallas, and Cleveland.

In light of such momentum, I was inspired to write this tequila primer. What most people know about tequila is that it's the wild child of the bar scene, the main component of a margarita, and that it packs a whopping punch when too much is consumed. It wasn't that long ago that a fraternity rite of passage was "lick, shoot, and suck"—in other words, take a lick of salt, shoot back some tequila, then suck on a lime. At about the same time, Jimmy Buffet wrote the famous song "Margaritaville" and the "lost shaker of salt." Since then, however, tequila has been transformed from something you down by the shot while chanting "one tequila, two tequila, three tequila, floor!" into a sophisticated libation slowly quaffed by the hip, urban professional. Who would have ever thought that we'd be doling out twenty bucks for a shot of tequila? People are drinking tequila on a greater variety of occasions, and they are experimenting with new labels outside the established names. They're learning that 100 percent agave tequila is pretty special stuff. And it's just the beginning!

A Drinker's Guide

The History

TALKING ABOUT TEQUILA without talking about the agave plant would be like talking about wine without discussing grapes. Unlike other distilled spirits, tequila doesn't come from a grain, nut, fruit, or vegetable. It is made from the blue agave plant, and its history hinges on the discovery and cultivation of this unique succulent. Blue agave, which thrives in the gentle hills of central Mexico, is often mistakenly believed to be part of the cactus clan, and its spiky, blue-green cactuslike leaves make this assumption understandable. But it is actually related to the lily family and to some aloe plants.

Of the approximately 136 varieties of agave grown in Mexico, the blue agave is the most prized. In 1753, Swedish botanist Carl Linnaeus classified the plant *Agave tequilana*, naming it after the Greek word *agavos*, meaning "illustrious," an apt description for such a magnificent and noble plant. In 1902, botanist Franz Weber categorized the species of agave for tequila making, naming it *A. tequilana* Weber var. *azul*. The origin of the word "tequila" itself is a mystery. It may have come from the Nahuatl-speaking inhabitants who have long lived in the area. The ancient word *téquitl* means "the place of harvesting plants," "the place of wild herbs," "place where they cut," "the place of work," or even "the place of tricks."

Indeed, to truly understand the history of tequila, one must go back thousands of years, to when the agave plant, or *maguey*, was much revered. The sap, also known as agave nectar or *aguamiel* (honey water), was fermented to produce a thick, white, mildly alcoholic drink with about 3 to 4 percent alcohol. The drink, called pulque, was considered a gift from the gods. The great civilizations of the Americas used it for several things: as an intoxicant for priests to increase their enthusiasm for sacrifice, as a relaxant for sacrificial victims, as a medicine for a variety of ailments, and as a libation to celebrate brave feats. The Aztecs attached such importance to the *maguey* that they even named one of their divinities Mayahuel, a goddess of fertility who was often depicted nursing babies with pulque from her many breasts while seated inside a *maguey* plant. Then, five centuries ago, the face of tequila changed.

Early in the sixteenth century, the invading Spanish recognized the potential of the agave plant. They tended to drink alcoholic beverages with their meals instead of water, which could be contaminated with disease-causing bacteria. Seeing that agave could produce a mildly alcoholic beverage, they concluded that perhaps it could be used to make something even more potent. The conquistadors, who had carried their copper distilling pots with them, applied their knowledge of alembic distillation to pulque, thereby bringing it one step closer to the tequila we know today.

In 1595, Phillip II banned the planting of grapevines in Mexico in an effort to keep the flow of Spanish wine and brandy coming into Mexico. For some reason, he didn't particularly care about agave. Five years later, Don Pedro Sánchez de Tagle, known as the Father of Tequila, took advantage of this loophole, cultivating agave and establishing the first tequila factory, in Jalisco. The product he made, called *vino de mezcal* or *mezcal tequila* (commonly spelled "mescal" in the United States), a rough-edged liquor fashioned from a variety of different agave species, was the first distilled spirit made in the Americas.

Early distilleries were located way out in the countryside in the agave fields, and since drinking glasses generally weren't available where mezcal was being made, it was initially served in the hollowed-out tip of a bull's horn, called a *cuernito* or *caballito*. Due to the limited supply of horns, the vessel was passed from one drinker to another. Because it was impossible to set the horn down without it falling over, shots were thrown back before the horn was passed along to the next drinker. Thus began the tradition of drinking of shots of mezcal and, later, tequila.

In 1636, Don Juan Canseco y Quiñones enabled tax collection on mezcal production by authorizing the distillation and manufacture of the spirit. Then, in 1785, due to the dramatic drop in sales of Spanish wines and brandy, the production of all spirits, including mezcal and pulque, was banned by Spain's Charles III. Officially, production was halted, but of course the manufacture of spirits continued underground. In 1792, new king Ferdinand IV thought that taxing the product would be a better way to control it, so mezcal was once again made legal. And the industry was reborn!

During the period from 1810 to 1821, Mexico gained its independence from Spain through the War of Independence. In the mid-1830s, Mexico tried to retake the province of Texas. Remember the Alamo? The Mexican army might have lost that battle, but in the process it introduced Mexican food, culture, and mezcal to the victors. Wagonloads of mezcal commonly followed the troops and soon became popular on both sides of the conflict.

During the U.S. Civil War, there was a serious shortage of American whiskey and moonshine. Smart tequila vendors from Mexico saw this as an opportunity to cross the Rio Grande and sell their mezcal to American soldiers. While they were in the United States, they picked up discarded whiskey barrels that were left over from making moonshine and took them back to Mexico, thinking that they would be perfect for storing mezcal. Thus began the aging of mezcal, and later tequila, in barrels.

Tequila wasn't officially named "tequila" until 1873. Mezcal producers in the town of Tequila wanted to distinguish their mezcal made in central Mexico from mezcal made elsewhere, especially what was being manufactured in southern Mexico. So, they named it "tequila," after the town of the same name. Later that year, three barrels of legal tequila were sent to the United States and sold there—and the tequila export business was established. A few years after that, exportation of tequila got a boost from a new railroad system that linked Mexico to its neighbor to the north.

It wasn't until 1903 that the first tequila bottling plant was built and tequila began to be sold in bottles. Then, beginning in 1918, an epidemic of the Spanish flu killed tens of millions of people in the United States, Europe, and Asia over the next two years. Believe it or not, this led to a tequila boom in Mexico, as doctors told their patients to ingest tequila, lime, and salt as a flu treatment. This could have been the beginning of the ritual of drinking tequila with lime and salt. The tequila available at the time wasn't as palatable as it is today, and the lime and salt probably masked the less-than-desirable flavor.

Between 1920 and 1933, tequila sales got a boost again, this time because of Prohibition. Strict laws limiting the sale and consumption of alcohol in the United States forced Americans across the border to buy "Mexican whiskey," as they called it. Again, during World War II, when whiskey was in short supply in the United States, Americans headed over the Mexican border to buy tequila.

The first efforts to regulate tequila manufacture began in the late 1940s and culminated in the establishment of the Norma Oficial Mexicana (NOM) in the 1970s, which specified both how the spirit could be made and the source of the agave, regulations that have been revised and updated over the years. Today, tequila can only be distilled from the sap of blue agave cores, or *piñas*, grown in zones in five north-central states of Mexico, and it must contain at least 60 percent blue agave. The NOM regulations were followed by two actions that guaranteed international recognition: the issuance of a Denomination of Origin (DOT), specifying that the production of tequila be applied to a specific geographical area of Mexico, and an Appellation of Control (AOC), which declared the word "tequila" the intellectual property of the Mexican government, thus preventing its use for any spirit made outside the government's jurisdiction.

Tequila and mezcal are the only two Denomination of Origin spirits produced in North America. The term "mezcal," which is often confused with tequila, refers not only to the agave-based spirits from the Mexican state of Oaxaca, but also to the whole category of distilled spirits created from the roasted agave *piña*. Tequila is actually a specific type of mezcal. Just as all cognacs are brandies but not all brandies are cognac (because cognac must come from the Cognac region of France), all tequilas are a type of mezcal, but not all mezcales are tequila.

There are many watchdogs over the tequila industry—and justifiably so. Founded in 1994, the Consejo Regulador de Tequila (CRT), or Tequila Regulatory Council, is a nonprofit organization made up of agave growers, tequila distillers, and government representatives that verifies the fulfillment of tequila standards. In short, the NOM ensures the protection of tequila's origin and name, polices production, and regularly revises standards to guarantee continued quality, while the CRT certifies that a tequila distillery has followed the laws of the NOM. When buying a bottle of tequila, check for the four-digit NOM number. It links the bottle to its distillery, which takes responsibility for the tequila in that bottle.

Discovering Tequila

TODAY, BY LAW, 100 percent agave tequila can only be produced using blue agave, or *agave azul*, grown in five areas in Mexico: the entire state of Jalisco and small parts of the states of Tamaulipas, Nayarit, Guanajuato, and Michoacán. Ninety-eight percent of all blue agave tequila is produced in Jalisco.

When you're in Guadalajara, you're in the heart of Jalisco. If you drive northeast from the city, you'll begin to see hints of red clay soil, a vibrant contrast against the steel-blue agave that covers the hills in the distance and reaches all the way down to the roadside. Continue on and you'll be in the Highlands, or Los Altos. A slow, steady climb will take you through Tepatitlán and Atotonilco, and by the time you reach Arandas, you'll be nearly seven thousand feet above sea level. This part of Jalisco is known for its red clay soil, the *tierra roja*. Rich in iron and full of nutrients, the soil produces a *piña*, or agave heart, with a higher-than-usual sugar content, of at least 27 to 28 percent. The *piña* can also weigh as much as 200 to 275 pounds. The colder temperatures at this elevation mean that it takes longer for the agave to mature, usually eight to ten years, and many say the cool temperature and richness of the soil result in an end product that is sweeter, more floral, and has a fruitier flavor.

Drive less than an hour from Guadalajara in another direction, toward the northwest on Route 15, and you'll arrive in the town of Tequila, the center of the Lowlands. Tequila shares its name not only with this tequila-producing town, but also with a tall volcanic mountain and the lowland valley. This area has a very different kind of soil than that found to the northeast. Here rich, jet-black volcanic soil, or *tierra negra*, is the result of a volcano that erupted 200,000 years ago. The volcano now looms over the town, with a peak of nearly ten thousand feet. Although this area is called the Lowlands, the elevation is still four thousand feet above sea level, and there are mountains everywhere. Unlike in the Highlands, where you are actually in the mountains, here in the Lowlands, you're in the valley looking at them. It is considerably warmer too, which means that the agave matures faster, sometimes in as few as seven years. The *piña* are smaller, 125 to 175 pounds, and have a lower sugar content, about 25 percent. Some tequila aficionados say that Lowlands tequila is drier, richer, rounder, and earthier. One thing is certain, though: the volume of tequila produced here is extraordinary.

The charming, easygoing colonial town of Tequila supports the tequila industry, and most of its residents work in the business. Battered old Buicks and Chevys share the narrow, cobbled streets made of black volcanic rock with rugged farmworkers, or *jimadores*, wearing sombreros and driving pickup trucks. They either work in the fields or in the distilleries (some of Mexico's largest are located here). The center plaza buzzes nightly with activity, as everyone comes to share it like a communal backyard. But Tequila isn't the only town with the drink in its blood. Nearby Arenal and Amatitlán produce some extraordinary blue agave tequila as well.

The Making of Tequila

TEQUILA IS THE only spirit that contains a whole life cycle. Grapes, potatoes, rye, and wheat all grow again, producing crops for wine, vodka, whiskey, and beer year after year—but every glass of tequila contains a whole life. Once the heart, or *piña*, is dug from the ground, the agave plant dies. A new plant must be grown to take its place. Imagine having to plan at least eight years in advance to produce a bottle of liquor!

At the beginning of the tequila-making process, a farmer starts with shoots called *hijuelos*, pups, or *mecuates*, which are produced at the base of the stem of a three- to five-year-old agave plant. When the shoots are a year old, they are removed and set aside for planting. Later, the female plant sends a tall *quiote*, or flower stalk, straight up out of the center of the plant, a signal that it is nearing maturation. The *quiote* is cut to prevent it from draining the sugars and nutrients from the mother plant. The plant continues to grow one more year, during which the sugar-rich nutrients ebb from the leaves and flow into the heart of the plant. It is now time to harvest the plant. The male plant is ready to be harvested when the leaves are taller than the *cogollo*, the spiky shoot that rises straight up from the center of the plant.

The cultivation of the agave plant is a long process, and the harvesting of it is laborious. The skillful *jimador* must be able to judge the perfect time to harvest the plant, determine whether a plant is diseased, and hack off each leaf, or *penca*, with a single blow. His job is an art, and often the skill is passed down from one generation to the next.

The *jimador* uses a long-handled tool called a *coa*, which has a round blade at the end that he continuously sharpens. When harvesting the plant, he starts at the bottom, pulling the plant, leaves and all, from the ground. Next he removes the leaves until he gets to the *piña*, which resembles a giant pineapple or pinecone. Until the *jimador* gets to the *piña*, he has no idea of its size, but it can weigh anywhere from eighty to three hundred pounds. He often uses his *coa* to cut the *piñas* in half right there in the field. The *jimador* then loads them into wire baskets strapped onto the backs of mules or into wheelbarrows, for transport to trucks that will haul them to the *fabrica*, or tequila distillery.

The Making of Tequila ▪ 11

Just like every chef or winemaker, every tequila distiller has his own way of doing things. But it's in the distillery that the magic happens. The *piñas* are loaded one at a time into steam ovens called *hornos*, which are fueled by coal or gas. Older ovens are lined with stone or brick, while the newer ones are pressure-cooker-like stainless-steel autoclaves that cook the *piñas* at much higher temperatures for a much shorter period of time.

The traditional *hornos* are huge and can accommodate up to fifty tons of *piñas*, which are steamed at temperatures between 140°F and 185°F for approximately forty-eight hours and then left to toast for another twenty-four hours as the natural carbohydrates and starches are converted into fermentable sugars. The end result is a soft, juicy, amber-colored edible *piña* with a taste of honey-dipped caramelized yam.

The *piñas* are then mashed to separate the pulp from the juice, though some traditional distillers keep them together during the fermentation. Traditionally, this crushing was done by a *tahona*, a

large wheel of volcanic rock weighing up to two tons, drawn slowly round and round in a cobblestone-lined pit by a mule or horse. (Today a tractor is often used.) Before the juices can be drained, the workers have to get into the pit and use pitchforks to remove the fibers. A few small distillers still do it the old-fashioned way, with the stone *tahona*, but they are few and far between. Now, most distillers crush the *piñas* with steel rollers or with mechanical crushers that resemble wood chippers.

The pulp is minced and washed with water, then strained to remove the *aguamiel*, or honey water. This liquid, called the *mosto*, is now ready for fermentation in very large wooden or stainless-steel

tanks or vats. Wild yeasts that exist naturally in the air—distilleries have lots of windows that are left wide open year-round—combine with the *mosto*, and sometimes brewer's yeast is added as well. As yeast consumes the sugar and converts it to alcohol and CO_2, the mixture bubbles and becomes warm. The CO_2 is released into the air, but the alcohol remains in the liquid. It is ready for distillation after 96 to 120 hours, when a white cap, called the *mosto muerto*, or "dead must," forms on the top of the liquid and the tank is once again cool. This process is very similar to making beer, and the fermenting *mosto*, which has an alcohol content of 4 to 7 percent, actually smells a little like beer.

Distillation is the next step in the process. Two distillations are required. Each time, steam is used to bring the liquid to a boil, which causes the liquid to evaporate and condense. Copper is the material of choice for stills. It reacts with the alcohol and releases ions that affect the flavor. Ever wonder why you don't get a headache after a night of consuming 100 percent agave tequila? The unique distillation process rids the tequila of the impurities and chemical compounds that the body can't metabolize.

The first distillation is called the "separation," as this process gets rid of the fibers, impurities, and chemical compounds that would compromise the final product. This takes about two hours. The distiller pours off the head and tail, or the beginning and end, of the distilled liquid and keeps the heart, or *corazón*, of the flow of tequila. After this first distillation you have *ordinario*, which is 20 to 28 percent alcohol by volume. This is the raw material for the second distillation.

The second distillation, or "purification," takes twice as long as the first—four hours—and the end result is 40 to 55 percent alcohol by volume. Even though the process is the same as for the first distillation, it's at this stage when the aroma, color, and authentic flavor of *blanco* tequila, the purest expression of the distiller's craft, are created. By the time both distillations are finished, about fifteen pounds of *piñas* have been used to make one liter of 100 percent agave tequila!

Types of Tequila

YOU CAN FIND two different types of tequila in the market today, *mixto* and 100 percent agave tequila—and only a fool would drink *mixto*! When buying tequila, beware. *Mixto*, or "mixed," (usually in bottles labeled simply "tequila") is a bastardized version of the real deal: a mix in which the fermented sugars are 51 percent blue agave and 49 percent from another source, typically cane sugar. This is a cheaper way to make tequila, and the results are much, much less complex in flavor. You're basically buying a headache in a bottle.

The proliferation of *mixto* began in the 1930s, when there was an agave shortage. Oftentimes called "gold tequila," *mixto* could also be called fool's gold! Its golden color isn't the result of aging, as one would think; it's added to imitate the color of aged agave tequila. This is the tequila that most beginners and college kids are familiar with, the tequila that often leaves you with a monstrous headache the next morning.

If you are a true tequila aficionado, you know that no matter which brand you choose, you must make sure it says 100 percent agave on the label. If you're at a bar specializing in tequila, ask the tequila sommelier or one of the bartenders to help you make a choice. There are hundreds of tequilas to choose from, and you want to get the one that's right for your palate. Tequila has an amazingly wide range of flavors, from spicy and complex to fruity. There's something there for everyone.

Today, with the steady growth in tequila consumption, many producers have opted for maximum purity and pride themselves on making 100 percent agave tequila. The CRT (see page 6), which certifies the quality of every bottle, recognizes four basic types of tequila: *blanco, reposado, añejo,* and *extra añejo.*

Blanco

Blanco, or white tequila, which is also known as *plata,* or silver, tequila, is produced and bottled immediately after the second distillation, without any aging. (In some rare cases, *blanco* spends thirty days in a "dead" tank—an oak tank that has been used so much that it imparts almost no flavor to the tequila—or up to sixty days in a stainless-steel tank.) It is crystal clear and looks just like water. Don't let it deceive you! Many tequila aficionados prefer *blanco* over aged tequilas because it captures the floral and vegetal flavors of the *agave azul* and expresses very purely what the distiller is trying to do. *Blanco* tequila ranges from fruity to spicy, from sharp to smooth. It is often described as subtly sweet, herbaceous, and peppery, with the flavor of fresh cucumber, lemongrass, and honey or caramel. The nice thing about *blanco* is that it can be drunk right away, straight out of the still. And if you drink it ten years or even fifty year later, there's no change in the flavor.

Reposado

Reposado, or "rested," tequila is the result of storing *blanco* tequila in oak containers of various sizes. They may be rather small barrels or large oak vats, some as large as seventy thousand liters, depending on how much flavor the distiller wants to impart to the tequila. It sits in these containers for at least two months and up to eleven months and thirty days. The oak imparts a warm amber color and rich aromas and flavors to the tequila. Because it is aged for less than a year, *reposado* tequila will be a pale gold and have a hint of oak and a little bit of smokiness. It will also have a slightly smoother taste than *blanco* tequila. The relatively short aging time yields a spirit that's nicely balanced between oak and the fruity flavor of agave.

Añejo

Añejo, or "aged," tequila sits in oak barrels no larger than six hundred liters for at least one year and up to two years, eleven months and thirty days (anything less than three years). *Añejo* is a deep caramel color, darker than *reposado*, with a more pronounced smokiness on the nose and woodiness and butterscotch on the palate. Toasty, long-aged *añejo*, which easily approaches the complexity, sophistication, and color of a fine cognac, is delicious quaffed at room temperature. But then again, so are *blanco* and *reposado*. It just depends on your mood!

Extra Añejo

In 2006, the CRT distinguished any tequila aged in oak for three years or more as *extra añejo*. *Extra añejo* is usually quite dark, almost mahogany, but the color all depends on how old the barrels used for aging were. This is a big guy that takes on flavor notes of peat, chocolate, caramel, leather, and wood. It's uncommonly rich and complex, and a bottle can set you back hundreds of dollars. If you want to taste the true flavors of agave, however, this might not be your best choice, since the heavy presence of wood alters the flavor of the plant, especially its more subtle notes.

Enjoying Tequila: Flights and Pairings

Tequila is more than just a drink. It's a quaint colonial town, it's an inactive volcano, it's a beautiful valley, it's a culture, and it's a symbol of Mexican identity. It speaks to tradition and heritage, families and feuds, land and politics, and even after hundreds of years, it still retains the magic of everything it stands for.

The ways tequila can be enjoyed are myriad. The best method to compare types is to taste them side by side in a flight, or a group of one-ounce pours. Many restaurants, bars, and events are starting to offer these, but you can also serve them at home with friends. Some prefer to taste tequilas in a traditional shot glass; others swear by tequila glasses, which are similar in shape to champagne flutes (see photo, page ii). Swirl and sniff a tequila before tasting it, and examine all the different flavors in the glass, just as you would with wine. When tasting tequila, leave a small sip in your mouth and let it get to body temperature, then swallow. Between tequilas, remember to cleanse your palate with water, crackers, or a bite of tortilla. You might even want to cover each of the tequilas with a coaster, to keep their aromas from interfering with your impressions of the one you are tasting at the moment.

One way of comparing tequilas is by doing a "vertical" flight, pouring different types—*blanco*, *reposado*, and *añejo*—from the same brand. Start with the *blanco*, to experience the clean, crisp flavor of the agave plant. In a way, *blanco* sets the stage for what the tequila maker is trying to do. Then move to the *reposado* and *añejo*, and even the *extra añejo*, if you're lucky enough to have some, to experience the full range of what aging and oak can do. If the tequila maker is good, there should be a logical progression from *blanco* to *reposado* to *añejo*.

Alternatively, if you're interested in a particular type of tequila, you can do a "horizontal" flight, pouring three to five shots of different brands of *blanco*, for example. This allows you to experience the variations in flavor among different producers of the same type.

Tequila can also be experienced with a wide range of foods and mixed with agave nectar, juices, and syrups to make a plethora of cocktails. The recipes that follow—some from my own repertoire, others from some of the top tequila bartenders in the United States—will get you started. When pairing tequila to sip with one of the dishes, remember to serve the same type of tequila that you used in the recipe. The Chorizo Hand Pies (page 77), for example, call for *blanco* tequila, which has a light touch and gives an extra zip to the spicy meat filling without overpowering the delicate pastry. The Market Steak Verde (page 107), on the other hand, pairs best with a smoky *añejo*. As you cook more with tequila and pay attention to the particular flavors, you'll develop a sense of which tequilas pair best with which types of food. And, in the end, it's not about right and wrong. Trust your palate and you'll soon be drinking and dining with the best of them. *Salud!*

Cocktails

The Margarita

For years, bartenders have been making margaritas with tequila, triple sec, and lime juice. Leave it to tequila expert Julio Bermejo to introduce a margarita sweetened with agave nectar. Agave nectar is the best natural sweetener for making the perfect margarita. It comes from the same plant as tequila, so why not?

1 1/2 ounces 100 percent agave tequila

3/4 ounce agave nectar

3/4 ounce water

1 ounce freshly squeezed lime juice

1 lime slice, for garnish (optional)

Combine all of the ingredients except the garnish in a cocktail shaker with plenty of ice. Shake vigorously for 5 seconds and strain into an old-fashioned glass filled with fresh ice. Garnish with a slice of lime, if desired.

Tore Margarita SERVES 1

This award-winning margarita, named after the mixologist's son, is chock-full of bright flavors. In the Yucatán, children love to climb trees in search of tamarind, which they mix with sugar for a candylike treat. Hopefully this will inspire the same kind of youthful excitement in you. You're a grown-up now, so enjoy! You can find tamarind pulp in Latin and Indian markets.

1 whole jalapeño, for garnish, plus 1/4 jalapeño, roasted and seeded (page 123)

1 golf ball–sized chunk seedless tamarind pulp

3/4 ounce freshly squeezed lime juice

1/2 ounce Cointreau or other orange liqueur

2 ounces añejo tequila

To make the garnish, holding the stem of 1 jalapeño, place on a cutting board. Cut away 2 strips of pepper and all of the seeds and membranes, leaving the top of the jalapeño and 2 pieces of pepper extending down, so the pepper can be balanced on the rim of a glass. Set aside.

In a cocktail shaker, muddle the roasted jalapeño and tamarind pulp for 20 seconds. Add the lime juice, Cointreau, tequila, and ice and shake vigorously for 15 to 20 seconds. Strain into a chilled old-fashioned glass filled with fresh ice (you may have to use a spoon to push the liquid through the strainer). Garnish with the jalapeño top.

Ronaldo Colli, Bar Americano
San Francisco, CA

Honey Margarita SERVES 1

Añejo tequila has notes of toasted almonds, butterscotch, and honey, so when you put it in a glass with sweet honey, tart pineapple, lime juice, and spicy jalapeño, it not only sings, it rocks. Add a burst of orange for a symphony in a glass!

1 lime wedge

Salt

2 ounces añejo tequila

1/4 ounce Cointreau or other orange liqueur

1 ounce freshly squeezed lime juice

1/4 ounce honey

1/4 ounce simple syrup

1 ounce pineapple juice

1 thin jalapeño slice

Moisten the rim of a cocktail glass with the lime wedge. Pour a thin layer of salt into a saucer, and dip the dampened rim in the salt, coating it very lightly. Combine the tequila, Cointreau, lime juice, honey, simple syrup, pineapple juice, and jalapeño in a cocktail shaker with plenty of ice. Shake vigorously for 5 seconds and strain into the prepared glass. Garnish with the lime wedge.

**Lucy Brennan, Mint
Portland, OR**

Cocktails ▓ 27

Peachy Rita SERVES 1

Somewhere between a Bellini and a blended tequila drink is where you'll find this soft-as-a-pillow creation. Make sure your sweet white peaches are ripe and your tequila is the finest *blanco* and you'll be as peachy as Rita.

1 ripe white peach, peeled, halved, and pitted, plus 1 paper-thin peach slice, for garnish

2 ounces prosecco

1 ounce blanco tequila

1/3 cup ice or 4 ice cubes

1/2 ounce agave nectar

Sugar

Cut a small piece from the peach and set aside. In a blender, combine the rest of the peach and the prosecco and blend until smooth. Add the tequila, ice, and agave nectar and blend until frothy.

Rub the small piece of peach around the rim of a champagne glass to moisten it. Pour a thin layer of sugar into a saucer, and dip the dampened rim into the sugar, coating it lightly.

Pour the blended mixture into the sugar-rimmed glass and float the thin slice of peach on top to garnish.

Orange Pineapple Crush SERVES 1

Save the expense of a tropical getaway and make yourself this sunny, refreshing cocktail. It is ready and willing to sweep you away to the islands, so prepare for the trip of a lifetime, in a glass.

2 ounces blanco tequila

6 (1/2-inch) fresh pineapple chunks (1/3 cup)

2 ounces freshly squeezed orange juice

1 ounce freshly squeezed lime juice

1 ounce agave nectar

1 very small pineapple wedge, for garnish

In a cocktail shaker, muddle the tequila, pineapple chunks, orange juice, lime juice, and agave nectar. Add ice and shake vigorously for 10 seconds. Strain into a Collins glass filled with fresh ice and balance the pineapple wedge on the rim to garnish.

Liz Baron, Blue Mesa Grill
Dallas and Fort Worth, TX

Phoenix Rising SERVES 1

Fresh cherries lend a fiery red hue to this bold twist on a tequila sunrise, which boasts a name that symbolizes dramatic rebirth. So mix it up— awaken your inner phoenix, and soar to new heights!

- 5 or 6 fresh cherries, pitted
- 2 ounces blanco tequila
- 4 ounces freshly squeezed orange juice
- 1 ounce agave nectar

In a mixing glass, muddle the cherries. Set aside. In a cocktail shaker, combine the tequila, orange juice, agave nectar, and ice and shake vigorously for 5 seconds. Strain the mixture into a Collins glass filled with fresh ice. Place the muddled cherries on the top of the drink.

**Liz Baron, Blue Mesa Grill
Dallas and Fort Worth, TX**

Surly Temple

When I was a kid, I thought *I* was Shirley Temple! It must have been my curly hair. I always ordered the drink in her honor just to make me feel a little closer to her. As I got older I wanted to order a more "adult" drink, so I invented this one. It will really make your hair curl.

1³/4 ounces añejo tequila

³/4 ounce freshly squeezed lemon juice

1¹/2 ounces purchased or home-made grenadine (page 121)

4 ounces club soda

2 thin lemon slices

Combine the tequila, lemon juice, grenadine, and club soda with plenty of ice in a cocktail shaker and stir gently for 15 seconds. Fill a Collins glass with ice. Press the lemon slices down into the glass. Strain the drink into the glass and serve with a couple of tall straws.

La Chupparosa

Chupparosa is Spanish for "hummingbird," and this floral, highly refreshing cocktail recalls the honey-sweet nectar that hummingbirds draw from flowers. The Sauternes, Meyer lemon juice, and agave nectar together bring out the honeyed notes of the tequila.

1 1/2 ounces blanco tequila

3/4 ounce Sauternes

1 teaspoon agave nectar

1 1/4 ounces Meyer lemon juice

2 dashes Fee Brothers grapefruit bitters

Combine all of the ingredients in a cocktail shaker with plenty of ice and shake for 5 seconds. Strain into a Collins glass filled with fresh ice.

Duggan McDonnell, Cantina
San Francisco, CA

Aperol Sunset SERVES 1

This cantaloupe-colored concoction looks lovely and inviting, like the sunsets over Zihuatanejo. Thanks to the bitter orange and rhubarb flavor of Aperol, this drink's delicate balance of sweet and bitter makes you feel like you're right there watching a bittersweet, slowly fading sunset.

2 ounces blanco tequila

1 ounce Aperol

3/4 ounce freshly squeezed lemon juice

1/2 ounce Grapefruit Syrup (page 121)

1/4 ounce Demerara Syrup (page 120)

1 edible flower, such as a pansy, daisy, or nasturtium, for garnish (optional)

Combine all of the ingredients except the garnish in a cocktail shaker with plenty of ice. Shake for 20 seconds and strain into a chilled cocktail glass. Garnish with the flower, if desired.

Audrey Saunders, Pegu
New York, NY

Nouveau Carré

This drink was among the most revered by my panel of "tequila testers," who loved its bold and slightly unexpected combination of *añejo* tequila, caramel, and herbs. There's a real complexity to this cocktail that only a truly daring bartender would create. You, too, must try this magnificence in a glass!

2 ounces añejo tequila
1 ounce Benedictine
1/3 ounce Lillet Blanc

2 dashes Peychaud's bitters
1 lemon twist, for garnish

In a cocktail shaker with plenty of ice, combine all of the ingredients except the garnish and stir until frost forms on the outside of the shaker, about 10 seconds. Strain into a chilled cocktail glass and garnish with the lemon twist.

Kacy Fitch, Zig Zag Café
Seattle, WA

Salud Mojito SERVES 1

Here is the ever-popular minty *mojito* and the limey margarita in one glass! This drink has all the makings of a margarita, plus a splash of club soda and mint. It's a light, refreshing take on two beloved classic cocktails.

10 to 12 fresh mint leaves
1 1/2 ounces blanco tequila
1 ounce agave nectar

1/2 ounce freshly squeezed lime juice
Club soda, for topping
1 lime wedge, for garnish

In a cocktail shaker, muddle the mint leaves. Add the tequila, agave nectar, lime juice, and plenty of ice and shake vigorously for 5 seconds. Strain into a Collins glass filled with fresh ice and top it off with club soda. Garnish with the lime wedge.

Jennifer Gordon, Salud Lounge
Chicago, IL

Sangrita SERVES 6

This fiery delight is traditionally served in a *copita*, a little Mexican shot glass, alongside a shot of tequila. Sometimes it's accompanied with a wedge of lime and coarse salt, but if you're using your best tequila (and you should), forgo the additional salt and lime.

1 ounce hot-pepper sauce, such as Tabasco or Cholula

1/2 ounce freshly squeezed lime juice

3 ounces freshly squeezed orange juice

1 ounce freshly squeezed grapefruit juice

1/2 teaspoon salt

1 teaspoon freshly ground black pepper

7 ounces tomato juice

1/2 jalapeño, seeded

100% blue agave tequila, for serving

In a pitcher, combine all of the ingredients except the tequila and stir until the salt dissolves. Let the mixture sit until it reaches the desired level of heat (it will get hotter as the jalapeño infuses the mixture), 15 to 30 minutes. Remove the jalapeño half and discard. Refrigerate until well chilled.

When you're ready to serve, pour the chilled mixture into *copitas* or shot glasses and serve with your favorite tequila straight up alongside.

Jacques Bezuidenhout, Brand Ambassador, Partida Tequila
San Francisco, CA

This pale diamondlike jewel displays all of the complexity you would expect from a cocktail based on mezcal It's at once sultry and complex, full-bodied and mysterious. Invite some corn chips and a smoky chipotle salsa to the party to make this sensuous experience complete.

1/4 ounce agave nectar

1/2 ounce mezcal

1 1/2 ounces reposado tequila

2 dashes Angostura bitters

1 flamed orange peel
(page 120), for garnish

Combine all of the ingredients except the garnish in a cocktail shaker with plenty of ice and stir for 15 seconds. Strain into a Collins glass filled with fresh ice and garnish with the flamed orange peel.

**Philip Brady, Death & Co.
New York, NY**

Curl up in the wintertime and warm yourself from the inside out. This creation looks and tastes like the classic old-fashioned but has a bold south-of-the-border twist.

  2 ounces añejo tequila
  1/4 ounce agave nectar
  2 dashes Bittermens mole
    bitters or Angostura bitters
  1 orange twist, for garnish

Combine all of the ingredients except the garnish in a cocktail shaker with plenty of ice and stir for 15 seconds. Strain into a chilled rocks glass and garnish with the orange twist.

James Meehan, PDT (Please Don't Tell)
New York, NY

Tea-Quila Highball SERVES 1

In this amber-colored concoction, the delicate flavors of the tea combine with the agave nectar and elderflower liqueur to create a refreshing summer beverage. Don't worry if lemon verbena isn't local to your area. It's widely available in teabags or online, and definitely worth seeking out!

4 ounces hot Lemon Verbena Tea (page 121)

1/4 ounce agave nectar

2 ounces blanco tequila

1/2 ounce St-Germain elderflower liqueur

1 lemon zest spiral (page 121), for garnish

Combine the tea and the agave nectar and set aside to cool. When cool, combine all of the ingredients except the garnish in a cocktail shaker. Fill with ice, stir for 10 seconds, and strain into a Collins glass filled with fresh ice. Garnish with the lemon spiral.

James Meehan, PDT (Please Don't Tell)
New York, NY

Suavecita SERVES 1

The next time you find yourself a little bored with the usual drinks or needing to smooth out the rough edges of your day, heal yourself with a smooth agave elixir—Suavecita!

2 ounces reposado tequila

1 ounce Aperol

1/2 ounce dry vermouth

1/2 ounce sweet vermouth

3 dashes orange bitters

1 lemon zest spiral (page 121), for garnish

Combine all of the ingredients except the garnish in a cocktail shaker with plenty of ice. Stir for 10 seconds and strain into a chilled cocktail glass. Garnish with the lemon spiral.

Dominic Venegas, Bacar
San Francisco, CA

This silvery green goddess is the essence of freshness. If you like cucumbers and mint, this drink brings the kitchen into the bar. It's like a Mediterranean picnic in a glass!

6 to 8 thin English cucumber slices

8 fresh mint leaves

Pinch of salt

3/4 ounce Simple Syrup (page 123)

3/4 ounce yellow Chartreuse

3/4 to 1 ounce freshly squeezed lime juice

2 ounces blanco tequila

In a cocktail shaker, muddle the cucumbers, 7 of the mint leaves, the salt, and simple syrup. Add the Chartreuse, lime juice, tequila, and plenty of ice. Shake for 5 seconds and double strain (page 120) into a highball glass. Float the remaining mint leaf on top to garnish.

Philip Brady, Death & Co.
New York, NY

Mexican 75 SERVES 1

This is a play on the French 75, a gin, champagne, and lemon juice
cocktail made famous by a Franco-American World War I flying ace.
It's unclear what makes the French 75 so powerful—but, whoo boy,
do you feel it when you down one! You can bet the same is true of its
Mexican cousin.

1 ounce blanco tequila

1/2 ounce Cocktail-Ready Agave
Nectar (page 119)

1/2 ounce freshly squeezed
lime juice

Champagne, for topping

1 lime zest spiral (page 121),
for garnish

Combine the tequila, Cocktail-Ready Agave Nectar, and lime juice in a
cocktail shaker with plenty of ice. Shake for 5 seconds and strain into
a champagne flute. Top it off with champagne and garnish with the
lime zest spiral.

Ashley Miller, Tres Agaves
San Francisco, CA

Drink Without a Name #2 SERVES 1

This drink doesn't need a name—the flavors speak for themselves. Orange oil graces the surface of this drink, lending the perfect acidity to its floral and tea notes.

1 1/4 ounces reposado tequila
1 ounce Qi White tea liqueur
3/4 ounce dry vermouth
2 Dukes Hotel orange twists (page 120), for garnish

Combine all of the ingredients except the garnish in a cocktail shaker. Add plenty of ice and stir for 15 seconds. Strain into a chilled cocktail glass. Squeeze 1 of the orange twists over the drink to spray the top with a fine mist of orange oil. Garnish with the remaining orange twist.

Joel Baker, Bourbon & Branch
San Francisco, CA

Shaken Novara SERVES 1

Novara, Italy, is the birthplace of Campari. In this cocktail, Campari is shaken up a bit with the addition of blood orange juice and *reposado* tequila. It's bitter, it's sweet, it's tart—all in one glass!

1 piece orange peel

1/2 ounce Campari

1 ounce freshly squeezed blood orange juice

1 ounce reposado tequila

1 thin orange slice, for garnish

Rub the inside of a cocktail glass with the colored side of the orange peel and chill the glass. Combine the Campari, orange juice, and tequila in a cocktail shaker with plenty of ice and shake for 15 seconds. Strain into the chilled glass and garnish with the orange slice.

Pancho's Punch SERVES 1

Pull up a lounge chair in your backyard, put up your feet, and find some shapes in the clouds drifting by—this drink will keep you company. Spicy but not overpowering, this tall drink is the perfect lazy-day companion.

2 ounces reposado tequila

1 ounce freshly squeezed orange juice

1 ounce Cocktail-Ready Agave Nectar (page 119)

Ginger beer, for topping

5 or 6 grinds freshly ground black pepper, for garnish

Combine the tequila, orange juice and Cocktail-Ready Agave Nectar in a cocktail shaker with plenty of ice. Shake vigorously for 5 seconds and strain into a 12-ounce pilsner glass filled with fresh ice. Top it off with ginger beer and garnish with the black pepper.

Dominic Venegas, Bacar
San Francisco, CA

La Paloma SERVES 1

Paloma translates as "dove," and this drink soars with the same lightness and grace. Also known as the lazy man's bubbly margarita, the Paloma is a fizzy, fresh, and very pretty drink. No wonder it's the *número uno* cocktail in Mexico.

1 lime wedge, for garnish

Salt

1 ounce freshly squeezed lime juice

2 ounces blanco tequila

1 (13½-ounce) bottle grapefruit soda, preferably from Mexico

Moisten the rim of a Collins glass with the lime wedge. Pour a thin layer of salt into a saucer, and dip the dampened rim into the salt, coating it lightly. Place a pinch of salt in the bottom of the glass and fill with plenty of ice. Add the lime juice and tequila. Top it off with the grapefruit soda and garnish with the lime wedge. Serve the rest of the soda on the side.

La Batanga SERVES 1

It doesn't get much more authentic than this drink, which was invented by Don Javier at La Capilla bar, in the town of Tequila. Be sure to use cola bottled in Mexico, where cane sugar is used instead of corn syrup as the sweetener. As your drink diminishes, top it off with the extra cola.

Pinch of salt

1 ounce freshly squeezed lime juice

2 ounces reposado or añejo tequila

1 (12-ounce) bottle Mexican cola

Place the pinch of salt in the bottom of a Collins glass and fill with plenty of ice. Add the lime juice and tequila. Top it off with the cola, and serve the rest of the cola on the side.

La Canterita SERVES 1

In Mexico, this popular drink is served in a deep-dish casserole called a *cazuela*. With lots and lots of hand-squeezed citrus and some grapefruit soda, it's almost like a punch, and suitable for slow, all-night sipping. But don't be fooled. There's a good splash of *blanco* tequila hiding among that fruit juice. This recipe yields just a single serving, but you can scale up the amounts to make a big pitcher and pour it with brunch.

1 1/2 ounces blanco tequila

1/2 ounce triple sec or other orange liqueur

1/2 ounce agave nectar

Juice of 1/4 ruby red grapefruit

Juice of 1/2 lemon

Juice of 1/2 lime

Juice of 1/2 orange

Assorted thin citrus slices, for garnish

Combine all of the ingredients except the garnish in a cocktail shaker with plenty of ice and shake for 5 seconds. Strain into a Collins glass filled with fresh ice and garnish with the citrus slices.

Ashley Miller, Tres Agaves
San Francisco, CA

La Flora Vieja SERVES 1

This drink is as romantic as its name: ethereal and sweet, it delicately bathes your senses in floral hues of orange and pink.

1 1/2 ounces blanco tequila

3/4 ounce maraschino liqueur

1/2 ounce St-Germain elderflower liqueur

1 dash Angostura bitters

1 flamed orange peel (page 120), for garnish

Combine all of the ingredients except the garnish in a cocktail shaker with plenty of ice. Stir together until frost forms on the outside of the shaker, about 5 seconds. Strain into a Collins glass filled with fresh ice and garnish with the flamed orange peel.

Tommy Schlesinger-Guidelli, Eastern Standard
Boston, MA

Rested Rosemary SERVES 1

This is a perfect winter drink, burgundy in color with a fresh sprig of rosemary growing out of the top like a Christmas tree. It has a kind of holiday sweetness but isn't cloying. So get out the Christmas carols and make a big batch of Rested Rosemary—it's time to celebrate.

    1 fresh rosemary sprig
  1/2 ounce agave nectar
1 1/2 ounces reposado tequila
    2 ounces pomegranate juice

Pull 10 to 12 needles off the bottom of the rosemary sprig and place the needles in a cocktail shaker. Add the agave nectar, tequila, and pomegranate juice and muddle. Fill the cocktail shaker with ice and shake vigorously. Strain into a highball glass filled with fresh ice and garnish with the rosemary sprig.

Steve Olson and Andy Seymour, wine geeks
New York, NY

All the King's Men SERVES 1

Tall, dark, and handsome, this thirst quencher is both herbaceous and viscous, offering layers of gentle tannin and fruit on the palate. If you like, garnish it with a few sweet, juicy blackberries.

1½ ounces reposado tequila

½ ounce Averna amaro

½ ounce ruby port

1 teaspoon agave nectar

1 ounce freshly squeezed lemon juice

1 to 2 ounces ginger beer

1 paper-thin fresh ginger slice, for garnish

Combine the tequila, Averna Amaro, port, agave nectar, and lemon juice in a cocktail shaker with plenty of ice. Cover and shake for 5 seconds. Simultaneously strain the mixture and pour the ginger beer into a Collins glass filled with fresh ice. Garnish with the ginger slice.

Duggan McDonnell, Cantina
San Francisco, CA

The Embarcadero SERVES 1

Sitting along the Embarcadero in San Francisco was the inspiration for this drink. Make it in a pint-sized glass because you're going to want plenty as you watch the boats go by and count the clouds. This refreshing afternoon drink is perfect when you're hot and thirsty and the sun is shining.

1 egg white

1 1/2 ounces blanco tequila

3/4 ounce orange Curaçao

3/4 ounce Aperol

1/4 ounce green Chartreuse

3/4 ounce equal parts freshly squeezed lemon and lime juice

1/4 ounce Simple Syrup (page 123)

1 lime wheel, for garnish

Combine all of the ingredients except the garnish in a cocktail shaker with plenty of ice and shake vigorously for 5 seconds. Strain into a pint glass three-quarters full of fresh ice. Garnish with the lime wheel.

Tommy Schlesinger-Guidelli, Eastern Standard
Boston, MA

Chaparrita Dorada SERVES 1

Thyme, vanilla, and *blanco* tequila are in perfect synergy here, dancing in tranquil harmony. The thyme and vanilla have that kind of smooth earthiness that makes you just want to kick back and relax. Garnish this sleeping beauty with a floating piece of lemon zest and a sprig of fresh thyme.

6 fresh thyme sprigs

1/2 ounce freshly squeezed lemon juice

1/4 ounce agave nectar

3/4 ounce vanilla liqueur

1 3/4 ounces blanco tequila

1 lemon zest strip, for garnish

In a cocktail shaker, muddle 5 of the thyme sprigs with the lemon juice. Add the agave nectar, vanilla liqueur, tequila, and ice and shake for 5 seconds. Double strain (page 120) into a chilled cocktail glass and garnish with the lemon zest strip and the remaining thyme sprig.

Ronaldo Colli, Bar Americano
San Francisco, CA

Prado SERVES 1

A *prado* is a grassy "meadow" or "field" in Spanish. This aptly named drink is the loveliest green. Airy and light, with a generous dose of agave, this cocktail is sure to impress. Its heavenly foam crown is most easily made by employing an interesting technique: remove the spring from your cocktail strainer and use it in the shaker as a whisk!

2 ounces blanco tequila

1 ounce freshly squeezed lime juice

1 ounce maraschino liqueur

1 egg white

1 flamed lime peel (page 120), for garnish

Combine all of the ingredients except the garnish in a cocktail shaker with plenty of ice and shake vigorously for 5 seconds. Using a whisk or the spring from the cocktail shaker, whisk the drink to create a little bit of foam. Strain into a chilled cocktail glass and garnish with the flamed lime peel.

Kacy Fitch, Zig Zag Café
Seattle, WA

The Jaguar SERVES 1

This drink will definitely appeal to anyone who enjoys a slightly bitter cocktail. Superior products from the United States, France, and Mexico come together to create an herbaceous mélange. Now, that's a world of good! If you can't find Amer Picon, you can substitute Torani Amer.

1 1/2 ounces blanco tequila
3/4 ounce Amer Picon
3/4 ounce green Chartreuse

3 dashes orange bitters
1 flamed orange peel
 (page 120), for garnish

Combine the tequila, Amer Picon, Green Chartreuse, and orange bitters in a cocktail shaker with plenty of ice. Stir until frost forms on the outside of the shaker, 5 to 10 seconds. Strain into a chilled cocktail glass and garnish with the flamed orange peel.

Tommy Schlesinger-Guidelli, Eastern Standard
Boston, MA

The Cinder SERVES 1

When you add the spicy seeds and membrane of the jalapeño to tequila and let it steep for a while, it makes a whole new spirit. The mezcal in this cocktail adds a smokiness that complements the spiciness of the peppers. The first time I had this drink, I just couldn't get enough—it's almost like food—so I had to order another!

1 lime wedge

Smoked salt (optional)

3/4 ounce Simple Syrup (page 123)

3/4 ounce freshly squeezed lime juice

3/4 ounce mezcal

3/4 ounce reposado tequila

3/4 ounce Jalapeño-Infused Blanco Tequila (page 121)

2 dashes Angostura bitters

Pinch of kosher salt

If desired, moisten the rim of a highball glass with the lime. Pour a thin layer of smoked salt into a saucer, and dip the dampened rim into the salt, coating it lightly. Combine all of the remaining ingredients in a cocktail shaker with plenty of ice and shake for 5 seconds. Strain into the salt-rimmed glass (if used) filled with fresh ice.

Philip Brady, Death & Co.
New York, NY

A pretty seductive name for a cocktail, isn't it? It has the oak flavors of *añejo* tequila, the herbaceous qualities of the green Chartreuse, and the smokiness of the mezcal. Put it all together in a glass with ice and you've got something sexy to be reckoned with.

$1/4$ ounce mezcal

2 ounces añejo tequila

$1/2$ ounce green Charteuse

1 flamed lemon peel
(page 120), for garnish

Combine all of the ingredients except the garnish in a cocktail shaker with plenty of ice and stir for about 20 seconds. Strain into a chilled cocktail glass and garnish with the flamed lemon peel.

Ronaldo Colli, Bar Americano
San Francisco, CA

Cable Car No. 2 SERVES 1

The sidecar, invented in Paris after World War I, was named for an eccentric captain who rode around in a chauffer-driven motorbike sidecar. The Cable Car No. 2, developed in San Francisco, takes the classic sidecar in a Latino and Caribbean direction with the flavors of rum, cocoa, and citrus.

1/4 orange slice

1 teaspoon unsweetened cocoa powder

1 teaspoon ancho chile powder

2 ounces añejo tequila

1 ounce Rhum Clément Créole Shrubb

1/2 ounce freshly squeezed lemon juice

Cut a slit in the orange slice and run it around the rim of a cocktail glass to moisten it. Put the cocoa and ancho chile powder on a small plate and mix thoroughly. Dip the dampened rim in the powder mixture to coat lightly. Set aside in the freezer.

Combine the tequila, Créole Shrubb, and lemon juice in a cocktail shaker with plenty of ice and shake for 10 seconds. Strain into the chilled cocktail glass.

H. Joseph Ehrmann, Elixir
San Francisco

The Mexico City SERVES 1

Served at San Francisco's Tres Agaves, this answer to the classic
Manhattan is maple-colored luxury in a glass that would be perfectly
at home in a gentlemen's club. Reeking of old money and the sweet
life, this drink is all grown up—and rich to boot!

2 ounces añejo tequila

1 ounce Heering Cherry Liqueur

1 ounce sweet vermouth

3 pitted French maraschino
cherries in kirsch, drained,
for garnish

Combine the tequila, cherry liqueur, and vermouth in a cocktail
shaker. Fill with ice, stir for 15 seconds, and strain into a chilled
cocktail glass. Skewer the cherries on a toothpick to garnish.

**Enrique Sanchez, Tres Agaves
San Francisco, CA**

Buenos Días SERVES 1

This is the ultimate hot coffee drink. It gets its spiciness from chipotle pepper, its richness from cream and Licor 43, and its sweetness from *piloncillo*, the cone-shaped unrefined brown sugar from Mexico. Serve this warming treat along with breakfast in bed and it will definitely start your day off just right. *Buenos días!*

2 ounces reposado tequila

4 ounces hot drip or French-press coffee

1 ounce Cinnamon-and-Chipotle-Infused Piloncillo Syrup (page 119)

Licor 43 Whipped Cream (page 122)

Finely grated orange zest, for garnish

Ground cinnamon, for garnish

Combine the tequila, coffee, and infused syrup in your favorite mug and stir to combine. Garnish with a big dollop of the whipped cream and sprinkle with orange zest and cinnamon.

Joel Baker, Bourbon and Branch
San Francisco, CA

Hurricane Mitch

While everyone else is out there freezing in the rain or snow, you can wrap your chilly hands around a big mug of this frothy hot drink. Smell the coffee and the Benedictine, an aromatic herbal liqueur, as they percolate together. Put on a pair of slippers, start a fire in the fireplace, and snuggle up with a good book. It might be cold outside, but you'll be warm inside.

1½ ounces blanco tequila

½ ounce Cardamom Syrup (page 119)

½ ounce Rock Candy Syrup (page 123)

6 ounces hot drip or French-press coffee

Benedictine Whipped Cream (page 118)

Combine the tequila, Cardamom Syrup, and Rock Candy Syrup in your favorite mug. Stir together. Add the coffee and top with a big dollop of the whipped cream.

Tommy Schlesinger-Guidelli, Eastern Standard
Boston, MA

Mulled Magic SERVES 1

This steaming cider will warm your bones as well as your spirits! The fragrant spices will make the whole house smell like a cozy autumn night, and the *añejo* tequila will add a smokiness reminiscent, ever so slightly, of far-off burning leaves. So bundle up and relax with your memories.

5 cardamom pods
10 whole cloves
6 allspice berries
2 cinnamon sticks
Pinch of freshly grated nutmeg

1 cup fresh apple cider
1 (4-inch-long) piece lemon peel, no white pith
1/2 teaspoon brown sugar
1 ounce añejo tequila

Place the cardamom pods, cloves, and allspice berries in a double layer of cheesecloth and tie with kitchen string to make a pouch. Place the pouch on a work surface and, with the bottom of a pan, tap the pouch gently to slightly crush the spices. Place the spice pouch, cinnamon sticks, nutmeg, apple cider, lemon peel, and brown sugar in a saucepan over medium-high heat and bring to a boil. Boil for 3 minutes, pressing the pouch of spices gently with a wooden spoon to release some of the flavors.

Remove the pan from the heat. Remove the cinnamon sticks from the pan and set them aside. Add the tequila and stir together. Strain through a fine-mesh strainer into a small glass coffee cup. Press the pouch to release all of the liquid. Place the cinnamon sticks in the cup and serve immediately.

Food

Spicy chorizo meets *blanco* tequila head on in these hot, flaky hand pies. If you have any leftover filling or you're pressed for time, skip the pastry, add some grated Monterey jack to the filling ingredients, and spread the mixture on top of toasted bread for zesty crostini. You also might want to keep a stock of these pies in your freezer for unexpected guests. All you have to do is take the frozen, uncooked hand pies out of the freezer and pop them in the oven.

2 tablespoons extra-virgin olive oil

1 yellow onion, minced

3 cloves garlic, minced

2 green bell peppers, seeded and finely chopped

1/2 pound chorizo sausage, casings removed

1/4 pound finely diced serrano ham, prosciutto, or Black Forest ham

Large pinch of saffron threads

3/4 cup peeled, seeded, and chopped tomatoes (fresh or canned)

5 tablespoons blanco tequila

1/4 cup finely chopped pimiento-stuffed green olives

1 teaspoon ground cumin

Salt and freshly ground black pepper

1 (10-ounce) package frozen puff pastry sheets, thawed

2 eggs

In a frying pan over medium heat, heat the olive oil. Add the onion, garlic, and bell peppers and cook, stirring occasionally, until soft, 7 minutes. Add the chorizo and ham and cook, stirring occasionally, for 5 minutes. Add the saffron, tomatoes, 4 tablespoons of the tequila, the olives, and cumin to the meat mixture and simmer, covered, for 10 minutes. Uncover and continue cooking until the moisture has evaporated, 4 to 5 minutes. Season with salt and pepper.

Preheat the oven to 350°F. On a floured surface with a floured rolling pin, roll the puff pastry into a rectangle 1/8 inch thick. Using a 3 1/2-inch round cookie cutter or a clean, empty can, cut circles from

continued

the pastry. Place a tablespoon of the filling on one half of each circle. In a small bowl, whisk together the eggs and the remaining 1 tablespoon tequila. Brush the edge on half of each circle with the egg wash. Fold the circle over, enclosing the filling, and seal the edges with your fingers or a fork. Place the hand pies on an ungreased baking sheet and bake until golden brown, 12 to 15 minutes.

NOTE: The turnovers can be made well in advance and stored in the freezer. When you're ready to serve, remove from the freezer, place on baking sheets in a single layer, and bake; they will take 5 to 7 minutes longer to cook. If they get cold before serving, reheat on the top rack of a 400°F oven.

Red Chile Pepper Pickles SERVES 6

These spicy little numbers can be eaten in as little as half an hour or left to pickle for up to a week. The longer they are pickled, the softer they will become. They can be set out to accompany many dishes, but my favorite way is to serve them is on the Tilapia Tacos with Citrus Salsa (page 95).

1 English cucumber, unpeeled and thinly sliced

2 tablespoons extra-virgin olive oil

1/4 cup white wine vinegar or champagne vinegar

2 tablespoons blanco tequila

2 teaspoons minced red onion

1 small fresh red chile, seeded and minced

Salt and freshly ground black pepper

Combine the cucumber, olive oil, vinegar, tequila, onion, and chile in a bowl and stir well. Season with salt and pepper. Transfer to a zippered plastic bag and let stand for at least 30 minutes, shaking the bag occasionally. If allowing them to soak for a day or more, transfer to a covered container and refrigerate.

Guacamole Soup SERVES 6

This smooth and elegant chilled soup is sure to add excitement to your table, and in a snap, too. Holy guacamole! This is the quickest route to nirvana.

2 large, ripe avocados

3 tablespoons minced yellow onion

1 clove garlic, minced

4 fresh cilantro sprigs, minced, plus extra sprigs for garnish

3 cups chicken stock

2 cups milk

1 cup water

1/2 to 1 serrano chile, seeded and minced

1 to 2 tablespoons freshly squeezed lime juice

1 cup heavy cream

2 tablespoons blanco tequila

Salt and freshly ground black pepper

Using a chef's knife, cut the avocados in half from top to bottom, going right around the pit. Twist the halves in opposite directions to separate. Tap the pit firmly with the knife blade, lodging it in the pit. Twist the blade and remove the pit. With a spoon, scoop the flesh from the skin into a blender, and add the onion, garlic, minced cilantro, chicken stock, milk, water, 1/2 of the serrano, and 1 tablespoon lime juice. Blend at high speed until very smooth. Add additional serrano and lime juice to taste. Add the cream and tequila and pulse 3 or 4 times until well blended. Season with salt and pepper. Cover and chill for at least 30 minutes before serving.

To serve, ladle the chilled soup into bowls and garnish each bowl with a sprig of cilantro.

Chilled Honeydew-Lime Soup SERVES 6

Is it a soup or is it a drink? Summer melons, tequila, and mint—look to these ingredients for a refreshing break, no matter how hot it may be outside. A splash of tequila in the soup and another served alongside, and who cares about the heat? Just pour yourself another bowl and relax.

1/2 large honeydew melon (2 pounds), peeled and cut into 1-inch pieces

8 fresh mint leaves

2 tablespoons freshly squeezed lime juice

1/4 cup blanco tequila

2 teaspoons honey

Salt

6 paper-thin lime slices

In batches, combine the melon, 2 of the mint leaves, the lime juice, tequila, and honey in a blender. Process on high speed until smooth and light, 2 minutes per batch. Season with salt. Cover and chill for 1 hour.

To serve, cut the remaining 6 mint leaves into very thin strips. Ladle the soup into chilled bowls and garnish with the lime slices and mint strips.

Gazpacho with Drunken Prawns SERVES 6

Gazpacho is the quintessential summer soup, perfect for cooling you down on a blazing hot day. Adding poached prawns marinated in tequila? Ingenious—and don't even think of throwing away the tequila after draining the prawns! Drizzle a spoonful on the top of the ice-cold gazpacho for a zippy variation.

GAZPACHO

1 pound large prawns, peeled and deveined

1 cup blanco tequila

1 cup fish broth or bottled clam juice

2 1/2 pounds fresh tomatoes, peeled, seeded, and chopped, or 1 (28-ounce) can Italian plum tomatoes, chopped, with juice

1 green bell pepper, seeded and coarsely chopped

1 red onion, coarsely chopped

1 large cucumber, peeled, halved lengthwise, seeded, and coarsely chopped

5 to 6 tablespoons red wine vinegar

3 large cloves garlic, minced

1 1/4 cups tomato juice

1/4 cup extra-virgin olive oil

1 slice bread, crust removed, soaked in water, and squeezed dry

Salt and freshly ground black pepper

GARNISHES

1 tablespoon olive oil

1 tablespoon butter

3 cloves garlic, crushed

6 ounces coarse-textured bread, crust removed and torn into 3/4-inch pieces

1/4 cup peeled, seeded, and chopped cucumber

1/4 cup diced green bell pepper

1/2 tomato, diced

1/4 cup diced red onion

In a large frying pan over high heat, bring 8 cups water to a boil. Season with salt. Add the prawns and boil for 30 seconds. Turn off the heat and let the prawns sit in the water for 10 minutes. Remove the prawns with a slotted spoon and place in a bowl. Add the tequila, stir together, and let sit in the refrigerator for 2 hours.

In a bowl, stir together the fish broth, tomatoes, bell pepper, onion, cucumber, 5 tablespoons of the vinegar, garlic, tomato juice, olive oil, and bread. In batches, process in a blender on high speed until very smooth, 3 to 4 minutes per batch. Strain through a coarse strainer. Season with salt, pepper, and the additional 1 tablespoon vinegar, if desired. Cover and chill for 1 hour.

To make the garnishes, preheat the oven to 400°F. Heat the olive oil and butter in a small frying pan over medium heat. Add the garlic and cook, stirring, until golden brown. Remove the garlic and discard. Place the torn bread pieces on a baking sheet and drizzle with the garlic-infused olive oil. Bake in the oven until golden and crispy, 8 to 12 minutes. Let cool.

Ladle the soup into chilled bowls. Drain the prawns, reserving the tequila. Divide the prawns among the bowls. Garnish with the cucumber, bell pepper, tomato, red onion, and croutons. Drizzle a teaspoon of the tequila on the top of each bowl of soup and serve.

Pineapple Carpaccio with Prawn and Pepper Salad SERVES 6

In this recipe, thin slices of golden pineapple are drizzled with fruity extra-virgin olive oil and coarse salt. All of this is topped off with tequila-poached prawns and crisp strips of colorful bell peppers tossed in a delicious tequila vinaigrette. Simple to prepare, this dish has a great "wow" factor when presented at the table.

1¼ pounds extra-large prawns, peeled and deveined

Kosher salt and freshly ground black pepper

1 cup plus 1 tablespoon blanco tequila

1 ripe pineapple, peeled, cored, and cut into ¼-inch-thick slices

6 tablespoons extra-virgin olive oil

1 teaspoon finely grated lime zest

2 tablespoons freshly squeezed lime juice

1 red bell pepper, seeded and cut into thin strips

1 green bell pepper, seeded and cut into thin strips

1 orange or yellow bell pepper, seeded and cut into thin strips

1 jalapeño, seeded and minced

1 tablespoon chopped fresh Italian parsley, plus sprigs, for garnish

Combine the prawns, 2 tablespoons salt, 1 cup of the tequila, and 1 cup water in a bowl. Let sit in the refrigerator for 10 minutes.

Meanwhile, arrange the pineapple slices in a single layer on a large serving platter. Drizzle 3 tablespoons of the olive oil evenly over the pineapple. Sprinkle with salt.

In a small bowl, whisk together the remaining 3 tablespoons olive oil, the remaining 1 tablespoon tequila, and the lime zest and juice. Season with salt and pepper. Set aside.

Drain the prawns, reserving the brine. Combine the brine and 1 cup water in a large frying pan. Bring to a boil. Add the prawns and simmer for 20 seconds. Turn off the heat and let the prawns sit in the

continued

Pineapple Carpaccio with Prawn and Pepper Salad,
continued

liquid in the pan until almost firm to the touch, 10 minutes. Drain and discard the brine. Let the prawns cool.

Combine the bell peppers, jalapeño, prawns, vinaigrette, and chopped parsley in a bowl and toss together. Mound the prawn salad on top of the pineapple. Garnish with parsley sprigs and serve.

Citrus and Avocado Salad with Honey-Tequila Vinaigrette SERVES 6

Salads don't have to be the old standby of lettuce, tomatoes, and cucumber. With the endless variety of produce available year-round, you may never again have to eat the same salad twice. But you might want to eat this one over and over—especially in the winter, when citrus and avocados are at their peak. Honey pairs magically with tequila, and the mint and red onions add just the right amount of color contrast and flavor. *Me gusta!*

1 grapefruit

4 navel or blood oranges

1 avocado

1/2 small red onion, cut into thin rings

1/4 cup extra-virgin olive oil

2 tablespoons freshly squeezed orange juice

1 tablespoon white wine vinegar

2 tablespoons reposado tequila

2 tablespoons honey

Salt and freshly ground black pepper

6 fresh mint leaves, cut into very thin strips, plus sprigs, for garnish

Lime wedges, for garnish

Grate 1 teaspoon grapefruit zest and 1 teaspoon orange zest and set aside.

Using a sharp knife, cut the top and bottom off each grapefruit and orange to reveal the colored flesh. Place one of the cut sides down on a work surface. Using a small, sharp knife, cut off the peel and white pith from top to bottom. Turn the fruit to the opposite cut side and remove any white pith. Cut the grapefruit and oranges crosswise into 1/4-inch-thick slices, and remove the seeds. Arrange the slices on a serving platter, alternating the grapefruit and oranges.

Using a chef's knife, cut the avocado from top to bottom, going right around the pit. Twist the halves in opposite directions to separate. Tap the pit firmly with the knife blade, lodging it in the pit. Twist

continued

the blade and remove the pit. With a large spoon, scoop the flesh from the skin. Cut the flesh into ¹/₄-inch-thick slices. Place the avocado slices on top of the sliced citrus. Sprinkle the onion on top of the avocado. Set aside.

In a bowl, combine the grapefruit and orange zest. Whisk in the olive oil, orange juice, vinegar, tequila, and honey. Season with salt and pepper. Drizzle the vinaigrette onto the citrus and avocado. Sprinkle the mint strips on top. Garnish with the lime wedges and mint sprigs and serve.

Smoked Trout and Tequila Quesadillas with Summer Tomato Salsa SERVES 6

The smokiness of these quesadillas comes from the smoked trout and the *añejo* tequila. Serve them with a cooling summer salsa and a glass of smoky *añejo* tequila shaken over ice and served straight up.

QUESADILLAS

- 6 ounces smoked trout fillet, skinned and broken into bite-sized pieces
- 1/4 cup añejo tequila
- 1/4 teaspoon pimentón
- 1 cup coarsely grated pepper jack cheese (about 3 ounces)
- 1 cup coarsely grated mozzarella cheese (about 3 ounces)
- 1 cup coarsely grated white Cheddar cheese (about 3 ounces)
- 5 green onions, white and green parts, thinly sliced
- 6 (8- or 9-inch) flour tortillas

SUMMER TOMATO SALSA

- 1 pound mixed yellow, orange, and red cherry tomatoes, quartered
- 5 tablespoons chopped fresh cilantro
- 3 green onions, white and green parts, thinly sliced
- 3 tablespoons freshly squeezed lime juice
- 1/2 to 1 jalapeño or serrano chile, seeded and minced

  Salt and freshly ground black pepper

In a bowl, gently stir together the trout, tequila, and pimentón picante. Let marinate for 30 minutes. Drain and reserve the liquid for the salsa.

To make the salsa, combine the tomatoes, cilantro, green onions, lime juice, and jalapeño to taste in a bowl. Add the reserved tequila mixture to taste. Mix well and season with salt and pepper.

To make the quesadillas, combine the trout mixture, the 3 cheeses, and the green onions. Divide the mixture among 3 of the tortillas, and top with the remaining 3 tortillas. Heat a nonstick frying pan over medium heat and cook a quesadilla on one side until the cheese melts and the tortilla is lightly browned, 2 to 3 minutes. Flip the quesadilla and continue to cook until the second side is lightly browned, 2 to 3 minutes. Repeat with the remaining quesadillas.

Cut each quesadilla into 6 wedges and serve with the salsa.

Bay Scallop Ceviche SERVES 6

In Mexico, the best hangover remedy is believed to be the juices from freshly prepared ceviche. When you're done with the ceviche, pop the juices into a shot glass—if they make it that far. People have been known to pour the juices straight from the plate into their mouths! Although this recipe calls for bay scallops, it can also be made with larger sea scallops. Just cut them horizontally into slices 1/4 inch thick before marinating them.

1 pound fresh bay scallops

3/4 cup freshly squeezed lime juice

1/4 cup blanco tequila

3 tablespoons extra-virgin olive oil

2 cloves garlic, minced

1/3 cup coarsely chopped fresh cilantro, plus sprigs, for garnish

2 jalapeños, seeded and minced

1/2 red bell pepper, seeded and cut lengthwise into 1-inch-wide strips

1/2 yellow bell pepper, seeded and cut lengthwise into 1-inch-wide strips

3/4 pound mixed yellow, orange, and red cherry tomatoes, halved

1/2 cup thinly sliced green onion, white and green parts

Salt and freshly ground black pepper

Lime wedges, for garnish

Remove the small white muscle from the side of each scallop. Combine the scallops in a bowl with the lime juice and tequila, mix together, and let sit for 1 hour.

Add the olive oil, garlic, chopped cilantro, jalapeños, bell peppers, tomatoes, and green onions to the scallop mixture. Season with salt and pepper. Mix well. The dish can be made up to this point up to 6 hours before serving. Garnish with the lime wedges and cilantro sprigs just before serving.

Bamboo Salmon with Mango-Avocado Salsa SERVES 6

Neat chunks of wild salmon, skewered on lime-infused bamboo and grilled until smoky—all they need is the perfect cooling salsa with a bit of attitude. This mango-avocado creation, infused with 100 percent agave *blanco* tequila, fits the bill. Once you've had it, you'll swim upstream for this dish, time and again!

BAMBOO SALMON

- 1/2 cup freshly squeezed lime juice (3 limes)
- 1 1/2 pounds fresh wild salmon, cut into 1-inch chunks
- 1 tablespoon olive oil
- Salt and freshly ground black pepper
- Lime wedges, for garnish
- Fresh cilantro sprigs, for garnish

MANGO-AVOCADO SALSA

- 2 large, ripe mangoes
- 2 ripe avocados, halved, pitted, peeled, and cut into 1/2-inch dice
- 1/2 to 1 jalapeño, seeded and minced
- 1/2 small red onion, diced
- 1 teaspoon finely grated lime zest
- 2 tablespoons freshly squeezed lime juice
- 1/4 cup freshly squeezed orange juice
- 3 tablespoons blanco tequila
- 1/4 cup chopped fresh cilantro
- 1 tablespoon olive oil
- Salt and freshly ground pepper

Place the lime juice in a container large enough to hold 12 bamboo skewers, each 6 to 8 inches long. Let soak for 30 minutes.

To make the salsa, working with 1 mango at a time, cut off the flesh from each side of the large, flat pit, to form 2 large pieces. Discard the pit. Using a knife, score the flesh lengthwise and then crosswise into 1/2-inch squares, cutting to, but not through, the skin.

continued

Now slip the blade between the skin and the flesh and cut away the flesh, directing the small cubes into a bowl. Add the avocados, jalapeño to taste, red onion, lime zest and juice, orange juice, tequila, cilantro, and olive oil. Season with salt and pepper.

Preheat a gas or charcoal grill. Thread the salmon chunks onto the skewers and brush with the olive oil. Season with salt and pepper. Grill the salmon, turning every 2 minutes, until cooked but still slightly pink inside, 5 to 7 minutes total. Alternatively, you can cook the skewers in a nonstick ridged grill pan over medium-high heat for about 10 minutes.

Place 2 skewers on each serving plate and scoop a large spoonful of the salsa alongside or on top. Garnish with lime wedges and cilantro sprigs and serve.

Tilapia Tacos with Citrus Salsa SERVES 6

Try saying the title three times fast! Anyone who can do it deserves a bonus pour of tequila. Another bonus—the salsa pairs equally well with fish.

CITRUS SALSA

- 3/4 cup freshly squeezed orange juice
- 2 oranges
- 1 tablespoon minced fresh cilantro
- 2 tablespoons minced red onion
- 1 tablespoon extra-virgin olive oil
- 2 tablespoons blanco tequila
- Salt and freshly ground black pepper

TACOS

- 12 (6-inch) corn tortillas
- 1/2 cup blanco tequila
- 2 tablespooons freshly squeezed lime juice
- 1 serrano chile, thinly sliced
- 1 1/4 pounds skinned tilapia fillets
- Salt and freshly ground black pepper
- 1 tablespoon vegetable oil
- 12 fresh cilantro sprigs

To make the salsa, place the orange juice in a small saucepan and reduce over medium heat to 3 to 4 tablespoons. Set aside. Using a vegetable peeler, remove the zest from the 2 oranges in strips. Mince the zest and set aside. Using a sharp knife, cut the top and bottom off each orange to reveal the colored flesh. Place one of the cut sides down on a work surface. Using a small, sharp knife, cut off the peel and white pith from top to bottom. Turn the fruit to the opposite cut side and remove any white pith. Cut along both sides of each section to free the sections from the membrane. Discard any seeds. Cut the sections in half and place in a bowl with the reduced orange juice and the zest. Add the cilantro, red onion, olive oil, and tequila and stir well. Season with salt and pepper. Set aside.

To make the tacos, preheat the oven to 400°F. Wrap a slightly dampened paper towel around 2 tortillas. Wrap tightly in foil. Repeat

continued

with the remaining tortillas, making 6 packets. Ten minutes before serving, place the tortilla packets on a baking sheet and place in the oven.

In a shallow bowl, combine the tequila, lime juice, and chile. Add the tilapia fillets and marinate for 10 minutes.

Remove the tilapia from the marinade, discarding the marinade. Season the tilapia with salt and pepper. Heat the oil in a large nonstick frying pan over medium-high heat. Add the tilapia fillets and cook, turning once, until opaque but still moist, 2 to 3 minutes per side. Remove from the heat and break into 1-inch pieces.

To serve, remove the tortillas from the oven. Discard the foil and paper towels and place 2 tortillas on each serving plate. Top with the tilapia and cilantro, distributing evenly. Pass the salsa on the side.

Quick Chick Mole SERVES 6

So you want to impress your friends with an authentic mole but you don't have the hours it takes to make it? This recipe will come to the rescue. The combination of tequila, authentic Mexican chocolate, and spices makes this unbelievably easy dish seem like you've been in the kitchen all day. In under an hour you've got yourself a dish to remember. Everyone at the table will be saying "Mmmmmm . . . Olé!" I mean, "Mole!"

2 tablespoons olive oil

6 skin-on, bone-in chicken breasts, about 3 pounds total

Salt and freshly ground black pepper

1/2 yellow onion, chopped

2 cloves garlic, minced

1 tablespoon chili powder

1 teaspoon ancho chile powder

1 tablespoon sesame seeds

1/2 teaspoon ground cumin

1/2 teaspoon ground cinnamon

1/4 teaspoon dried oregano

2 tomatoes, chopped

1 cup chicken stock

1/2 cup canned tomato sauce

1/2 cup reposado tequila

3 tablespoons raisins

1 ounce bittersweet Mexican chocolate, such as Ibarra, finely chopped

1/4 teaspoon cayenne

Toasted pumpkins seeds, for garnish

Warmed flour tortillas, for serving

In a large frying pan over medium-high heat, warm the olive oil. Add the chicken, skin side down, and cook until lightly browned, 5 minutes. Turn the chicken, season with salt and pepper, and cook on the other side until lightly browned, 5 minutes more. Transfer to a platter and cover with foil. Set aside.

Add the onion to the pan and cook, stirring occasionally, until it begins to soften, 2 minutes. Add the garlic, chile powder, ancho chile powder, sesame seeds, cumin, cinnamon, and oregano and cook, stirring constantly, for 30 seconds. Stir in the tomatoes, chicken stock, tomato sauce, tequila, raisins, chocolate, and cayenne. Return the

continued

chicken to the pan. Bring to boil, reduce the heat to low, and simmer, turning occasionally, until the chicken is no longer pink in the center, about 15 minutes. Transfer the chicken to a platter and cover loosely with foil. Simmer the sauce until slightly thickened, 5 to 6 minutes. Season with salt and pepper.

To serve, spoon the sauce over the chicken. Garnish with the pumpkin seeds and serve at once with tortillas.

Grilled Tequila Chicken with Black Bean and Corn Salsa SERVES 6

Marinating chicken breasts in tequila overnight both tenderizes them and gives them a smoky flavor. The next day, fire up the barbecue! And if you don't have time for the whole marinating and grilling thing, just throw together the salsa and eat it with some tortilla chips. Don't forget a little glass of tequila alongside.

GRILLED TEQUILA CHICKEN

- 1/2 cup reposado tequila
- 1 cup freshly squeezed lemon juice
- 1/2 cup freshly squeezed orange juice
- 1 teaspoon chili powder
- 1 tablespoon seeded and chopped jalapeño
- 3 cloves garlic, minced
- Large pinch of red pepper flakes
- Salt and freshly ground black pepper
- 6 boneless, skinless chicken breasts
- 2 tablespoons extra-virgin olive oil

BLACK BEAN AND CORN SALSA

- 2 tablespoons freshly squeezed lime juice
- 3 tablespoons extra-virgin olive oil
- 1 clove garlic, minced
- 1 teaspoon ground cumin
- 2 tablespoons reposado tequila
- Salt and freshly ground black pepper
- Kernels from 2 ears corn
- 1 1/2 cups cooked black beans
- 1/2 cup finely diced red onion
- 1/4 cup chopped fresh cilantro or Italian parsley, plus sprigs for garnish
- 1/2 jalapeño, seeded and minced

In a shallow, nonreactive dish, combine the tequila, lemon juice, orange juice, chile powder, jalapeño, garlic, red pepper flakes, 1 teaspoon salt, and 1 teaspoon pepper. Add the chicken breasts, turn to coat, and refrigerate overnight.

Preheat a gas or charcoal grill. Remove the chicken from the tequila marinade and pat dry with paper towels. Brush the chicken with the olive oil. Set aside.

continued

Grilled Tequila Chicken with Black Bean and Corn Salsa, continued

To make the salsa, in a small bowl, whisk together the lime juice, olive oil, garlic, cumin, and tequila. Season with salt and pepper. Add the corn kernels, black beans, onion, chopped cilantro, and jalapeño and mix well.

Place the chicken on the grill and grill until golden on one side, about 5 minutes. Turn the chicken, season with salt, and continue to grill until the chicken is cooked through, 6 to 8 minutes. Transfer to a serving platter. Top with the salsa and serve immediately, garnished with cilantro sprigs.

Cha-Cha-Cha Chile Lasagna

My favorite thing about lasagna is all the different layers. I love to mix things up a bit, and this version, made with corn tortillas, a spicy bean stew, and gooey melted cheese hits the mark. The best thing about this dish? It's vegetarian, but you won't miss the meat!

1 (15-ounce) can pinto beans, drained

2 yellow onions, minced

3 cloves garlic, minced

2 small green bell peppers, seeded and chopped

1 (14 1/2-ounce) can diced tomatoes, with juice

1/4 cup plus 2 tablespoons blanco tequila

1/4 to 1/2 teaspoon cayenne (optional)

6 tablespoons chile powder

1 tablespoon ground cumin

Salt and freshly ground black pepper

8 (6-inch) corn tortillas

2 cups coarsely grated Cheddar or Monterey jack cheese (about 6 ounces)

2 tomatoes, coarsely chopped

2 cups coarsely chopped crisp lettuce

1/2 cup sour cream (optional)

In a large frying pan over medium heat, combine the beans, onions, garlic, bell peppers, canned tomatoes, 1/4 cup of the tequila, the cayenne to taste (if using), chile powder, cumin, and salt and pepper to taste. Slowly simmer until most of the liquid has evaporated, 5 to 10 minutes, then add the remaining 2 tablespoons tequila and turn off the heat. Set aside.

Preheat the oven to 350°F.

Spread one-third of the bean mixture on the bottom of a 3-quart baking dish. Top with half the tortillas, overlapping them evenly, and half of the cheese. Repeat with the remaining ingredients, ending with the bean mixture. Cover with foil and bake until hot and bubbling around the edges, 35 minutes.

To serve, top with the fresh tomatoes and lettuce. If you like, spoon a dollop of sour cream on top of each serving and serve immediately.

Mexican Spaghetti and Meatballs

Who doesn't love spaghetti and meatballs, the ultimate Italian comfort food? But Italians don't own the dish. In this recipe, little meatballs, called *albóndigas* in Spanish, are stewed in a lively tequila-tomato sauce, tossed with spaghetti, and sprinkled with Parmigiano-Reggiano. Get ready for a killer dish! The meatballs and sauce can be refrigerated for up to 2 days before serving.

1 1/2 cups dry bread crumbs

3/4 cup milk

1/2 pound ground pork

1/2 pound ground beef

1/2 pound ground veal

6 cloves garlic, minced

1 1/2 teaspoons ground coriander

1 1/2 teaspoons ground cumin

1/4 teaspoon ground pimentón

Large pinch of cayenne

Salt and freshly ground black pepper

1/2 small yellow onion, finely minced

3 tablespoons extra-virgin olive oil

5 cups peeled, seeded, and chopped plum tomatoes (fresh or canned)

1 cup water

1/2 cup blanco tequila

3 tablespoons tomato paste

Large pinch of red pepper flakes

1 teaspoon sugar

1 1/2 pounds spaghetti

1 cup grated Parmigiano-Reggiano cheese

Preheat the oven to 350°F. In a bowl, combine the bread crumbs with the milk and stir together to moisten the bread crumbs completely. Squeeze the bread crumbs gently, removing some, but not all, of the moisture. Discard the milk. In a bowl, combine the moistened bread with the pork, beef, veal, half of the garlic, the coriander, cumin, pimentón, cayenne, 1 1/2 teaspoons salt, and 1/2 teaspoon pepper. Using your hands, form the mixture into balls 1 1/4 inches in diameter and place on an oiled baking sheet. You should have about 30 meatballs. Bake until they are firm and brown on the outside

continued

but not cooked in the center, 10 minutes. Remove from the oven and set aside.

Purée the tomatoes in a blender and set aside. Heat the olive oil in a large soup pot or saucepan over medium heat. Add the onion and cook until soft, 10 minutes. Add the remaining garlic and cook, stirring, until slightly softened, 30 seconds. Add the tomatoes, water, tequila, tomato paste, red pepper flakes, and sugar and simmer slowly for 30 minutes. Add the meatballs to the tomato sauce and continue to simmer slowly until the sauce has reduced slightly and the meatballs are cooked through, 30 minutes. Season with salt and pepper.

Meanwhile, bring a large pot of salted water to a boil. Add the spaghetti and cook until al dente, 8 to 10 minutes. Drain and toss the spaghetti with the tomato sauce and meatballs. Transfer to a large heated serving bowl and serve immediately, sprinkled with the Parmigiano-Reggiano.

Slow-Braised Pork with Tomatillos and Tequila SERVES 6

When I get the urge for Mexican food, I always crave slow-braised pork, or *carnitas*. Imagine pork braised for hours and hours with tangy tomatillos and smoky tequila. I love to serve it rolled into warm, fresh corn tortillas topped with sour cream, green onions, and sliced avocado, or as the filling for burritos.

2 tablespoons vegetable oil

2 pounds boneless pork shoulder (Boston butt), cut into 2 large pieces

Salt and freshly ground black pepper

1 yellow onion, chopped

1 small green bell pepper, seeded and chopped

2 jalapeños, seeded and minced

4 cloves garlic, minced

1 tablespoon ground cumin

1/2 teaspoon dried oregano

1 cup chopped tomatillos (fresh or canned)

1/2 cup añejo tequila

1 cup water

6 lime wedges, for garnish

Cilantro sprigs, for garnish

Heat the oil in a large, heavy Dutch oven over medium-high heat. Season the pork well with salt and pepper. Add the pork to the Dutch oven and brown, turning occasionally, until golden brown on all sides, 20 minutes total. Remove the pork from the pan with a slotted spoon. Reduce the heat to medium-low, add the onion, bell pepper, and jalapeños, and cook, stirring occasionally, until the onions are soft, 10 to 12 minutes. Add the garlic, cumin, and oregano and cook, stirring, for 1 minute. Add the tomatillos, tequila, water, and pork and bring to a boil. Reduce the heat to very low and simmer, covered, turning the pork occasionally, until the pork is very tender, about 4 hours. Remove the cover, increase the heat to medium, and simmer until the sauce thickens and about 1 cup of the liquid remains, 10 minutes.

Remove the pork from the Dutch oven and let cool. When it has cooled enough to handle, shred the pork into large pieces. Place on a platter and garnish with the lime wedges and cilantro sprigs.

Market Steak Verde SERVES 6

Chipotles, which are dry-smoked jalapeños, lend a delectable flavor to the sauce. Thanks to the grilling of the steak and, of course, the addition of *añejo* tequila, this dish has a triple shot of smokiness.

3 boneless market (rib-eye) steaks, trimmed (about 2½ pounds total)

Salt and freshly ground black pepper

4 tomatillos, husks removed

2 cloves garlic, crushed

½ ripe avocado, pitted and peeled

6 fresh cilantro sprigs, plus more for garnish

1 to 2 tablespoons freshly squeezed lime juice

1 teaspoon hot-pepper sauce, such as Tabasco or Cholula

½ to 1 teaspoon minced chipotle pepper in adobo sauce

3 tablespoons añejo tequila

1 tablespoon extra-virgin olive oil

2 cups cherry tomatoes, halved

Season the steaks with 1 teaspoon salt and ½ teaspoon pepper and allow them to come to room temperature.

Bring a pot of water to a boil over high heat. Drop the tomatillos into the boiling water and cook for 3 minutes. Drain and rinse under cold running water until just warm to the touch. Using a paring knife, remove the cores. Cut the tomatillos in half and place in a food processor along with the garlic, avocado, cilantro sprigs, 1 tablespoon lime juice, hot-pepper sauce, chipotle, tequila, and salt and pepper to taste. Purée until smooth. Season to taste with more lime juice, hot-pepper sauce, salt, and pepper, if needed. Set aside.

Preheat a gas or charcoal grill or a ridged cast-iron grill pan. Rub the steaks with the olive oil and cook until medium-rare, 4 to 6 minutes per side. Transfer to a warm serving platter and allow to rest for 10 minutes.

Meanwhile, transfer the sauce to a saucepan and warm, stirring constantly, for 1 minute. Remove from the heat.

Cut the steaks on the diagonal into thin slices and return to the platter. Pour the sauce over the top and garnish with the tomatoes and sprigs of cilantro.

Cinnamon Panna Cotta with Apple Caramel SERVES 6

Just a little slice of heaven west of nirvana—a silky *panna cotta* infused with tequila and cinnamon, accompanied by an apple-caramel sauce.

CINNAMON PANNA COTTA

- 2 cups heavy cream
- 1/2 cup milk
- 1/4 cup sugar
- 5 cinnamon sticks
- 1 3/4 teaspoons granulated unflavored gelatin
- 2 tablespoons reposado tequila
- Pinch of salt

APPLE CARAMEL

- 3 cups apple juice
- 1/4 cup sugar
- 1 tablespoon unsalted butter
- 1 tablespoon heavy cream
- 2 tablespoons reposado tequila

Combine the cream, milk, sugar, and cinnamon sticks in a saucepan over medium heat and heat until very hot but not quite boiling. Remove from the heat and let steep for 1 hour. Discard the cinnamon sticks.

In a small bowl, sprinkle the gelatin over the tequila and set aside to soften for 5 minutes. Combine the cream mixture and salt in a saucepan. Bring to a boil over high heat, reduce the heat to medium, and boil for 1 minute, stirring constantly. Remove from the heat and whisk in the gelatin mixture until dissolved. Divide the mixture among six 5-ounce ramekins and chill for 3 hours.

To make the apple caramel, place the apple juice in a saucepan over medium heat. Cook until the liquid is reduced to 1 cup and looks syrupy, 10 to 15 minutes. Watch it closely so it doesn't scorch. Remove from the heat and whisk in the butter, cream, and tequila. Let cool for 10 minutes before serving.

Just before serving, run a small knife around the inside edge of each ramekin. Dip the bottom of each ramekin in boiling water just until the panna cotta loosens, then turn out onto a serving plate. Spoon the sauce over the top and around the edges.

Añejo Truffles MAKES 5 DOZEN TRUFFLES

Mexico is the birthplace of both chocolate and tequila, so what could be better than the marriage of these two great treasures? These truffles, inspired by a recipe from my friend Dorothy Kinne, are chocolaty, silky, and smooth, with a mellow punch of smoky *añejo* tequila. They freeze well, so tuck some away for a rainy day when you need a snappy, creamy pick-me-up.

12 ounces milk chocolate, chopped

4 egg yolks, at room temperature

1/3 cup añejo tequila

6 tablespoons unsalted butter, at room temperature, cut into small pieces

1 cup unsweetened cocoa powder

Place the chocolate in a heatproof bowl. Rest the bowl in the rim of a saucepan over (but not touching) barely simmering water. Stir constantly until the chocolate melts and is smooth.

Whisk the yolks into the chocolate; this will make the chocolate firmer and somewhat grainy. Whisk in the tequila; the mixture will separate. Add the butter, a few pieces at a time, and whisk constantly until the mixture is well blended and smooth, about 3 minutes.

Transfer to a 1-quart baking dish, cover with plastic wrap, and refrigerate until set, 3 to 4 hours.

Remove from the refrigerator and let soften at room temperature for about 15 minutes. Using a spoon, scoop the mixture into grape-sized balls. Mold them with your hands into spheres. Just before serving, place the cocoa powder in a bowl, and roll the truffles in the powder, coating evenly.

Tequilamisu <small>SERVES 9</small>

Who said that tiramisu can only be made with rum? Italians don't have tequila, but that doesn't mean we can't shake things up a little bit. Tiramisu means "pull me up" in Italian. Make it with tequila in place of the rum and you've got its Mexican cousin, *tequilamisu*. I promise you, you're going to love this one. *Ay, caramba!*

2 cups very strong espresso

3/4 cup granulated sugar

3/4 cup añejo tequila

4 eggs, separated

1 pound marscapone

1 teaspoon vanilla extract

3/4 cup heavy cream

1 tablespoon confectioners' sugar

2 ripe but firm bananas

36 to 40 excellent-quality ladyfingers

1 1/2 cups excellent-quality grated bittersweet Mexican chocolate, such as Ibarra

In a bowl, combine the espresso, 1/4 cup of the granulated sugar, and 1/2 cup of the tequila. Set aside.

In a separate large bowl, using an electric mixer, beat the egg yolks and the remaining 1/2 cup granulated sugar until very light. Add the marscarpone and beat until smooth. Add the remaining 1/4 cup tequila and the vanilla and stir to combine. Set aside.

In a separate bowl, whip the cream until it forms soft peaks. Whisk in the confectioners' sugar. In a separate bowl, beat the egg whites until they form stiff peaks. Fold both the whipped cream and the beaten egg whites into the mascarpone mixture.

Just before assembling, thinly slice the bananas and set aside.

To assemble, dip half the ladyfingers, one at a time, into the espresso mixture and line the bottom of a 13 by 9-inch baking dish. Spread half of the mascarpone mixture over the ladyfingers. Arrange the bananas in an even layer on top of the mascarpone mixture. Repeat with the remaining ladyfingers and mascarpone mixture. Spread the chocolate in a thick layer on top. Refrigerate for at least 2 hours before serving.

Mexican Chocolate Soufflés with Tequila-Chipotle Crème Anglaise SERVES 8

I love to play around with sweet and spicy combinations in desserts. The hint of pepper in the soufflé and the smoky chipotle in the crème anglaise produce an unexpected twist on this classic after-dinner delight! And, of course, there is the distinctive kick of tequila in every bite.

TEQUILA-CHIPOTLE CRÈME ANGLAISE

- 1/2 cup heavy cream
- 1/2 cup milk
- 1/2 cup granulated sugar
- 1 cinnamon stick
- 1 tablespoon reposado or añejo tequila
- 1 teaspoon minced chipotle pepper in adobo sauce
- 1/4 vanilla bean, split lengthwise
- 3 egg yolks

MEXICAN CHOCOLATE SOUFFLÉS

- 10 ounces excellent-quality bittersweet Mexican chocolate, such as Ibarra, finely chopped
- 3/4 cup heavy cream
- 1/4 cup granulated sugar, plus extra for dusting
- 2 tablespoons unsalted butter
- 2 tablespoons reposado tequila
- 1 tablespoon vanilla extract
- 2 teaspoons ground cinnamon
- 1/2 teaspoon cayenne
- 1/4 teaspoon salt
- 6 large eggs, separated
  - Pinch of cream of tartar
  - Confectioners' sugar, for dusting

To make the crème anglaise, in a small saucepan, combine the cream, milk, granulated sugar, cinnamon stick, tequila, and chipotle. Using the tip of a knife, scrape the seeds from the vanilla bean into the cream mixture and then add the pod. Place over medium-low heat and heat until very hot but not quite boiling. Remove from the heat and let steep for 15 minutes.

In a bowl, whisk together the egg yolks. Whisking constantly, slowly add the hot cream mixture to the yolks. Return the mixture to the saucepan. Cook over medium-low heat, stirring constantly, until the custard begins to coat the back of a spoon and the temperature registers 170°F on an instant-read thermometer.

Strain the mixture immediately into a clean bowl and whisk to incorporate some cool air. Allow to cool for at least 30 minutes before serving. If you are not using it immediately, cover the bowl with plastic wrap and refrigerate. Bring it to room temperature just before serving.

To make the soufflés, combine the chocolate, cream, granulated sugar, butter, tequila, vanilla, cinnamon, cayenne, and salt in a heavy saucepan. Stir over low heat until the chocolate melts and the mixture is smooth. Remove from the heat and let cool to lukewarm. (The soufflés can be made up to this point up to 1 day ahead, covered and refrigerated. Stir over low heat until lukewarm before continuing.)

Preheat the oven to 350°F. Butter eight 12-ounce ramekins and dust lightly with granulated sugar. Whisk the egg yolks into the lukewarm chocolate base. In a large bowl, using an electric mixer, beat the egg whites and cream of tartar until stiff peaks form. Fold one-third of the egg whites into the chocolate base, then repeat with the remainder in 2 batches. Divide the soufflé mixture evenly among the prepared ramekins, and place the ramekins on a baking sheet. Bake until the soufflés are puffed but still moist in the center, about 15 minutes.

Dust the hot soufflés with confectioners' sugar and serve immediately. At the table, make a hole in the center of each soufflé and pour some of the crème anglaise into the center.

Coco Loco Tequila Cupcakes

MAKES 2 DOZEN CUPCAKES

These soft, moist, and very coconutty cupcakes should come with a warning! Not only can you not stop after eating just one, but these adult-only cupcakes provide enough kick to make you feel like you are on vacation south of the border. The inspiration for this recipe comes from my friend Tina Gherzi, who loves tequila and coconut as much as I do.

CUPCAKES

- 2 cups all-purpose flour
- 2 teaspoons baking powder
- 1 teaspoon baking soda
- Large pinch of salt
- 1 cup unsalted butter, at room temperature
- 1 cup sugar
- 2 eggs
- 1 cup unsweetened coconut milk
- 2 tablespoons fresh grated ginger
- 1 teaspoon coconut extract
- 1/4 cup 100 percent agave tequila
- 1/2 cup buttermilk
- 1 cup shredded sweetened coconut

COCONUT CREAM FROSTING

- 1/2 pound cream cheese, at room temperature
- 2 tablespoons unsweetened coconut milk, or more as needed
- 2 tablespoons 100 percent agave tequila
- 2 teaspoons coconut extract
- 3 cups confectioners' sugar, sifted, or more as needed
- 1 cup shredded sweetened coconut

Preheat the oven to 350°F. Butter and flour two 12-cup cupcake pans or line with paper liners.

Sift the flour, baking powder, baking soda, and salt into a bowl and set aside.

In a large bowl, using an electric mixer, cream together the butter and sugar until fluffy. Add the eggs one at a time, occasionally scraping down the sides of the bowl and mixing well after each addition. Add the coconut milk, ginger, and coconut extract and beat for 1 minute

continued

at high speed until well blended. In a measuring pitcher, stir together the tequila and buttermilk. Add the dry ingredients in 3 batches to the egg mixture alternately with the buttermilk mixture in 2 batches, beginning and ending with the dry ingredients and mixing well after each addition. Fold in the shredded coconut.

Fill each cupcake well about three-fourths full with batter. Bake until a toothpick inserted into the center of a cupcake comes out clean, 20 to 25 minutes.

Let the cupcakes cool in the pan for 10 minutes. Turn out onto a rack and let cool completely before frosting.

Meanwhile, to make the frosting, using the electric mixer, beat the cream cheese on high speed until smooth. With the mixer on high speed, slowly add the coconut milk, tequila, and coconut extract. Continue beating until thoroughly combined and smooth, about 5 minutes. Add the confectioners' sugar and continue beating on high speed, occasionally scraping down the sides of the bowl. The frosting should be smooth and spreadable. Adjust with more coconut milk if the consistency is too thick, or more confectioners' sugar if it is too runny.

To assemble, spread the frosting on the cooled cupcakes and sprinkle with the shredded coconut.

Margarita Granita

Some people like their margaritas blended, some like them on ice. Some like them with salt, some without. If you happen to like yours blended, you will love this Italian slush! Serve in chilled margarita or martini glasses. Salt optional.

1 cup water

1 cup sugar

2 tablespoons grated lime zest

2 cups freshly squeezed lime juice, strained

1/4 cup blanco tequila

1/2 cup kosher salt

1 large wedge of lime

2 teaspoons agave nectar

8 thin lime slices, for garnish

Combine the water and the sugar in a saucepan, place over high heat, and heat until the sugar dissolves. Remove from the heat and add the lime zest and juice and the tequila. Pour the mixture into a shallow 13 by 9-inch metal baking pan. Freeze until ice crystals begin to form, 1 1/2 to 2 hours. Whisk with a fork to break up the crystals and return to the freezer. Repeat every 30 minutes until the mixture is the consistency of slush, about 2 hours more.

Meanwhile, place 8 margarita or martini glasses in the freezer. Place the salt on a large plate.

To serve, rub the lime wedge along the rim of a chilled glass to moisten it. Dip the dampened rim into the salt to coat lightly. Repeat with the remaining glasses. Spoon the granita into the glasses and drizzle each serving with 1/4 teaspoon agave nectar. Cut a slit in each lime slice, and balance a slice on each glass rim. Serve immediately.

Glossary and Basics

Agave Nectar Natural liquid sweetener extracted from the agave plant. It has a lower glycemic index than sugar or honey, and is often organic and kosher.

Amer Picon French liqueur flavored with bitter oranges, quinine, and spices. Difficult to find in the United States, but the similar U.S.–made Torani Amer can be substituted.

Angostura Bitters Dr. J. G. B. Siegert created Angostura bitters, also called aromatic bitters, in 1824. It is made from a secret recipe of herbs and spices, including gentian root, in an alcohol base. Spicy, with strong clove characteristics, Angostura bitters are used in aperitifs and as a digestive, as well as in cocktails and cooking.

Aperitif An alcoholic drink that is served before a meal as an appetizer, either with or without food.

Aperol An aperitif with a bitter orange flavor, derived from orange, gentian, rhubarb, and a proprietary blend of herbs and roots.

Averna Amaro Also known as Averna bitters, this Italian liqueur was first made in 1868; the highly guarded formula garnered many awards on its inception. Can be served as a digestive, aperitif, or in mixed cocktails.

Benedictine An herbal liqueur with a cognac base, made from a secret recipe of twenty-seven plants and spices.

Benedictine Whipped Cream

1/2 cup heavy cream
1 tablespoon Benedictine

In a bowl, whip the cream to soft peaks. Add the Benedictine and continue to whip until soft peaks form again. Makes enough for 4 hot drinks. Leftovers can be stored in the refrigerator for a day. Also good on hot cocoa or over ice cream.

Bitters Generally used as aperitifs or digestives, and some can be used as both. There are two types of bitters: aromatic bitters and bitter liqueurs. Aromatic bitters are used in tiny quantities in mixed drinks, and are usually sold in small bottles. The bitter liqueurs have been sweetened and can be enjoyed on their own.

Campari An alcoholic drink simultaneously classified as an aperitif, liqueur, and Italian bitter. Made from a secret recipe created in 1860 by Gaspare Campari. Detectable flavors include anise, bergamot oil, bitter orange, ginseng, licorice, rhubarb, and quinine.

Cardamom Syrup

1/2 cup sugar
1/2 cup water
1/2 teaspoon ground cardamom

Combine all of the ingredients in a small saucepan over medium-high heat and bring to a boil, stirring until the sugar melts. Remove from the heat immediately. Makes 1 cup. Store any excess in the refrigerator for up to a month. Cardamom is traditionally added to coffee and tea in the Middle East and Turkey. Try this syrup in your own morning beverage for a snappy alternative to sugar.

Chartreuse, Green An all-natural process results in an intensely flavored, bright green herbal liqueur. Made from a highly secret recipe that blends 130 plants.

Chartreuse, Yellow Milder and sweeter than its green counterpart. Also contains no artificial colors, flavors, or preservatives.

Cherry Heering Liqueur This dark red, black cherry cordial was developed in Denmark in the early 1800s. One hundred years later, it finally found its fame with the introduction of the Singapore Sling. It's full flavored, mildly sweet, and smooth.

Cinnamon-and-Chipotle-Infused Piloncillo Syrup

1 cup plus 2 tablespoons water
6 ounces piloncillo
4 cinnamon sticks
1 chipotle pepper in adobo sauce, mashed

Combine all of the ingredients in a small saucepan over low heat. Simmer until the sugar dissolves and the cinnamon and chipotle flavor is just becoming apparent when the mixture is tasted, about 15 minutes. Makes 1 cup. You can also add this to your morning coffee for a spicy treat.

Citrus Wedges Used as both a garnish and an ingredient in many recipes. To create, wash the citrus with soap and water, rinse well, and dry. Cut in half vertically, then vertically again, repeating until the wedges are the desired thickness.

Cocktail-Ready Agave Nectar

Combine 1 part each agave nectar and water and stir to dissolve.

Cointreau A premium brand of triple sec, Cointreau is made in Angers, France. This clear brandy is flavored with sweet and sour sun-dried orange peel.

Demerara Syrup

1/2 cup water

1 cup Demerara sugar

Combine the water and sugar in a saucepan over medium heat and heat just until the sugar dissolves. Do not boil. Makes 1 cup. Store any excess in the refrigerator for up to a month. Can be used as a substitute for simple syrup in almost any cocktail.

Digestive An alcoholic drink enjoyed after a meal.

Double Strain To give a drink a clean, clear, and bright look, first pour the drink through a Hawthorne Strainer (a traditional bartender's strainer), and then through a fine-mesh (tea) strainer, to remove any pieces of ice, pulp, or herbs.

Dukes Hotel Twist To create, use a vegetable peeler to remove a wide band of zest from an orange, ensuring there is no pith.

Fee Brothers Grapefruit Bitters

Fee Brothers has a long American history as a producer of several different kinds of bitters, created using secret formulas. The Grapefruit Bitters have a very concentrated grapefruit flavor with hints of spiciness and are used in place of grapefruit juice when a bartender is trying to avoid the bulk or color impact.

Flamed Citrus Peel Remove a 2- to 3-inch-long piece of citrus peel using a sharp knife or a vegetable peeler. To flame the peel, light the end of a toothpick or bamboo skewer with a lighter. Hold the burning toothpick or skewer about 2 fingers above the rim of the glass and warm the outside of the peel. Then, holding the peel just above the flame, sharply squeeze it, propelling the oil from the peel through the flame and into the glass. Drop the flamed peel into the cocktail.

Ginger Beer A nonalcoholic carbonated drink made from the fermentation of ginger, sugar, lemon, and water.

Glassware, Champagne Flute Tall, thin, and tapered, the flute holds between 7 and 11 ounces and is perfect for preserving the bubbles in champagne cocktails.

Glassware, Cocktail/Martini A Y-shaped glass, perfect for 3- to 6-ounce drinks. Also known as an "up" glass.

Glassware, Collins A tall, slender tumbler with an 8- to 12-ounce capacity. Generally interchangeable with the highball glass, which is slightly wider.

Glassware, Highball A large tumbler, usually with an 8- to 12-ounce capacity. Generally interchangeable with the Collins glass, which is slightly narrower.

Glassware, Margarita Typically

12 to 20 ounces in capacity, with a large surface area about 5 inches across. Also available in a jumbo 60-ounce version!

Glassware, Old-Fashioned

A short tumbler holding 5 to 10 ounces. Also known as a lowball or rocks glass.

Glassware, Shot Glass A standard

shot is 1$\frac{1}{2}$ ounces, but check yours, because shot glasses often come in different sizes. The glass is made with a thick base to withstand the inevitable slamming of it back onto the bar. In Mexico, the traditional straight-sided shot glass is known as a *caballito* or *copita*.

Grapefruit Syrup

1 cup plus 2 tablespoons water

1 cup superfine sugar

Zest of 1 grapefruit

Combine the water and sugar in a small saucepan over medium heat and warm just until the sugar dissolves. Do not bring to a boil. Let cool. Add the zest to the syrup, transfer to a sealed container, and refrigerate for 24 hours. Using a fine-mesh strainer, strain the liquid, pressing down on the zest to extract as much flavor as possible. Makes about 1$\frac{1}{2}$ cups. Store any excess in the refrigerator for up to a month. You can combine a few tablespoons with soda water for a refreshing Italian soda.

Grenadine

$\frac{1}{4}$ cup pomegranate juice

$\frac{1}{4}$ cup cranberry juice

2 tablespoons sugar

6 tablespoons water

Combine all of the ingredients in a small saucepan and bring to a boil over medium heat. Reduce the heat to low and simmer for 5 minutes. Makes about $\frac{3}{4}$ cup. Store any excess in the refrigerator for up to a month.

Jalapeño-Infused Blanco Tequila

3 jalapeños

1 cup blanco tequila

With a small, sharp knife, separate the flesh of the peppers from the seeds and membranes. Reserve the flesh for another use. Combine the seeds and membranes with the tequila in a bowl and let steep for 1 hour. Strain the tequila, discarding the seeds and membranes. Makes 1 cup. Store any excess in the refrigerator or freezer.

Lemon or Lime Zest Spiral Using

a vegetable peeler, remove the zest from a lemon in a strip about 4 inches by $\frac{1}{4}$ inch. Wrap the strip around the stem of a cocktail stirrer and hold for 10 seconds. Slide the curl off the stirrer to garnish a cocktail.

Lemon Verbena Tea

$\frac{1}{2}$ cup fresh or dried lemon verbena leaves (12 to 15 leaves), or 2 teabags

1 cup boiling water

Put the leaves in a heatproof cup. Pour the boiling water over the leaves and let steep for 3 to 5 minutes. Strain the tea, discarding the leaves. Makes 1 cup. If you have any left over, serve as hot or iced tea.

Licor 43 Named for the number of ingredients used to make it, Licor 43, also known as Cuarenta y Tres, has been produced in Spain since 1923. It is pale and golden, with the flavors of vanilla, spices, fruit, and citrus.

Licor 43 Whipped Cream

$1/2$ cup heavy cream

1 tablespoon confectioners' sugar

1 teaspoon vanilla extract

2 tablespoons Licor 43

Place the cream in a bowl and whip until it forms soft peaks. Add the sugar, vanilla, and Licor 43 and whip just until evenly mixed; do not overbeat. Makes about 1 cup. This is best used immediately to top a Buenos Días (page 70), a cup of hot cocoa, or a bowl of ice cream.

Lillet Blanc Known as "the aperitif of Bordeaux," this French quinine-fortified aperitif wine was created in 1887 as a tonic. It contains a proprietary blend of fruit liqueurs and wines exclusive to the Bordeaux region.

Maraschino Liqueur Not to be confused with the juice from maraschino cherries, this clear liqueur is made from Marasca cherries and their pits, which lends it a complex, slightly almondlike flavor.

Mole Bitters Inspired by the mole sauce common to many Mexican recipes, this specialty bitter is not yet available at markets. Check www. bittermens.com for updates, or visit Alembic or Coco 500, in San Francisco; No. 9 Park or Eastern Standard, in Boston; or Tailor, Death & Co. or Milk & Honey in New York to taste it. For the Jalisco Old-Fashioned (page 41), you can substitute Angostura bitters.

Muddle To muddle is to press or crush ingredients—usually fresh fruit, citrus wedges, or herbs such as mint—with a muddler to extract their flavor.

Muddler A pestle, usually made of wood and shaped like a small baseball bat. The flat end, which often has a rough texture, is used to crush ingredients in a mixing glass or cocktail shaker.

Peychaud's Bitters An aromatic red bitter with the flavors of anise and gentian root. Created in the 1830s by Antoine Peychaud.

Prosecco Italy's answer to champagne, this sparkling wine is the star of the famous Bellini cocktail. It's produced primarily from prosecco grapes, although it may also contain a small amount of pinot blanc or pinot grigio. Most bottles should be enjoyed within three years of their vintage, though finer ones can be aged for up to seven years.

Qi White Tea Liqueur Made from oranges, herbs, spices, and white tea buds, and sweetened with honey, which makes it less sweet than many other orange liqueurs.

Rhum Clément Créole Shrubb A blend of white and aged rum, sugar cane syrup, tropical Caribbean spices and sun-bleached bitter orange peel gives a nice balance of bitter and sweet to this orange-gold spirit made in Martinique.

Roasted Jalapeño Place a whole jalapeño over a hot grill or, using tongs or a long fork, hold it over a stove's gas flame. Turn it occasionally, until the skin is black and blistered.

Rock Candy Syrup

- 1/2 cup sugar
- 1/2 cup water
- 2 teaspoons vanilla extract

Place all of the ingredients in a small saucepan over medium-high heat. Bring to a boil, stirring until the sugar dissolves. Remove from the heat immediately. Makes 1/2 cup. Store any excess in the refrigerator for up to a month.

Ruby Port Ruby port is a young port aged in neutral oak or stainless-steel tanks for two to three years in an effort to maintain the ruby color and intense fruit flavor while being fortified with grape juice during fermentation, and sometimes blended with older wines. The most affordable and widely produced type of port.

Sauternes Sauternes is both a region in France and a sweet, unctuous wine. Golden and honey-sweet, Sauternes gets its flavor from a beneficial mold called noble rot, or botrytis, a sooty film that develops on the grapes as they age on the vine. Often paired with desserts and enjoyed as an after-dinner drink with cheese.

Shaker/Strainer Vessel and strainer used to mix cocktails that call for a "shaken" and/or "strained" preparation. The shaker is filled with ice and various juices and liquors, then shaken with the lid on, usually for about 10 seconds. The liquid is then poured through the strainer into a glass. The tiny slivers of ice created by shaking continue to melt and keep the drink cool. Sometimes the ingredients for a drink are combined in a shaker, but are stirred, rather than shaken. The Boston shaker is used with a separate strainer, while the cobbler shaker has a built-in strainer.

Simple Syrup A syrup used to sweeten mixed drinks. It is made by combining equal parts sugar and water and heating until the sugar dissolves.

St-Germain Elderflower Liqueur A mildly sweet liqueur made in France from hand-picked elderflower blossoms.

Triple Sec Refers to a variety of orange liqueurs, including Curaçao, Grand Marnier, and Cointreau, that are flavored with the dried peel of Curaçao oranges. Triple sec sounds like "triple dry" but actually it means "triple distilled."

Vermouth Created in the eighteenth century in France, vermouth is a fortified herbal wine. There are many varieties, from dry to sweet. Dry vermouth is usually used as an ingredient in cocktails; sweet vermouth is sometimes served as an aperitif.

Sources

HERE IS A SAMPLING of my favorite brands of tequila. I've included web addresses for those that have their own webpage. For a more thorough list of tequilas, you can visit www.tequila.net or www.tequilasource.com/tequilabrands. Happy hunting!

1800
www.1800tequila.com

1921
www.tequila1921.com

4 Copas
www.4copas.com

7 Leguas
www.tequilasieteleguas.com.mx

Amate
www.amate.com

Arette

Asombroso
www.asombrosotequila.com

Cabo Wabo
www.cabowabo.com

Casa de Oro

Casa Noble
www.casanoble.com

Cazadores
www.cazadores.com

Centinela
www.tequilacentinela.com.mx

Chamucos
www.tequilachamucos.com

Chinaco
www.chinacotequila.com

Corazon
www.tequilacorazon.com

Corralejo
www.tequilacorralejo.com

Corzo
www.corzo.com

Cuervo
www.cuervo.com

Don Camilo

Don Eduardo
www.doneduardo.com

Don Fulano
www.donfulano.com

Don Julio
www.donjulio.com

Dos Manos

El Charro
www.elcharrotequila.com

El Diamante del Cielo
www.HandCraftedTequila.com

El Jimador
www.eljimador.com.mx

El Tesoro
www.eltesorotequila.com

Espolón
www.tequilaespolon.com

Fina Estampa
www.finaestampatequila.com

Frida Kahlo
www.doradopizzorniandsons.com/
tequila

Gran Centenario
www.grancentenario.com

Herencia de Plata
Herradura www.herradura.com

Hornitas

La Cofradia
www.tequilacofradia.com

La Fogata

Los Abuelos
www.losabuelos.com

Milagro
www.milagrotequila.com

Ocho

Oro Azul
www.oroazultequila.com

Partida
www.partidatequila.com

Patrón
www.patronspirits.com

Penca Azul
www.pencazul.com

Pueblo Viejo

Pura Sangre
tequilapurasangre.com

Tapatio

Tezón
www.tequilatezon.com

Tonala

Trago
www.trago-tequila.com

Tres Generaciones
www.sauzatequila.com/3G

XQ
www.tequilaxq.com

Index